bound

HONOR BOUND: BOOK TWELVE

ANGEL PAYNE

This book is an original publication of Waterhouse Press.

Cover Design by Waterhouse Press, LLC
Cover Photographs: Shutterstock

Paperback ISBN: 978-1-64263-306-1

bound

HONOR BOUND: BOOK TWELVE

ANGEL PAYNE

WATERHOUSE PRESS

For my Thomas.

Bound to you for life and loving the ride, baby.

Thank you for the safety of your strength,
and the gift of your heart.

CHAPTER ONE

"Help us! Help *him*! Please!"

Jayd Cimarron had waited too damn long to shriek the words. Every moment of the flight between Paris and her home island of Arcadia had been a torturous eternity. Only after they put down on the thin tarmac outside of Sancti and then taxied to the far end of the runway, where medical and military personnel waited, did she realize that the plane ride was just the beginning of this ordeal.

The beginning?

Perhaps it was just easier to think of it all that way now. Jayd's brain had no extra bandwidth to keep processing all the events that had led to her premature homecoming to the kingdom in which she had once been a well-loved princess. Now, she was just a woman arriving in the island's capital, hoping King Evrest would extend his mercy to her.

More importantly, to the man in her arms.

The force of nature she had not yet known for twenty-four hours.

The human who had been her rescuer, protector, teacher, and lover—and, just before this plane had left the ground at Bourget Field, her self-sacrificing savior. The three bullet wounds in his massive body proved that with horrifying clarity.

The body that had direly needed medical attention long ago.

That was clinging to life—by a thinner thread than she

wanted to admit.

No. You will not die today, Maximillian Brickham!

She repeated it in a desperate rasp, pressing her jaw against his thick stubble while ramming her lips against his ear. "Do you hear me? Do you? You shall not dare, damn it—unless *you* want to be the cuffed and helpless one."

She was rewarded for that by a weak grunt from the man, which hit her like the chorus of a grand symphony. She watched as her tears spilled off her cheeks and onto his.

His cheek . . . still too pale. Still too taut.

Still hanging on by that terrible thread . . .

"Creator on high," she muttered to herself as a pair of medics in red shirts and khakis approached.

They were flanked by two members of the palais guard force—soldiers she had known since childhood but who now acted as if she were barely there. She cared not. They could believe what they wanted to, courtesy of the alerts that had likely been sent from the City of Paris prefecture. In the eyes of the foreign police force, Brickham was naught but the treacherous soldier who had accompanied her on a quest to meet her biological father, only to kill the man as she watched.

They knew nothing. None of them. Subsequently, neither did the Arcadian warriors who glared down at him now.

Jayd tuned them totally out.

She redirected every ounce of her concentration onto the medics who now knelt in front of Brickham and her.

"He . . . he was trying to get me onto the plane," she stammered. "On the tarmac . . . back at Bourget. But then . . . they came from everywhere . . . and they were shooting, and—"

"Highness." The responder closest to her, a tall girl with huge brown eyes and mocha skin, enforced her interruption by gently patting Jayd's forearm. "We see how important he is to you. We will not let any more damage come to him. You have my word."

Jayd merely nodded, her throat too tight for speech now. Worse, her royal title also felt so wrong, even less than a week after the proof that it had never been hers to begin with. But she did not want to ruin the rightness of everything else in the woman's assurance.

"*Merderim*," she finally forced herself to whisper, letting the gratitude stand on its own so the pair could focus on Brickham. She held on to him as long as she could, but they were soon asking her to scoot back so they could fully assess the ugly gash across his broad forehead.

Anxiously, Jayd pushed back. Ozias Demos, Brickham's friend and leader of the mission to retrieve her from Paris, had been certain it was just a graze—but Jayd knew better than to breathe easy about that. A bullet wound was a bullet wound. Brickham could end up just fine or as a barely functioning vegetable. She prayed for the former but told herself to brace for the latter—especially as Brickham stirred and moaned again.

"Mr. Brickham?" said the male medic, who leaned over and flicked a penlight beam into Brick's eyes. "Are you with us? Can you hear me?"

His response was a string of nonsensical mumbles. Jayd could only discern every third or fourth phrase, which happened to be "got me," "keep her safe," and "Duck, Pixie, duck."

The clog in her throat grew heavy and tumbled to the breadth of her chest. She clamped her fist over the slicing pain in her heart, though it did little to help the agony of her every breath.

"Will he be all right? Tell me. Please. *Please*. Brickham? Can you hear me?"

The woman, who turned enough to let her see a name badge reading *Lyza*, secured her with a steady gaze this time. "*Desonnum*, Highness—but when you speak, his pulse rate jumps. We need to keep him as calm as possible for transport to the palais."

"Surgeon Sevyal is already standing by at the infirmary," stated the man opposite her, with a tag reading *Alyx*. Not that Jayd noticed it after his assertion.

"Sevyal?" she exclaimed. "Surgery? *Why?*" Damn it, she would command the information out of them if she had to, though Lyza already seemed to perceive that and cut her off with a raised hand. It did not escape Jayd's attention that the woman's white latex glove was stained with a lot of bright-red blood.

"The bullet in his shoulder is in the joint," she said. "And that could lead to lethal migration, as well as a lot of pain."

"Shit." The virulent sound gushed from the pit of her throat. No. From the bile that lurked even deeper. "Shit, shit, shit!"

"Highness." It was Requiemme this time, crouching protectively next to her. "He is going to be all right. Lyza and Alyx know what they are doing. But the more you remain here and fret, the less their ability to do their jobs."

"She's right."

Once more, neither of the medics spoke it. Jayd gasped, consumed by joy, when recognizing the beautiful baritone emanating from Brickham's chest. A torso for which she was now feeling peevishly protective, since the medics had to slice open the front of his Henley and one leg of his jeans for access to his wounds.

"L-L-Listen to them, Pixie," he said with shocking pronunciation. "They know th-th-this fire d-d-drill."

Jayd swooped her face back over his in an earnest rush. *Just a few seconds.* She begged it of the Creator, despite grasping the selfishness of her action. But after this, they were taking him away from her. Into *surgery*. If the everlasting decided it wanted him now, then his last memory of her would be the smile she forced across her lips.

And then the tender kiss she pressed across his.

She ignored Emme's reacting gasp. She also cared not about the startled hums exchanged by the medics.

What she could not toss off so easily, especially as Alyx and Lyza transferred Brick to a stretcher and carried him to the waiting gurney on the tarmac, was the man they passed on their way out. A male who pivoted back into place and then damn near filled the aperture of the plane's door.

A warrior who looked not a speck pleased about what he'd just witnessed.

"*Bon sabah*, brother."

At least she thought it was morning, with the sky behind Samsyn's head glowing with soft peach light. The breeze smelled right too, aromatic with brisk sea wind and morning glories. But the scents soured in her stomach once Syn fully boarded the plane, having to duck down to get all the way in.

"Well, it *was* good." Nothing missed the scrutiny of his sweeping glower, from the dings in the plane's bulkhead to the dirt and blood splotches across the floor. "Creator's filthy balls, Jayd."

She rocked back with her arms folded. "Well, mince no words on *my* account."

Her snark, which usually had her brother smirking, brought her only his darker grimace. "No time for mincing at the moment, since you have deemed it necessary to bring chaos to our front door."

Nothing sealed the deal on a girl's messy morning more than even more mess, especially when brought on by her own brother. *No.* Not her brother anymore. That was the absolute truth now, was it not? The revelation that had made her flee Arcadia in the first place. That has sent her on the wild quest to find the man who had truly sired her.

The mission that had brought them to this painful mess.

And turned Samsyn into a stranger.

It mattered not that Evrest, their eldest sibling, had assured her nothing would ever change as far as he, Shiraz, and Samsyn were concerned. Because it seemingly had. Maybe Syn really gazed upon her now and saw not his little sister, but a half-blood pretender.

She shook her head, refusing to believe it. Samsyn was a warrior who led warriors, not an *imbezak* who led fools. More than anyone, he should understand that truths were not always what they appeared, even when security camera footage and global headlines declared otherwise.

"He has a name, and it is not Chaos." She accessed the dredges of her strength to plant hands on her hips. If Syn was in the mood for a brawl, she would be happy to give him at least a verbal version. "This is Maximillian Brickh—"

"I know who he is, damn it," he growled. "Just like everyone else who has seen the European news feeds for the last hour, wondering why one of their most beloved princesses has made off with a man who stalked her across Paris and then murdered a poor old man before her eyes."

"None of that is true!"

He grimaced, dropping his nose between two fingers. "I am not the enemy here, Jayd."

"Really? Could have fooled me." But her confident fire fizzled fast. "Samsyn? *Rerda?* Do you not remember talking to me last night? You do not believe any of those allegations for a second, do you?"

As he raised his head, she already knew he had barely slept in the last couple of days. Perhaps the last *week*. "I know *you* believe differently, sister. And yes, I also know that you were there for all of it. But the camera footage they have released everywhere . . . is damning at best, *fembla*."

"And at worst?" she retorted. "Samsyn?"

He pushed out heavy air through his nose. "I just need to understand. Why has no one else from the scene come forward and—"

"Perhaps you'd be getting some of those answers for yourself, mister—if you'd cut the ogre act for a minute or two."

The comeback, flung with feminine snark that Jayd unabashedly envied, was accompanied by a sight she welcomed with as much gratitude.

Brooke Valen-Cimarron made a lithe leap into the cabin, her leggy physique clad in battle gear that nearly matched her husband's. Jayd wanted to hug the woman but had to rely on an indebted glance toward Brooke. The woman could temper Syn in ways no one else could.

"Damn it, woman. I told you to stay outside and supervise things on the ground."

Then again, maybe not.

"You mean the near-nothing that's going on down there?" Brooke gestured to the calm that had taken over the tarmac now that Brickham was on his way to the palais. "Not the way I roll and you know it. But what *does* fire up my blaster bank? Knowing you were likely in here chapping your sister's hide before totally hearing her out." She stepped over, driving a knuckle into Syn's bicep with wince-wielding precision. "So do it, damn it."

"A very good idea."

The endorsement was brandished by Jagger, who had been notably quiet since Samsyn came on board. Syn eyed his lieutenant with eyes turned to slits, resurrecting the competitive energy that sometimes rose between them. Jayd had wondered about that stuff for a while, even exploiting it back in the day when she toyed with a few flirtations with Jagger.

But needling Samsyn had been less important than supporting Jag after she learned his deeper secrets, which were not so subterfuge now. As Jagger stepped forward, he kept one hand firmly clasped with that of Ozias Demos, the obvious center of his world.

"I will stand for Maximillian Brickham on the weight of my honor in Your Highness's service," he declared.

"Bloody oath, that," Oz inserted. "He's giving it to you straight, mate—ermmm, Highness." As soon as Syn scowled, the Aussie persisted, "Come on, man. You and I have dined on a lot of dirt in a lot of trenches together. You know this isn't my sunshine up your anus, Samsyn."

Her brother growled. "I want nothing from you up my anus, Demos—sunshine or otherwise."

"Fuck me," Jayd muttered.

"Creator help us all," Brooke said at the same time. As soon as she bopped Syn again, he pushed out a heavy sigh.

"Fine," he gritted. "Set me right, then. I seem to be missing some important details here." His stare stayed glued on Oz. "You had a safe house secured in Paris, right?"

Oz pulled in a breath through flared nostrils. "Since you were paying the tab on it, you likely already know that answer."

"So Brickham had one job after he delivered Jayd to that door. To help you keep my sister secure until you were able to arrange a smooth exit out of the city."

Poor Oz. He was all but squirming in place. "I believe we're all on *that* same page, yes," he said cautiously.

"So why the *hell* was he dragging her into a bar in Pigalle, well past midnight—"

Jayd stomped forward. "You mean why was he letting *me* drag *him* in there?"

"Not a detail that helps his case, *fembla*. The man was supposed to be sheltering you, not following you to some seedy *tavane*, where you were fully exposed to every manner of gutter flotsam in the city—"

"You mean like Trystan Carris?"

"Also not helping his case, sister."

She gritted her jaw. "You know what else would have been bad for his case, *rerda?* Allowing me to go out to that meeting by myself—because in that moment, I was stupid and desperate enough to believe Louis LaBarre had actually sent that message himself and meant every one of those sweet words. I would have gotten on the train and met that drug-addled lizard in the ghetto, if that is what he asked."

Oz resolidified his own stance. "Brick made the same call I would have picked. He could've tried tying down the princess, along with chaining every window in the apartment, or going with her on the hope that she'd get what she actually came to Paris for."

For the first time, Jayd was grateful for her brother's fume. As Syn wound up a comeback, she seized the chance to drop her head and hide every pore that broke out in a furious blush. Okay, Brickham had not officially *tied her down,* but the reference was still too close for comfort.

And Creator's toes, how she missed all her lover's deliberate *dis*comforts…

"Fine," Syn finally muttered. "The tactical logic makes sense. And there was no way of knowing, given the short notice, how far Carris was willing to slither for this win."

"All the way up the Paris Prefecture's chain of command, apparently," Jagger inserted, twisting his lips.

"Which still makes no damn sense," Brooke replied. "At a federal level, we enjoy a healthy relationship with France's forces. Why didn't those choads think to—hmmm, let's see—maybe pick up the phone and call Syn directly about everything?"

Oz tick-tocked his head a couple of times, shoulder to shoulder. "Might've crossed *our* minds a few times, out on the tarmac at Bourget."

"But there was not exactly a pause to stop for a full debrief at that point," Jagger added. "Considering the lead confetti we were dodging, courtesy of our *friends* in the Gendarmerie."

Jayd shot him a warning glance, hoping he caught her meaning. His snark was blooming in not-so-small proportions—not a wise selection of composure, given the thin rail upon which Syn was already skating. *Damn it, Jag. Please think of other things. Puppies. Pies. The power loader scene from* Aliens. *Making out with your boyfriend…*

"So we do apologize, Highness. We were a little

preoccupied with ensuring your sister was shepherded to safety without a bullet in her skull. Only a few small priorities to juggle there, right?"

Damn it, really? The guy knew the power loader scene by heart. But so much for Jag listening to her telepathic hint.

And so much for hoping Syn was going to be less of a raging *bonsun* about it.

"Do. You. Actually. Dare?" His face, following his wife's prediction, became the timeline photo for Ogres-R-Us. "*Do you* dare, *cheeky* soldask*?* You, the sneaky fuck who abetted my sister's flight from this island to begin with?"

Creator's mercy. That was just it.

Jayd let the ire in her belly fill the fists she shoved at her brother's chest. "He abetted nothing, damn it. He *helped* me because he is my friend and I was getting no answers from anyone—answers that should have been coming from you, Evrest, and Shiraz! Instead, Ev locked all the files away as if I were seven again, begging to watch George Romero instead of Nickolodeon. At the same time, you and 'Raz were practicing on the war drums and rallying your troops for violent antics I do not want to know about."

Syn snorted. It was less ogre and more stubborn ox this time, not that the new image altered Jayd's ire. "*Mmmph.* Antics," he repeated. "Now listen here. I do not engage in *antics,* sister. I am not some child, playing with—"

"A plastic toy?" She dropped her fists but arched her brows. "Then stop treating me like one."

"I am not—"

Brooke slid in, planting a hand between the slabs of Syn's chest. "Would you let her finish at least one freaking thought?"

The woman, obviously well-versed in dealing with

hotheaded Cimarrons, even shaved off some of Jayd's vexation.

"I may have spent much time looking like a dressed-up doll, but Syn, I *am* a human being. The human being you are still calling sister—for which I am deeply grateful—but a person just the same, with thoughts and reactions and feelings. Feelings that were mired in lost confusion last week after Trystan and Fortin Santelle left the palais."

So much for the gentler emotions. Just mentioning that afternoon, now seeming much further away than five days ago, pushed stubborn tears behind her eyes. She was able to knock them back by notching her chin half an inch higher.

"I needed answers," she asserted. "*So many answers,* brother. And waiting around for someone to offer them was not appearing like the brightest idea."

Samsyn jerked up his own jaw. "So you picked the most perilous one instead?"

"All right, then. Tell me what *you* would have done. Paced around in your gilded tower, hoping someone would show up to tell you Evrest had finally given in and promised twenty years of your life to a Pura *prispoul*? Or that he had opted to give up his throne entirely? Would you have laid your delicate head on your downy pillow, entertained by the possibility that your *other* brother was likely concocting plans for a civil war because of it?"

His gaze, already the shade of a storm on the sea, intensified. "Not one of those has happened!"

"Not *yet.*"

"So you still have no trust in your brothers? You do not believe we were working as hard as we could for a reasonable solution to the crisis? Something *besides* those catastrophes?"

"I am not a seer, Samsyn. How would I know what you

three were doing except for what my logic informed me? None of you were *communicating* with me. I had very few alternatives left to explored."

She was baiting the ox, tempting him to become a full bull, and she knew it. But the fires in Syn's eyes now told her something else too. She was pushing on his truth. The very heart of it. That was why she did not flinch when Brooke shifted forward, speaking into the silence in his stead.

"You could have come to me," the warrior princess offered. "I thought we were more than relatives, Jayd. I'd do anything for you, as your sister *and* friend."

"Indeed?" Jayd folded her arms. "Including keeping the secret about my plans, even to the man you work and sleep with?"

The question mark was a silly addition. She already knew that answer, and Brooke did too.

Still, the woman murmured, "We could've found a better way."

"Concepts that do not matter now," Samsyn muttered. He reached up for the bulkhead, stretching his uniform tight over his massive chest. "Much like me grilling her about why the fuck Brickham was brought here."

Brooke rolled her eyes. Jayd barely held back from grabbing for both her brother's orbs and tossing them to the birds on the tarmac. But what would that accomplish? It was the *imbezak's* pompous tongue that fed her fury so steadily.

"Have you listened to anything we have just relayed to you?" she spewed. "Jagger, Ozias, and myself? Brickham risked his life for mine! And not just that one time on the tarmac at Bourget. The information in the media is not even half the story. Damn it, Syn! You of all people should know—"

"And he does." Brooke again, inserting a tone of reason when it was most needed. "And for what it's worth, I do too. I really believe you, Jayd. About all of it."

"You do?" It was pathetic and desperate, but she cared not. She needed the balm on her severely bruised spirit.

"Senator's daughter, remember?" her sister-in-law said. "Ratings points, story spins, and viral posts were like milk on our morning cereal. The media can be your best friend or your worst enemy. And as long as we're on *that* subject"—she swung her gaze toward Oz and Jag—"do you guys have any clue about where Carris could be slinking now?"

While the guys shook their heads with remorse that could not be feigned, Samsyn decided to try some of his humanity on for size. "Well, the man is a mongrel, and those filthy beasts eventually get their due," he reassured to everyone. "I have called in some extra favors across Paris, hoping to rouse the proper hounds for the job. They all relocated to the city for reasons that would not have me entrusting them with a search for my sister, but this is different."

Brooke frowned. "How so?"

"This time, I do not care if they kill the target." His rough grunt was hardly necessary for punctuation. Her brother was serious and everyone knew it. He growled harder before going on. "What I am more concerned about is containment. Those gutter dogs love their gossip more than all the palais hens combined. But I have also offered ample compensation to those who can supply us with the right whispers about Carris's escapades. Let us be like the rubber tree plant and have high hopes that it buys some discretion, as well."

Thankfully, Brooke chuckled on behalf of them all. "Yo mister . . . you mean an ant, right?"

"Ants?" Samsyn jolted as if she told him a velociraptor had landed behind him. "What? Where? Are they the big red fuckers? Damn it, Brooke. *Where?*"

As Brooke gave her husband a calming hug and a full explanation of his misquoted song, Jayd yearned to indulge the same laughs as everyone else. Instead, her belly twisted tighter and her head ached worse. She hated this. Hated how *her* damning secret was reducing her big, bold brother into a stress ball who freaked about ants.

It was not fair. Nor acceptable.

Conclusions that lent new boldness to her tongue.

"All right. What if we took discretion out of the picture? I mean it," she insisted, knocking back at Syn's incredulous glower. "What if we just stopped all this silly secrecy and beat the Pura at their own game? Right now?"

Amazing, how her brother could narrow his stare but pack a harder wallop with it. "By doing exactly what?"

"You know what," she countered. "By breaking the news ourselves."

His expression got darker. Struck back harder. "Are you fucking *fougin*?"

"Seriously?" Brooke's new stance was just as stubborn. "She might be the only one who isn't. Just lock down the frown, Cimarron, and listen to her for a second. Is it that crazy to think about taking back the control on this from the Pura *without* flying bullets? I mean, do you think those assholes aren't already expecting you to storm their bunkers? So that means they've already stowed the originals of their documents in other places. So guess where that lands everyone after you're all done taking target practice at each other?"

"Sounds like square one to me." Ozias offered the sanction,

though he embellished it with a deferential shrug. "Not that I don't enjoy a good brass-up from time to time. But in this case, seems the dirty laundry on open hangers is better than leaving it in the closet to grow mold."

Syn scrubbed a hand down his face. "And if that dirt strips my sister of her title? What about her standing in the palais? In the hearts of the whole kingdom?"

Jagger weighed in with his own rough grunt. "And I thought the Palais Players were the only melodramatic ones." His sanguine smirk took over fast enough. "With all due respect, Highness, Jayd's place in her people's heart is secure."

"And you know this fact?" Samsyn challenged. "Had time to do a casual poll while you were out and about in Paris these last few days?"

"I simply know that your citizens are not fools. None of this was Jayd's direct fault, and surely the Arcadian people would understand that. They would listen if you explain things and are transparent about the story. Creator's toes, she has been as blindsided by this as you, Ev, and 'Raz. As for her rightful place in the palais, or even as a legitimate Cimarron princess anymore, I cannot say. There are likely some official policies about all that . . ."

"There are," Syn inserted. "In dusty old books, as fragile as the dead bones of their creators."

"More outdated rules than the Pura is fighting to uphold," Jagger groused.

Samsyn tilted his stare back at Jayd. "Right now, if we went public about this, you would have to move out of the palais. Your crown, and all its privileges, could not go with you. You would become a commoner."

"Albeit a well-loved one," Jag reiterated.

Jayd emulated her brother's pose, without his growly tone. "Actually, that sounds quite lovely."

"Fuck," her brother spat. "Creator help me."

And there went her concerted effort to be nice. "I think the Creator needs your breath for assistance on better matters," she volleyed. "In case it has missed your attention, I got all the way to Paris and survived there without you for more than a day. Without Ev, 'Raz, or a hundred keepers, either. "

"And have returned with a criminal within an inch of INTERPOL's watch list."

"His name is Maximillian Brickham." Now she was done trying to be civil, as well. "And if you call him a criminal one more time, I shall remind you of the truth by carving it across your testicles."

She could have declared she was piloting the plane back to Paris and get a less stunned stare from Samsyn. Though he had always been more demonstrative than Ev or 'Raz, the reaction was more than she expected and doubly satisfying to savor.

Good thing she did, since the moment was over as soon as Brooke interceded again. "As a high-stakes interest holder in the future of those gonads, I'm calling recess on you both." She clamped a hand over the ball of Syn's shoulder. "Big Cimarron, it's time for some rest." And then over Jayd's. "Little Cimarron, same for you." Her gaze swung to Jag, Oz, and Requiemme. "And you three, as well—but Emme, only after the infirmary rechecks your knee. What the hell happened, anyway?"

Requiemme Farre, the lady's maid brave enough to accompany Jayd on her quest to Paris, gave Brooke a jittery smile. "A long tale, Your Highness."

A very long tale.

Four quick words that stood for eons of events and a

thousand different meanings. Not even a week had passed since her life had been upended, but Jayd felt years older. Like she had returned home as a new person.

In many ways, she was.

In one important way, she definitely was.

But for now, that was her secret alone. No matter how badly she wanted to sit down with Emme or Jag, or maybe both, and confess about every beautiful, passionate moment she had shared with Brickham, her life was still perched on shifting sands. The man who had taken her to the stars was now riddled with bullets. He had followed her into a trap, yet her own brother was ready to lock him in the palais dungeons. He had saved her life, only to have his hunted by half the world.

And the *bonsun* responsible for all of it was still roaming free.

She had to fix this.

She *would* fix it.

She had no idea how, but she was positive about one place to start. Certainly not arguing with her brother in the middle of the Sancti tarmac. Wrong place, wrong time.

And in so many ways, the wrong brother.

After faking acquiescence with Brooke's demand for detente with Syn, she waited until Emme was loaded into a non-emergency medical vehicle and then climbed into a smaller van with Jag and Oz.

Only then, alone in the car's back row, did she finally slip out her phone. The battery indicator was reading red, but she prayed the power held out long enough for her text to reach Evrest.

Can we please talk? As soon as possible?

CHAPTER TWO

Max Brickham rarely remembered his dreams. That was probably by choice, since most of them wound up being nightmares. As a result, he'd trained his mind to ditch its subconscious adventures the second he woke up.

But this slumber sojourn wasn't going to go gently into the good night. Not by a fucking longshot.

He was holding Jayd Cimarron. The woman who, in the space of one night, had etched herself deeper into his psyche than any female with whom he'd tiptoed into more extended arrangements. By extended, he meant longer than a month. And *arrangements* were in the form of paper contracts with club submissives who understood he'd focus on them inside Bastille's walls only. Seattle was a major city, but the kink world was a smaller universe inside it. Bleeding boundaries weren't his thing.

He'd bled a lot for Jayd already. Outside and in.

And holy fuck, how he craved another hemorrhage.

So in his dream world, he clutched her too damn tight and too damn close. He kept doing it, even knowing they were about to say goodbye for once and for all. The wind was warm but sharp across Bourget's tarmac, making her huddle closer against him. He gripped back, inhaling the mist and myrrh of her hair, the honey and amber of her skin.

Fuck.

He had to fight the pull of her. Needed to keep his shit

together. He'd already been through this a thousand times. This was no different than muting his growling stomach while hiding from the Seattle truancy teams or pretending he didn't care about sleeping outside when Cashmere and Zelda had clients for the night. Like then, he forced himself to remember the same ancient adage.

It could be worse.

Except now, with his pixie's whisper at his neck. With her little body in his arms. With her arms latched so desperately around him.

Worse didn't feel so far away anymore. It was right the hell here, in the heaviness of his heart and the pain of each breath.

That was before the dream became a nightmare.

With the lights and the noise, the shouts and the blasts. And then—

Oz?

It was Demos all right, yelling something about Christmas. And juice.

Things were muddled after that. Jayd disappeared. He heard her voice, but that was it. He was lost. No. Worse. He was lost and lachrymose. And shit, did his head hurt. But that pain wasn't as awful as the anguish. It was overwhelming…

Until the next bizarre cameo in his head.

Asha was there.

What the hell?

The girl didn't look anything like he remembered. She was no longer lying in the Afghanistan cave in which they'd been imprisoned. Her big brown eyes were happy, not fading from the wound she'd gouged into her own chest.

He reached for her but couldn't seem to get near. That didn't seem to upset her, so he chilled out too. Suddenly, they were above ground in Bamiyan, and they were going over the plan for how he'd smuggle her out of the shithole. She was thanking him for the hundredth time, and he was telling her to save it until they got to the other side.

She replied with words that made no sense.

But Brickham . . . I am *on the other side.*

He shook his head, baffled by what she meant.

I am here and I am happy, all right? And you do not have to worry about me anymore.

But he did exactly that. Still consumed by confusion, he lunged for her again. She'd already disappeared. The chaos and noise were back again. And the pain. Holy fuck, the pain.

Bourget. He was on the tarmac at—

But he wasn't.

He was in a plane, but then not. He was on a stretcher, but then not. There *was* on a tarmac at some point, but Paris was no longer on the horizon. There were palm trees and flowers and an ocean . . .

What the hell?

What the hell?

What the—

"Hell?"

He jolted as if someone had dunked him in ice water. He jerked his eyes open, only to slam them shut just as fast.

"Shit!"

Light. Once more, way too much of it. But it was accompanied by a breeze that smelled like a trip to Fantasy Island. Palm trees and freesia, ocean salt and cloves. Damn. If Asha had really been walking him up to heaven, the place smelled better than he'd anticipated.

It looked different too. *A lot* different.

After several heavy blinks, attempting to moisten the three-ton potato chips doing service as his eyelids, he was able to focus on his surroundings.

Not a tarmac.

He was in a bedroom. A damn fancy one. Not the-sheik-on-steroids kind of fancy. More like old money meeting new but not needing to broadcast that fact. None of it matched the medical monitoring equipment to which he was tethered in several places. But he didn't linger long on the anomaly. There was still a hell of a lot to figure out here. Or so he'd try.

He was resting against a dozen downy pillows in a bed that could easily accommodate a Hummer. Maybe two. The thing's four posts were wrapped in flowy white fabric that matched the drapes in front of the massive windows, waving gently with the crisp wind off the water. To his left, a wide stone archway led to a stone balcony with bougainvillea-wrapped columns. Beyond the balustrades was an endless ocean, looking like blue satin encrusted with a million diamonds. As if on cue, a pod of dolphins cavorted by.

At once, an important recognition hit.

He'd been asking the wrong question. No way could this be hell.

Then where exactly was he?

"Ah. You are awake. Thank fuck for small miracles."

Maybe he'd tossed off that hell theory too fast.

Between the mountain of a human who stalked into the room and the take-no-prisoners look across the guy's formidable features, that much was adding up just as quickly. And much too accurately.

"Define awake."

He felt safe enough about rasping the jibe, which was

only half a joke. He'd been beat to a pulp on many occasions, for reasons both noble and nasty, and felt only slightly worse than this. He was fairly certain that wasn't the case this time, though the exact details were fuzzy. Logic wasn't giving him any hints. He was housed like a sultan but being glared down like a convict.

Shit...

"Fair question," the giant muttered, bypassing a couple of nearby chairs to reposition himself at the foot of the bed. Of course. Establishing more control by maintaining his elevation. "Since my surgeon dug three bullets out of you just as many days ago."

"Three bullets? Just as many d—" He choked, reaching for a cup of water on the plastic tray nearby. After glugging the liquid, he managed, "Okay, what the actual fuck?"

The hulk barely flinched either brow. "What is the last thing you remember?"

Brick ignored him with matching intention. "Three days," he muttered. "Shit."

"*What* do you remember?"

"Okay, okay. I heard you." But could he trust the stranger? The inquisition certainly wasn't small talk. Then again, he wasn't even cuffed to the bed. Maybe the guy already knew that moving more than an inch was like inviting a thousand knife throwers to take target practice through his gut. And his left arm. And his head. *Damn it,* his head.

But he had to try the whole remembering thing. For both their sakes.

"Paris," he stammered. "Yeah. I was there... helping a friend out."

"Ozias Demos."

He took a chance on lifting his gaze, grimacing against the ruthless glint off the sea. "That's right." No harm in declaring what the guy obviously knew.

"He asked for your assistance in locating Princess Jayd Cimarron."

Jayd.

It killed him, physically and mentally, to keep his reaction sheathed this time. So help him God, if this dickhead was in cahoots with Trystan Carris and had handed her into that asshole's hands . . .

"You care about her."

He didn't waste more seconds playing dumb. It'd only piss off the not-so-jolly giant, and he still had no idea who the fucker was. Worse, who he was working with or for.

"She was the asset. I found her. That's it."

"Bullshit."

Brick chuckled. Good Christ, it hurt. "Oh, goodness me. Thank God I don't have any state secrets to spill. Ooo, you're so big and frightening, I might just tell you *everything*."

The guy flared his nostrils. Beyond that, there was no sign Brick had tread on sensitive territory. The observation was weirdly frightening.

"I do not have time for *everything*," he countered. "But I *do* have all the fucking time in the world to hear why my little sister threatened me with interesting physical harm while defending your honor."

And there went all the good intentions of holding on to his poker face. Fortunately, his surprise from the hulk's first revelation covered well for his second. "Your little sister. Well, damn. Jayd is your—" He peered around with fresh focus. "Jayd is your sister, and this . . . is Arcadia."

His new friend cocked his head. "You do not remember anything at all about getting here?"

He dared half a smirk. "Remember that whole *define awake* question?"

"Fair point."

The guy's small olive branch had Brick examining the giant with new understanding. "You're Samsyn," he said. "Right? The brother who runs the security forces. We called you on our way out of Paris."

Hell's fucking bells. He wanted to clock himself for not seeing it sooner. The soldier's hair, tumbling over his shoulders, was the same mix of black and mahogany as Jayd's. He had a bolder nose than his sister, but their proud jawline was strikingly similar. Most blatantly, he stood with the same noble posture that she did—right before emulating her gift for noble indignation.

"Were you listening in?" he demanded.

"Were you not aware we *all* were?" Brick returned. "To our side, at least," he qualified. "We were in an SUV, buddy, not a private jet. Not until Bourget, anyway."

Once the declaration was out, some switch in his brain got flipped. Memories tumbled in, one after the other, exploding with fire and urgency and violence.

"Fuck," he grated. "Bourget."

And then fear. Holy crap, so much fear. Thankfully, there were more thoughts on top of that. Anxieties that hogged all the normal placeholders for panic attacks. "Christ," he blurted. "Is everyone okay? I mean, did everyone . . ." He slouched back into the bank of pillows. "Sorry." He pushed out a shallow cough. "Everything just hit me now. Goddamned PTA."

Post-traumatic amnesia. It wasn't anything to be fucked

with. He of all people should know. After they'd hauled him out at Bamiyan, it had taken a full twenty-four hours for him to remember everything. Even then, the PTA had hit him in strange little spurts.

Nothing about the shit at Bourget came back as a spurt.

But now, the odds were different. Now, the odds involved Jayd.

"Understandable." Another small truce token from the prince at the end of the bed. "And partially relatable."

The prince provided no more details. Fine by Brick. Every soldier had their secrets, some more easy to stow than others. So far, he'd been able to get along with the occasional ghosts of Bamiyan with the help of magic tablets in a nifty orange bottle—that was now thousands of miles away, in his abandoned room at the Ritz Paris. While he was certain the panic would mind its manners as long as the Arcadian doctors were keeping him full of pain meds, he had no concrete plan for what to do after that.

Shit, shit, shit.

Or maybe not.

Hopefully, he was correctly interpreting Samsyn Cimarron's new scowl. The expression that said this island's security commander wanted him on a plane back out of here as soon as humanly possible.

Once again, fine by him. But not just because leaping dolphins and hibiscus breezes couldn't take the place of his medication. There was only one thing on this island remotely capable of accomplishing that.

Only one *person.*

The woman he didn't dare touch again. Didn't take the chance of ever seeing again.

"Jayd."

For that matter, outlawing her name from his head was probably a good idea too. But he'd consider that only after this part. The most vital part of all.

"She's okay?" he asked Samsyn. "Just let me know that. I won't pray about anything else. I got her on the plane. I recall that much. But those bastards from the tarmac… They didn't…"

"No," the warrior replied. "They did not. She was tired and bruised in a few places, but she arrived in one piece. Physically, at least."

His pause before those last three words wasn't lost on Brick. Nor was the slight lift of the man's right eyebrow.

"Meaning what?" Wasn't it best to just cut to the chase? If he made Samsyn dick around with coy hints, they might be here until fucking midnight.

"Oh, that is definitely for *you* to tell *me*, Mr. Brickham," the prince replied smoothly.

"Meaning *what*?" Brick spat. "You're not really Sherlocking all over me on this because your baby sister had a fleeting crushie-crush on her rescuing knight, right? You know how this stuff happens, man. Shit goes down, adrenaline kicks in, endorphins go wild. She'll get over it. She probably already has."

He had no way of knowing if the explanation worked. Seemed Samsyn *was* jonesing to be cagey about things, dragging out one moment and then the next while pacing back to the side of the bed.

"Yes. Probably," the guy finally answered. "Which thoroughly explains *that*, yes?"

Brick followed the guy's directional nod upward, toward

a far corner of the room. The spacious nook housed three black-and-white security monitors. One screen displayed the wide, empty balcony outside the bedroom. The second was a random hallway, which Brick assumed to be the chamber's outer corridor. It was also empty.

But the third monitor wasn't.

It showed another angle of the same hallway. Walking along it, looking five thousand kinds of gorgeous in a long silky dress, was his beautiful little Pixie. She was smiling, even radiant. She was also in a hurry.

"That makes her third visit today," Samsyn offered. "On top of the five she paid you yesterday."

Brick swallowed. Couldn't be helped. But his answering tone could be. "Huh. Well, she's got a good soul," he rushed out. "Probably just worried. Once she sees I'm fine, she'll move on."

Samsyn grunted softly. "From her . . . *crushie-crush*."

Thank God he had fake chortles down to an art form. "Right? You *do* get it, then."

"Of course." The guy flashed a just-between-us-bros kind of look. It was weirdly freakish. "I have certainly had my fair share of a few of those," the prince remarked. "This one female, in particular . . . I would even say that her crushie-crush extended into a smashie-smash."

"Yikes." Brick frowned and meant it. "How did you handle it?"

Samsyn angled his head down again—this time to bore his gaze directly into Brick's. His pupils were darker than his sister's—and as intense as his low, firm reply.

"I married her."

CHAPTER THREE

As Jayd approached the door to Brickham's room in the infirmary wing, she ordered her lungs to take in full breaths. Maybe the measured air would help to slow the wild gallops of her heartbeat and lend to the sophisticated air of the dress she had carefully picked out for this moment. Granted, her selection process for the garment was about more than impressing Brickham, though that goal never left the top of her list.

But rounding out the list were many more intentions.

No. She had to be honest about this. Not intentions. They were more like reactions. Peeved ones.

Funny how the attitudes of three "caring" brothers could do that to a girl.

She was certain their hearts had been in the right places—at *some* point. But from the moment she had reentered the palais three days ago, to be greeted by Ev and 'Raz together, her nerve endings were turned into spooked porcupine quills. Their high noon standoff had *not* been the goal of her text from the tarmac, which had been to steal a quiet heart-to-heart with Ev.

After the ambush in the vestibule, they escorted her into one of the high council's conference rooms. Sure enough, several members of the island's chief governance body were already waiting inside—which had turned her quills to icicles. She was positive she would be shown right back out the door, but their surprise was larger than that. They wanted to grill her about everything that had happened in Paris. More specifically, about what had happened with *Brickham* back in Paris. By then, they had obtained more observation footage than what the media had. Much more than what the cameras at the pub had picked up.

Creator help her, so much more.

From a roof across the narrow passage in Montmartre, they saw her and Brick ducking into the doorway at the hidden sex club.

From a spot near the Moulin Rouge windmill, they saw him tugging at her close in the middle of Place Blanche, his face nuzzled into the back of her neck.

From a desktop camera in the undertaker's office at the Montmartre Cemetery, they watched him break into the office and then help her do the same.

As they replayed each piece of footage, one conclusion had become increasingly clear. They had already tossed their eggs into the same basket as Samsyn's. The basket engraved with Brickham's name, filled with the eggs decorated in a single word.

Guilty.

She had not remained in that conference room for long. What good would it have done? She left her brothers there, with their assumptions that their sister had fallen for some charlatan spy and not a selfless warrior who had given her the world in one night, and aimlessly paced her chambers while waiting for word of Brickham's progress.

Sometime, in those seemingly endless hours, she had gone to her closet and pulled out this dress from the back. She had done so in anticipation of this exact moment. The dark azure garment was more fitted on top than she normally wore, with a deep V neck that descended into layers of fluid skirts. Those were the dress's ultimate deception. Only a few of the gauzy panels were actually sewn together. That meant, if she moved the right way, she had the opportunity to expose a great deal of her legs.

And perhaps, if Brickham liked it, a lot more.

Oh, how she prayed he would like it.

How she wanted to know, at last, if everything they had shared in Paris was not just a collection of random memories for him. Not all the running and hiding and shooting and fear, of course. But everything else. Absolutely everything else.

Every electric tangle of their gazes.

Every wet mesh of their lips.

Every frantic fusion of their bodies.

By the Creator and all his angels, especially that.

All the moments she had ordered herself to toss away as they had raced to the outskirts of Paris. With every mile they had gotten closer to the tarmac at Bourget, she'd focused on pushing all those stolen moments to similar environs of her mind. Not all the way out, because she already recognized that impossibility, but far enough away that her spirit would cease panging from them and her heart would stop demanding more of them.

But then the world itself had exploded.

And mere minutes later, as bullets ricocheted off the hull of the private jet that Samsyn had arranged for them, a new realization had drilled into her.

Brickham was going home with her.

Which meant the memories no longer had to hide.

For the last three days, she had practically been living on

them. They had been her strength during the days, her succor during the nights, her hope for the agonizing transitions between each.

But none of them compared to the pure wonder of this moment. Of walking into the room and finally getting to embrace the joy of her reality again.

He was truly awake. And even sitting up!

She took her same path in from the door, nearly a direct line to his bedside, but had to halt after three steps. That was the instant Brickham turned his head.

And their eyes met.

A moment she had been fully preparing her senses for—or so she had thought.

She was *not* ready. Not by the smallest fraction. The truth . . . it bared her in a thousand unseen ways. The miracle was filled with so many more details. The sculpted magnificence of his torso against the bed's downy pillows. The rough glory of his thick stubble. The proud lift of his formidable jaw. The powerful pierce of his oceanic blues.

"Brickham." She finished with a gulp. It hurt in all the best ways. Not the same during all the moments that crept by, weaving an increasingly uncomfortable silence between them.

"I—they told me you were awake and talking." Uncomfortable became unnerving. "I had to come see for myself."

Thank the saints, that part was less of a stutter. She also managed to leave off the part about leaping up in the middle of lunch with Camellia, her brother's wife and anointed queen, once she received the update text from the infirmary medic. After a fast stop in her chambers to slip into the special dress, she had almost taken the hallways at a full sprint.

"Your Highness Jayd." His voice was a little scratchy, but his unmistakable undertone of command was still there. "Forgive me for not standing, but under the circumstances…"

Oh, yes, still completely there, despite his gruff attempt at a laugh. Creator's toes, how she longed to join him in that blessed insertion of mirth, and then use it as a gateway to letting more of his energy flow through more of her.

But she was not the only one in the room who had heard the man's rumbling nuance. The fierce grooves that appeared between Samsyn's brows proved that already.

Damn it.

"Mr. Brickham." She wrapped her own tone in irritation while throwing a terse glance toward her brother. "That is not necessary, and you know it."

A beat of silence. Two more. Neither man moved, though she finally looked over at Samsyn again.

"Brother."

"What?"

"Surely you have someplace else to be now?"

Syn stiffened, clearly ready with a retort. But, thank the Creator, a procession of pings broke out from the radio on his hip instead.

"Fuck." Syn eyed the message in the radio's window. While replacing the device into its belt holder, he was equally concise about the look he gave Brickham. "I will make it back later. We can pick up the conversation from there."

Three seconds and a matching number of strides later, he was gone.

Jayd regarded the closing door, debating whether to let out the next words in her head. Perhaps it would be all right if she forced a lighthearted laugh first. "And what conversation might *that* be?"

But her smile faded fast, as soon as Brickham averted his gaze. Since he did it while she closed the remaining space to the bed, she was not hesitant about her new expression.

"He basically asked me what was going on between us."

"He—*what*?" It was as sharp as her backside plunking to the mattress. Thank the stars every bed in the infirmary had extra-firm foam toppers.

"Not in those exact words," Brickham offered. "Not yet, at least."

Jayd twisted her lips to the point of pain. "How can he *think* to possess such gall? I was already clear with the *prispoul*. Brooke backed me up!"

She craved an answer to that less than an explanation about her bigger worry. Why was Brick handling this with the tranquility of a mystic on meth? All right, some of the tubes in his arms were feeding him decent pain inhibitors, but he was speaking coherently—and now, even cocking a lucid grin at her.

"He actually led off by mentioning that fun little reunion you two shared. Something about turning his balls into your arts and crafts project—using my initials?"

She could not tell if he was being admiring or admonishing. The mystery was no help for her irritation. "He was being an utter *imbezak*. Branding you before he knew you. Taking the news feeds as fact instead of believing me, Jagger, *and* Oz about—"

"Whoa. Hold up." His calm countenance was suddenly, violently eclipsed. Though Jayd was used to such ferocity across his bold features, she had only ever watched the storm take over him in stages. This was an alarming tempest. "News feeds? They took the story wide?"

A new gulp thudded down her throat. *Damn it.* Why had she gone and spouted off without thinking about it? Of course Brick knew naught of the media's shenanigans over the last few days—and instead of breaking it to him with care, she had become the man's cardio shock paddle. One glance at the leaping lines on his bedside monitor were awful proof.

"How wide?"

As he asked it, the electric jolts bounced higher.

"Across Europe?"

Then faster.

Jayd's heart rate lurched the same direction. Her chest was a hollow tympany. Sweat broke out on her forehead. But not once did she consider lying to him. Fifteen minutes into their relationship—friendship, partnership, whatever this was—they had been on the run and trapped in a situation both strange and amazing. A circumstance too dangerous for lies. Further, she had given him one of the rawest forms of her honesty. Her orgasm beneath his fingers. Mere hours after that, she had given him her virginity too.

She regretted none of it. Not even now. She did not hold back from letting Brickham see it either. With a determined snap, she lifted her head to directly meet his troubled gaze.

Then she said, "Across the world."

She had not a clue of what to expect for his reaction. Though she was not stunned by the continued neutrality of his face, the intensifying *bleeps* from his monitor conveyed a fuller story.

After another three seconds, they were joined by a loud *whump,* as a medic raced into the room.

"Creator's mercy." The woman's big green eyes were wide and terrified. The sparkling stud in her nose looked ready to pop free. “What on earth is—*oh*!” She skidded to a stop and dropped into a curtsy. “Your Highness Jayd. *Desonnum beaupek*. I had no idea you had arrived in the wing.”

“I am the one with the apologies, Twylah.” She turned, gritting out a smile. “I did not check in with any of you. I was hoping to ease Mr. Brickham’s recovery with a few humorous stories. Seems I might have overdone it a bit.”

“Ermmm...” Twylah sneaked a puzzled glance at Brickham’s thunderous profile as she reset the monitors. “All right, then.”

Jayd grabbed the medic’s hand with a reassuring squeeze. “Thank you for your concern. If we really do need help, I shall hit the call button. But perhaps it is best if you turn off the alarms for now?”

“Of course, Highness.” Twylah’s inflection was friendly but reverent. She was a newer member of the palais medical staff, so she had not yet learned that Jayd and her brothers were only flesh and blood, like everyone else. Jayd started to hope the woman would get it sooner than later, though that depended on just how *much* later. As lovely as the woman was, the infirmary was not Jayd’s facility of choice for casual afternoon hangouts. As soon as Brickham could be safely moved out of here, she planned on making it happen.

Better plans and higher hopes for a later time.

Definitely after she could properly clean up *this* mess.

As soon as Twylah was gone, she directed her remorseful grimace to Brickham. “I was not tactful about that. I am very sorry about the bomb.”

She reached over and nestled her hand atop his.

He pulled away at once.

So now they were even on the bombs.

"Nothing to be sorry about," he said past tight lips. "Sometimes it's just good to open the curtains and let the light in."

The analogy fit. Jayd was speared by emotions that might as well be blinding lights. Frustration and fury. Sadness and helplessness. Weirdly, not even losing her father to Trystan's bullet had felt this desolate. But in reality, she had only known Louis LaBarre for a few moments. No matter what, she would carry Maximillian Brickham in her soul for a lifetime.

But she refused to let Brick see all that. What good would it do him now? She had better information for him. More useful truths.

"All right, then. Here is more light." She leaned over, leaving her abandoned hand right where it was. "All three of my brothers believe *your* side of the story."

He grunted. "How magnanimous of them."

"You could say that," Jayd volleyed, "since they are not men of idle commitments." She paused, letting her censure set in. It was petty, but he was not giving *her* much to be magnanimous about. Still, she wanted to pierce something helpful into his stubborn gray matter. "Shiraz has a technical team tearing apart the incident video from the bar, as well as every inch of footage from surveillance cameras across Montmartre. Evrest has already reached out to the Prime Minister of France, proposing a special forces alliance in tracking down Trystan and his *soldasks*."

That sparked at least one bolt in his Frankenstein brood. "And that worked?"

She nodded. "Samsyn is also working on some things. He has connections working the Paris underbelly. A number of them have confirmed Trystan was, and still is, allied with some key factions of *Le Milieu*."

"The French mob," Brickham interpreted with a brutal scowl. "Who are comprised of some dangerous motherfuckers. Do they all really know what they're up against here?"

"Enough to be excited about an alliance to take some of them down."

"That's not enough," he snapped. "These are career criminals. They steal rare jewelry and artwork, not slushies at the Shop-n-Gulp. They're into extortion and human trafficking. They recruit *kids*—"

"Brickham." She matched her command to his, not giving him a choice about the hand clasp anymore. "They are not proposing a cut-and-paste operation on the *bonsuns*. And Samsyn may have all the polish of a battering ram sometimes, but he knows the subtleties of criminal minds." She paused and reared back her head. "And why am I *bragging* about that?"

"Goddammit." Brick's expression only got bleaker. "It'd just be easier for him to just turn me back over to the Gendarmerie."

And exactly why did she think her update would *cheer* him? Instead, rage swirled up like a fire funnel, singeing every canyon of Jayd's psyche. She sensed the pressure building, ready to explode all the way out.

And it did.

Two seconds after unhitching her hand from his, she flung it hard across his face.

Her palm stung worse than the backs of her eyes. But her tear ducts caught up as soon as Brickham rendered his reaction. Well, lack of one. Her tears, full of guilt and embarrassment, spilled forth. Dire conflict had her choking on them.

The man had saved her life. Taken three bullets for her.

But did that give him the right to give up now? To be so morose and mad and flippant, discounting his very existence?

"I stood my ground for you." Every word of it came out as a low, thick accusation. "I *ordered* Samsyn to accept your presence here, damn it. I *told* him you were worth the chance. Worth his trust."

"I know." It was a rasp on his lips, defying the new determination in his hold. "And I'm grateful for that, Jayd, but—"

"I stood up to my own brother for you," she bit out. "For *you*, Brickham. Not Jag and Oz's soldier friend who got Emme and me away from those *bonsuns* in that alley. Not the man who became my friend too, who came with me to meet my father, only to be set up by a lunatic and misaligned by the media. I was standing up for both those men, but most of all for the man I truly believed in. The man who, in the space of a few hours, had made me believe in *myself*, in so many new ways. Who made me see myself from different eyes."

"Different eyes."

Brickham's repetition was stripped of her earnest inflection. But his gruffness did not alter his hold in hers. Maybe he had heard her now. Maybe he really understood!

"What if those eyes were looking through mottled glass, Princess?"

Her hope dissolved. Fizzled away in a fresh vat of fury.

Princess. The nickname he had used on her right after they met, painting her in the same derisive colors the rest of the world did. But he had soon re-ordained her as Pixie. Yes, because circumstances had given him no choice—but by the time they ran across the tarmac at Bourget, it was all different. The designation had become his own choice.

Or so she had thought.

So damn stupidly.

"So that is how you want *me* to see things, then?" she rasped. "Is that how you want me to remember everything we said in Paris? Everything we did? Like a distortion? A mistake?"

His lips thinned. "It wasn't a mistake, damn it. *Nothing* about you is a mistake, Jayd."

She stabbed out a bitter laugh. "'Twould seem everything about my life is a mistake, Sir—starting with my birth."

And leading directly to this moment, in which she assumed fate had given them an unexpected gift. The time they had gotten so little of in Paris. Granted, it had come in bizarre wrapping, but she would take it swaddled in barbed wire.

Until Brickham declared it had never been a prize in the first place.

Until his razor line of a jaw and his stiff pylons for shoulders gave glaring proof of that.

Enough proof to push her heart back into aching agony and then her whole body off the bed.

Or so that was the idea.

She had made a huge error, thinking painkillers and stitches would hamper her force of nature. His reflexes were as sharp as the moments he had wrested her from both Gervais and Trystan. But unbelievably, there was twice as much rage across his face. She knew that clearly, considering the man hauled her back all the way against him. Yes, to the point their noses were a centimeter apart. Yes, with her chest slamming down so solidly, he grunted in pain from the pressure on his shoulder wound.

But also to the point that she caught every bright fleck

of light in the depths of his gaze. Flecks that could only be reflections from one source.

Pure steel.

"You are *no* goddamned mistake." His lips were just as taut, with his snarl erupting from the depths of his chest. Jayd flinched without thinking, only to find out her range of motion was not a range at all. Not with Brick's other hand now sprawled at the middle of her back.

"Okay," she uttered, twice as shaky and freshly impatient. What if she was doing him more harm? What if his stubborn dominant side was helping that cause? "*Okay,* Brickham. I heard you. *Unnnhhh!*"

Her gasp became a moan as soon as he snatched at the ends of her hair and twisted it in his fingertips. More anxiety reached in. He was doing that with the hand that corresponded to his wounded shoulder, but nothing changed except the rapid beeps of his fluctuating vitals. Thank the Creator she had told Twylah to turn off the alarms.

"Why don't you try telling me that again, sweet girl?"

The intention behind his challenge was clear. She could not have been more elated.

"I said . . . I heard you fully, *Sir.*"

More low thunder from the center of his chest. More gorgeous gleams in his powerful, persistent stare.

"Hmmm. Better . . . but not quite good enough."

That should have hiked her hackles at once. But his statement, so insolent and even a little judgmental, aroused more than her hackles. So many parts that trembled for him again. That ached for even more of his brutal touch.

That longed, more than anything, to be good for him. *So good . . .*

"How can I be better, Sir?"

She finished with a shallow sigh, which Brickham pulled into himself with slightly parted lips. The sight held her in thrall. Was this really happening? Was he really savoring the very air she breathed?

"Don't just tell me that you heard me, Pixie," he finally said. "Repeat it all back to me. Word for word. 'I am not a mistake.' Say it, girl—and mean it."

Jayd flinched, yearning to rear back. But Brickham barely moved—save for the area directly between his thighs. Though his legs barely shifted, that magnificent part of him certainly did. She would probably not have even noticed the change, if not for how her thigh had fallen against his crotch when he pulled her over. But her awareness was unmistakable now. And unignorable.

And so unquenchable . . .

Which slammed her with more confusion.

He was not flexing down there for her sake, was he? Nor even his. Males, especially those on a cocktail of pain medications, were not able to just turn that kind of thing on and off at will, right? But the fact that he even had it *on* was cause for shock. Granted, the pleasant version of the stuff.

Oh, saints and stars.

Perhaps a little more than pleasant.

For three days, she had committed to *dis*remembering this man's aroused glory. In less than five minutes, her efforts were unraveled. He was not even at full mast yet, but with nothing but his infirmary smock and a couple of sheets between them, her imagination swiftly filled in the rest.

Her imagination . . . and her hope.

"*Brickham.*" She scooted her leg over, fitting it better

against his groin. Despite their fabric separators, his surging cock felt like a baked gavel against her leg. The comparison fit, since his whole face was now filled with judicial pique. She cared not. "Brickham. Sir. How I have missed you."

His sharp intake was nearly synchronized to hers. Nevertheless, he rebutted, "And how you've forgotten what I'll do to you as well? For being this disobedient to a direct order from your Sir?"

"Oh, I have not forgotten." She could not help her impish croon, which originated in the joyous well through her spirit. All of this was like a dream come true, only better. Back in Paris, even her wildest imaginings had not included a plot with Brickham returning to Arcadia with her. Now, her force of nature was not just in her homeland but in her *home*. Better yet, he had brought all the best of their memories from Paris with him. Best of all, he seemed ready to relive them. At least certain parts of his body did.

"Goddammit." His utterance betrayed equal parts confusion and amusement. "What am I going to do with you?"

"I imagine whatever you feel... up to... Sir." She swung up and over until she fully straddled him. Best and worst idea ever, since her most sensitive parts were now slotted so intimately—so perfectly—along his burgeoning length. "The monitor alarms are all off. If you go into full arrest, I'll be right here for the mouth-to-mouth resuscitation efforts."

She preened just a little, proud of her suggestive banter. But it was useless for wiping away the far-off scowl on Brick's face: an expression that had been there since the end of his own growled question. It was so firmly implanted, she restrained another naughty comeback. And then fully dismounted from him.

Something in her instincts, now blaring in place of the silenced monitors, sluiced through her veins like ice.

She climbed the rest of the way off the bed.

"Well, I have provided a personal suggestion for your answer, but it seems you have your own ideas about how this conversation should be going, Sir."

Brickham had the grace to shake his head. "Jayd? What the hell? What are you—"

"Some excellent queries," she returned. "Perhaps you should now ask them of the man in the mirror. Maybe *he* can tell you what to do with me, since my very own ideas do not seem to be the right *fit*."

She was grateful, however morbidly, that Brickham respected her enough not to hide how accurately her comment had landed. He floundered not for some stuttered apology either. The man was direct until it hurt, complete with his unblinking gaze and folded hands. But how did he make the pose look so forceful and alluring, while she still felt like a fidgety school marm?

"Jayd." The supports beneath his tone were as stern as his posture. "I'm sorry, okay? This is all just... unexpected. And complicated. *Really* complicated."

"Complicated." Letting him off the hook for that last mumble was not a mercy she felt like granting. "Of course. I understand."

And if he believed that, she would toss aside princess duties and become an actress. *Gold statuette, here I come.*

Oh, why did she *not* understand?

He had not asked to be brought here. So maybe he truly did not *want* to be here. Maybe he would have preferred being left behind on the tarmac at Bourget, taking his hideous chances with several battalions' worth of the French Gendarmerie. And maybe—all right, quite possibly—he would have survived and escaped.

Which meant *complicated* was probably an understatement in his book.

Which meant she had to accept the truths tucked so conveniently into the corners of her mind.

One: the only reason they met at all was that the man was a contract soldier in the right place at the right time.

Two: he had been treated like a visiting nobleman at the kink club where they went hiding. The club in which he had played her body like a musician with an instrument he knew all too well.

Three: he had not had an easy upbringing, nor even a peaceful adulthood. He carried the mental scars from both. Scars that, in certain places, tore his mind away from reality.

She even wondered if this moment might become one of them—until he uttered, "No, Pixie. I don't think you do understand." His lips twisted. "And if you ever really did, I'd be terrified."

Thankfully, the man was not hoarding all the grimaces in the room. The frustration in Jayd's soul swiftly spread across her face. She unfurled it in full, letting him see every inch as she fought to construct a diplomatic reply to his noble words.

But her heart was nowhere near a benevolent bend. Not when another truth daggered its way into her conscience.

"Terrified." As she paused, waves slammed along the beach below the palais. Funny how similar they sounded to the disappointment drowning her heart. "Well, we cannot have *that* happening."

"Damn it. I'm serious, Jayd."

"Of which I am well aware, Brickham."

"So what's the problem?"

She shifted her weight before nervously tapping a foot. *What is the problem?* Besides how he had pulled her so close, making her beg for more of his addicting touch, before shutting her down with his cryptic crisis of conscience—or whatever this was? Besides how he tried to cover for it with his overprotective puffery instead of his heartfelt truth? Truth he had already given to her, in so many beautiful ways, during their hours in Paris?

But not in every way.

She knew that already. Three nights ago, she had even accepted it. Had signed off on that clear but silent condition, just as Brickham had signed off on hers.

That while they were together, in every way fate had gifted them, they could step free of themselves. Live free of their boxes. Feel everything they craved. Be anyone they wished. She had not just given him her virginity. She had surrendered all her inhibitions and limitations. All the boundaries in which she had been stuffed her whole life by her parents, her brothers, her people.

The box he was now jamming her back into. As fast as he possibly could. She could nearly see his mental packing tape too, at the ready to box her in. On the top of the thing, he might even scrawl a hasty mental note.

Paris Princess Rescue. Clingy. Crazy. This End Up. Keep Sealed!

Well, she would save him the effort. By doing it for herself.

By taking all her hope and anticipation and turning it into packing shreds.

By ripping out her heart and nestling it in the center.

By quickly closing the box around it and sealing it with long lengths of mortification.

Emotion that she somehow managed to strain from her breeze of an answer to the *bonsun*.

"There is no problem, Brickham. Everything is fine. Just . . . fine."

"Fine?" But he was at a full spit, causing her a mental double-take. "Jayd, *damn it*."

But not enough of one to go back to square one with him. To listen to more of the puffery and shallow excuses. She was back in the box now. Could he not see that? And why was it not making him happy? It was what he wanted, right? It was what *everyone* wanted.

She just had to convince her soul of that now.

"Mayhap you should get some rest, Brickham." She congratulated herself at that strong keel, as well. "The afternoon grows long, and the evening will be chilly. I should get out of this dress."

And after that, she would burn it.

CHAPTER FOUR

"Fuck."

It had earned the repetition on Brick's lips. Probably a hundred more too, but he reined it in to the single spew.

"Real slick, asshole," he grumbled to himself.

That had all gone as well as a night mission with broken goggles. Replaying it all in his head was no salve for the feeling. If anything, it made things worse.

Everything is fine, *Brickham.*

Oh yeah, she'd really gone there. But goddammit, he'd been the one to lead her to that path first. He could sit here and fume about that, deflecting blame to his painkillers as well as the three-day nap from which he'd just roused, but he wasn't that brand of dickhead.

But how he *had* handled it was just as shitty.

Jayd hadn't missed a whiff of the stench, either.

"Fuck."

All right, only ninety-nine repetitions now. His frustration was worth the ration. And who was he kidding about that? He was conscious now, which meant the panic was just getting itself dolled up for this tasty feast. Every ingredient was here. A strange new setting. A room he couldn't easily leave. A situation he didn't have a shred of control over. A lot of miles between here and his meds. *A lot* of miles.

Oh, yeah. Any . . . second . . . now . . .

He gritted back the dread as the door opened again.

Goddammit. It was surely Samsyn again, ready to pounce in where their bizarre exchange had left off.

Thankfully, he was wrong. The little nurse Twylah bustled in on him instead. The woman had probably been born with her comforting smile, but it was also clear she'd been kind to Jayd over the last seventy-two hours, so he owed her some surface-level cordiality.

"Hi there. Twylah, right?"

Her smile hitched a little higher. "Yes! Thank you for remembering."

"Still don't think that makes us even on the kindness scale for the week."

She flashed a wry glance while checking his monitor readings. "Oh, indeed. Because you have been such a bear of a patient to tend."

"Spoken like a dedicated nurse," he returned. "But I know a downplay when I hear one. And I have a feeling that in this case, the visitors were more high maintenance than the patient."

"You saved Her Highness Jayd's life. She, as well as the rest of us, are beyond grateful."

"I wasn't referring to the princess."

His rebuttal was clearly not expected. The woman didn't have a free second to conceal her sudden stiffness. "Well, your arrival *has* put King Evrest in an interesting position," she admitted. "Though he has certainly been in those before."

Brick settled deeper against the pillows, absorbing that revelation as the downy cushions cradled him. Once more, he cautiously perused the room, attentive for any details he might've missed on the first sweep. But there were no motion detectors on the door frames, security cams in the corners, or cuff scuffs on the bed rails.

Still, he couldn't be dissuaded from asking, "So am I being detained?"

Twylah startled. "Stars and saints, no! You are a *guest* of Arcadia." Her eyes widened. "Forgive me. I should have made that point clearer, I suppose."

"Fuck. I—ermmm—I mean, *no*, you've been great. Honestly. I was doing some conclusion jumping, just considering the circumstances."

"Perfectly understandable," the nurse soothed before her demeanor perked. "Are you feeling ready to get up for a bit, then? Would you like to sit on the balcony or take a walk around the wing? We probably could not go much farther since the marble floors in the main vestibule have been newly waxed. Her Highness Jayd would skin me alive if you fell—"

"Oh, I wouldn't be too sure about that anymore."

"Pardon?"

"Never mind."

He was glad he'd gotten morose and mumbled that in the direction of his navel. But eventually the acrimony would pass and he'd get to the reward on the other side. The part where he'd be sure about doing the right thing. Nipping this thing with Jayd in the bud before it could shoot up and become a rampant living thing again. But this time, it wouldn't be a planter full of gorgeous Paris roses. It'd be a carnivorous pod thing, ready to swallow them both whole.

He'd made the right call. He had to believe that, even if it was impossible to envision it.

"So . . . not a detainee," he finally said. "Does that mean I can have access to a phone?"

"Absolutely!"

Twylah was all too eager to find a device and get it into his hand, but his original impetus for the request had gone to a weird place. He dwelled in that strangeness for several minutes, staring at the phone like it started to gawk back. In many ways, it probably was.

He wasn't new to the game. He knew this thing was likely hotwired in a bunch of different ways. A gang of Arcadian spy guys were likely in some bunker right now, just waiting for him to dial. Ready to track where he called, whom he asked for, everything they said, and every detectable cadence in their voices…

So why was he letting that matter?

He had to be okay with this. More importantly, he had to be okay if *Jayd* ever listened to this. But not once had he'd lied to her about who—or what—he really was. About how he made his living and had chosen to align his lifestyle.

That didn't mean he'd been totally up-front about it either.

"Fuck it," he muttered, hitting the green button on the device.

If she found out like this, maybe that was for the best. Maybe it would be the agonizing but galvanizing ax into her heart. With any luck, the blade would hack down the pedestal upon which she'd flung him.

He'd just have to deal with the torment of the fall.

Pain he couldn't think about right now. There really was that little thing called his real life to check in on. The staff who'd expected him Stateside by now. Shit, even his house and neighbors—the term being loose, of course. Nobody bothered each other too much on his end of Whidbey, but they did keep casual tabs every once in a while.

There was a familiar musical tone in his ear. He jolted

from his reverie, not recalling having dialed the US country code and the private digits in Seattle. Christ. What kind of a pharmaceutical cocktail were they dripping into him?

"Thank you for dialing the administrative offices of Bastille, a Seattle nightclub for discriminating tastes. Please note that we do not take private playroom reservations via this line. Public dungeon space is available every night on a first-come, first-serve basis. Additionally, new member interviews are only conducted in person, and only after a full application and background check have been completed. If you'd like more information about joining or playing in Bastille, please consult our webs—"

Brick punched the seven key, which was Z's office extension. Despite the hour—his sketchy math told him it had to be two or three in the morning in the US Northwest—he knew his night owl friend would likely still be awake and busy.

He'd met Zeke Hayes on a mission neither could ever speak about, in what seemed like another life. Their philosophical and spiritual approach to kink had strengthened their friendship, but none of that meant as much as Z's earnest outreach to him after the failed mission with Asha. Ops weren't the same after that, a confession he'd also entrusted to the guy, leading to them actually talking about the reality of the Bastille club. It didn't take them long to find a space in Seattle's warehouse district in which they quickly built out to their kinky hearts' desires.

Helming Bastille's grand opening and daily operations was exactly what Brick needed during those dark, unpredictable months. Once Zeke decided to step back from active service, it felt right to start sharing the Dungeon Master duties. Life had gotten into something resembling normalcy—whatever that even was when a guy transitioned from spies and subterfuge to whips and safe words—meaning he actually had free time for the first time in his life.

It wasn't all it was cracked up to be.

Sort of like this little R&R break, courtesy of the French military and his Arcadian hosts.

Which was why, as soon as Z's voicemail filled his ear, Brick jabbed at the key to be rerouted to the club's front desk.

He'd have better luck now. He was sure of it. Somebody was probably still in the building, though they had likely wrapped up playtime across the dungeon around midnight. He'd have preferred to speak straight to Zeke, but the guy was the father of an infant now, and sometimes "midnight snack" carried myriad new meanings.

"Bastille, front desk."

Bingo.

As soon as the bright female voice filled the line, a grin spread across his face. If he couldn't get Z, Caressa Fimmel was a damn close second. During the two years the woman had been the definition of indispensable for Z and him, he'd never heard a note of irritation or exhaustion in the woman's voice. On top of that, she was a true Irish redhead with one of the most luscious figures he'd ever seen. If he was the kind of guy capable of mixing business with pleasure, he'd have likely booked her for weekly sessions at the end of his crop—and other interesting toys—but the woman had already seen the professional equivalent of his underwear drawer, and just the thought of dropping those walls for her was more bizarre than an episode of *Space Force.*

"Carey," he said, rubbing a hand on his chest to ward off a fresh wave of discomfort. He'd been purposeful about using her nickname, but not because it was his usual preference. Suddenly, he felt like he had something to prove. A secret password, proving he wasn't the big bad wolf tromping on her phone line in the middle of the night. "Hey . . . uhhh . . . it's—"

"Holy. *Shit.*" The second syllable was such a giddy shriek, he was shocked not to hear tortured dog howls in the background. "Max fucking Brickham. What the hell? Is it honestly you?"

"Sure hope so." As his grin suffused his words, the boulders in his chest dissolved. "How are *you*? And everyone else? What's going on?"

"Oh my God," she exclaimed. "Are you freaking serious right now? *How are you?* he asks. *What's going on?* he also asks. Shooting my shit like there's not a three-ring media circus right now, revolving solely around *him*, and—"

"All right, all right. I've been made aware of the crazy train. But in my defense, I only found out an hour ago, and—"

"No, *no*. Crazy won't cut it," she volleyed. "They're rabid wolves, Brick. Thankfully not around here, since the club's behind a corporate name. But at both ferry stops over to the island, as well as all over Whidbey itself, it's open hunting season."

He clenched his jaw, shifting again. His chest was still manageable, but it was because the rocks went ahead and plummeted to his gut.

"Fuck me sideways," he growled.

"Oh, I think they're already doing so," Carey rejoined. "Probably a few other fun positions, as well. Not that any Dom through these doors cares to test my knowledge about the subject . . ."

She trailed off as he ramped up another low snarl. Damn

it, how he yearned to launch into Papa Brick mode at her. To tell her not to give up—that there was a Dominant out there destined to make all her kink dreams come true. But he couldn't. He was still locked up at the slew of daunting details she'd just revealed.

There were reporters on the ferries and traipsing all over Whidbey? *Why?* Unless Samsyn and Jayd had it wrong, every European media outlet had confirmed he left France on a plane likely headed for Arcadia. So what was their game in *Seattle*?

Shit.

Unless the story had blown bigger than they knew or he assumed and the reporters were desperate for any scoop at all. Unless they were all really sniffing around his home turf, hoping to unearth whatever new angle they could.

Shit, shit, *shit.*

That meant it was only a matter of time before someone sniffed harder than the rest. Until they connected him back to Bastille.

Forget fucking him sideways. This time, they'd be ramming him up the ass without a drop of lube.

That kind of media glare would turn Bastille into everything it wasn't. A scandalous curiosity. A sordid sin pit. A place where "unnatural" people went to indulge their "perversions."

The safe haven Zeke and he had created would be exposed beyond repair.

And that wasn't the worst of it.

Eventually, Jayd would see those reports too. She'd watch those talking heads and believe all their judgments. She'd listen to the shame they spread in the name of link clicks and ratings and instantly see her own kink experiences in a new light. Every experience she'd known with *him*.

Not. Acceptable.

If memories were all that either of them could cherish from those magical hours in Paris, then he would protect them with a vengeance.

Actions that had to happen *now*.

"Carey." He felt crappy for cutting into her happy chatter, especially because her excitement about the newest streaming zombie series was practically contagious. "Hey, I can't wait to hear more about this. You know I'm always down for some epic brain scarfers . . ."

"But you need to talk to Z," she filled in before his mind finished the thought.

"You're getting scary good at that, woman."

"I'd totally own that if he hadn't just run up here like he hasn't peed all day."

Brick winced, already anticipating the price his sutures would pay for his laughter. Fortunately, his wounds held to under five on the pain scale. Whatever they were doing to train their medical teams around here, it was the stellar choice.

"Well, Kermit the Frog on a fucking camel."

Zeke's voice blasted across the line like a Sirocco wind from the terrain he'd just taken in questionable vain. But if a matching dose of gravity was what he was after from Brick, the dude would be left hard up.

"Hold up. You mean in a carnal sense? Because I'm not sure Kermie's into camel kink. You think Marisol would know?"

"Leave my kid out of this," Z barked. "I know your deflections like the backs of both hands, asshole."

"Not deflecting." Since he was confident the guy knew his straight shots as well as the famous deflections, he gave it no embellishment beyond his sincerity. "Probably trying to dilute things with humor, maybe... Yeah, that's likely it."

"Things?" Zeke retorted. "What *things*, exactly?" Scuffling noises scratched up the line, giving away his friend's abrupt movements. Big dork was probably trying to eyeball the phone's screen for an origin number. Brick had no idea what was showing up, if anything. "Where the fuck are you?" Z demanded. "Are you even aware of what's going on? They've caught some dipwad on camera in Paris, drilling a guy in a bar between the eyes and then making off with the princess of Arcadia. The footage is grainy enough that they're pinning it on a certain brick with feet."

"Don't know anyone with that rap sheet, man. Sorry. Can't help you."

"Not fucking around about this, buddy. This is now an international manhunt. To make shit worse, the crackpot led all the uniforms out to Bourget, where he stirred some bullet stew with the national police. And *that* was before—"

"He made a suicide run across the tarmac with the princess? And then escaped onto the bird behind her?"

New gruff static from his ended, this time because of Z's chuff. "So you do know. But why'd you go dead air on us? Especially when we all knew you'd hung back in Paris for some R and R. Then when days went by, and you didn't call or show..." Another brutal sound, more like the beginnings of a full choke. "Christ on toast, man. You don't want to know all the scenarios I created. Everything from some crazy mob getting their hands on you, to you going feral somewhere in the French countryside, to a faction of the Arcadian government itself hunting you down—what?" He bit it out as soon as Brick pushed a rough snort into the rant. "Tell me. You *owe* me, fucker."

"The Arcadians, and their . . . hunting skills." He cleared his throat. "That's not a half-bad guess."

"What?" Z spat. "Why?"

"Because I *was* the dipwad on the footage. And also the idiot on the tarmac at Bourget, and in the plane."

"*What?*"

"Well, the plane ride wasn't part of the plan. But that got changed courtesy of a few knocks of lead, courtesy of the Gendarmerie that an Arcadian asswipe called out on us. Since one of them grazed my dome, I wasn't exactly snapping the right Legos together, and—"

"Wait. Fuck." He really choked this time. "Want to connect me from one to ten in a logical line this time?"

"Depends on what you want to define as *one*," he returned. "There's the part about Jayd Cimarron sneaking off of Arcadia in the first place. Then there's the part where they learned she'd made it to Paris, but nobody could find her there."

"I assume the girl had a good reason besides wanting to grab the limited-edition Louis Vuitton boots?"

"It's so terrifying that you know shit like that now."

"Whatever keeps my woman happy. So stop evading."

He clamped an automatic snark-back into silence. The guy was right. It was best to just get on with shit. "Oz Demos got pulled in on the search efforts. And once he heard I was in the city too—"

"The wizard?" Z cut in. "*He* was just strolling through Paris too?"

"Not exactly." Keeping his original assumption in play,

that there were Arcadian bunker rats listening to their every word, he jumped ahead to evade the reasons—more specifically, *one* reason, named Jagger Fox—behind Oz's involvement with the mission. He hadn't been awake long enough to nail the extent of the Arcadians' knowledge about Jagger and Oz's relationship. "Anyhow, he chased me down. Gave me all the air in the balloon. They were basically hanging in the wind, with a misplaced princess also being hunted by some nasties from the kingdom's Pura rebel group."

"Crap." Z punctuated it with a harsh grunt. "Never had the pleasure of waltzing with those guys, but I've heard tales. Why'd they want to get their paws on her?"

"Tale for another time." To others, the toss-back was a casual enough write-off line. Between Zeke and him, it was a deeper code standing for more layers of the story. Just not the stratagem he was free to reveal right now.

"Whatever," Z muttered, playing along with the dodge. "Just clears the deck for the question I'm more interested in asking."

"Save it." He went kneejerk because he had to. There was no need to squeeze harder on his Asha-sized wound. Between his woo-woo brain lapses back in Paris and even his painkiller-inspired dreams, he'd done a fine job of that already, thank you very much. "For the record, I hesitated plenty. Even told Oz I'd have to think about it and tried walking off the cobwebs to think clearly. Also for the record, he was offering a truckload of flow for the gig."

"Because that's always been your deciding factor . . . how? Further, because you didn't make enough off of the job for Reece Richards a couple of weeks ago?"

"Hmmm. Good point and even better point."

"But you're still a wuss for a damsel in distress."

"Distressed wasn't exactly how I found her."

And *now* he earned all the points for clever evasion. Better yet, without lying. Though so many words rushed to mind about his first face-to-face encounter with Jayd Dawne Cimarron, none of them came close to the descriptor. He'd just peeled a shithead off her who clearly hadn't been after a sweet little courtship in the alley behind the Hotel Particulier. And she'd been so . . .

Defiant.

Dazzling.

Brave.

Beautiful.

"So what happened, then?"

So unspeakably beautiful . . .

"Brickham? Shit. Max? Did I lose him? Why do I still hear him breathe—"

"Everything." He forced it out, despite accepting it as another shitty stand-in for the words that really belonged. Or perhaps the words that would never be enough. "It was just that . . . *everything* happened."

"Everything." The guy repeated it with such deliberation, it sounded like he'd hit slow playback mode. "Which means exactly what?"

But slow hadn't robbed Z's ability to stab in with a distinct bite. It nipped Brick from his reverie, driving his free hand over his skull in a nervous sweep. Goddammit. He hadn't had a chance to run a razor over this shit in more than a week. His hand was going to come back as a bloody stump.

"You already know what," he snapped. "Aren't you the one who just told me it's all over the news?"

"And are *you* the one who expects me to buy that crock?" Zeke flung. "Shit. You're being as cagey as Taylor Swift fretting a breakup. You, the king of *nothing* happening, ever. Not with any woman you've seen or subbie you've screwed in the last two years. So you're counting on me buying your story when that's *not* part of your narrative?"

"Hayes."

"Sometimes it's all about what's *not* there, buddy."

"*Zeke,*" he finally bit out. "Jesus *fuck*."

He pushed up straight until his wounds actually did pang, only to hunch over with new awareness of their possible—probable—audience. The bunker buddies were probably tossing grins while frantically writing down the time stamp for this part of the exchange, unless fate decided he was owed a miracle and the Arcadians just assumed Z's *crock* was a slow cooker and his *subbie* was a long sandwich filled with twelve varieties of pastrami. None of it framed Brick in a flattering light, but at least they wouldn't assume he'd been messing with their princess in that way.

"Fuck what?" Z volleyed, hanging on to his hound dog side—only with his wolfish mode on. "I mean . . . did you?"

"Did I what?"

"Fuck her. Your new little . . . asset."

"You mean the official *princess* of a complete country with which our government is allies?"

Or so he was assuming, about that official stuff. But he'd been out cold for three days now. Many coups had happened in half that time. And though neither Samsyn nor Jayd had said anything to the contrary, it wasn't like the subject had conveniently rolled around.

Still, he persisted, "Honestly, man. You really think I'm

that special brand of idiot?"

Zeke sighed. It was long and contemplative. "I think you're the guy who was doing his buddy a solid and found yourself in a high-octane situation with a grateful, gorgeous girl, and—"

"Woman." He bit it out like the Doberman *he* now felt like.

"Ermmm . . . huh?"

"Jayd Cimarron is a *woman,* Z, not a girl."

And God help the Doberman who barked without thought. Right away, Z was pouncing like the words were juicy T-bones. "Ohhh, damn." And relishing the feast with a hefty chortle. "You really did get biblical with her."

"Fuck you." But it sounded as desperately angry as it felt. The frantic pounds of his heart were ample confirmation.

"Ohhh, you completely did. And aww—now you're being all prom-night coy about it. That either means you *really* liked that dance, or you can't wait to flip the punch table and get out of the gym."

He drew in a breath, ready to order the guy to go fuck himself again. But Z was already on a take-charge roll.

"Because that's all fixable, just in case you've forgotten. One call to Colton, and he'll have one of his corporate jets on the Sancti tarmac faster than you can say—"

"*No.*" Regret slammed as soon as the rebuttal spewed. "No calling Dan. No involving him or any of the other guys in this."

"Whoa. Chill out," Z reprimanded. "And why the hell not?"

"Because the guy isn't a spook anymore, and this mess isn't some random secret op gone to shit. Eventually, that bird would have to put me down somewhere—meaning Colton Industries and its good name would instantly be dragged through the mud. It'd be no different once the media identified any of you guys—and now it's about way more than just you, as well. Hawk, you, Tait, Kell, and Shay are all fathers now. And how long until they link any or all of us to Franz? He's engaged to the fucking president."

"You really think he'd let that make a difference?" Zeke snorted. "You think any of us would? Wait, let me ask this differently. If it were any of *us* at the center of this insanity, would it make a difference to *you*?"

"Goddammit. It's not the same."

"The hell it isn't. Ohhh, *snap*." The roll hit a bump, but not the kind Brick had hoped for. This was a bigger, bolder snag. "Unless it really is. Unless all of this really *is* different for you . . ."

"Okay, at ease with that shit too. I only mean this has the potential to royally blow up in my face, pardon the crappy pun. If I let you guys just jump in without making sure you've thought about the ramifications, it'd be—"

"Exactly what *you* did, helping me slip out of town when every member of Seattle's PD was ready to chomp on my ass."

"Almost five damn years ago," Brick volleyed. "In one city, in one country. This is crazier and you know it. It's involving a lot of Europe and beyond. You can't risk it. Not anymore. Your life isn't about just you anymore, man."

At last, thank God, there was a resigned sigh over the line. "Fine," Zeke conceded. "Roger that, loud and clear."

As he spoke it, the words blended in with a dark techno beat. The guy must've walked into Bastille's main bar and adjoining playroom station area. Zeke quickly switched off the music, but Brick wished he'd kept it on. More than that, he yearned to be right next to his buddy, hashing this out together between the spanking horse and the submissive stockade.

But if he was, they wouldn't be throwing down about this at all. Because it would also mean he'd never have met Jayd. She'd be nearly seven thousand miles away. She'd also be a complete stranger.

Though right now, wasn't it the same difference?

And wasn't that exactly what he wanted?

Yes.

Yes, damn it.

Things were better this way. The way they were supposed to be from the start between a globally loved princess and a mentally wrecked soldier. Their night of crazy coincidences was electrified by a crackling physical attraction, underlined by dangerous circumstances and raging adrenaline. No wonder they'd caved so quickly to temptation. And then *again.*

Hormones and happenstance.

Impulses and opportunities.

Not a life-changing bond.

Damn it, he wasn't the long-term choice for anyone. Not for his parents, who decided a vanishing act from society was better than watching him grow up. Not for any of the kids in school, who figured his thrift store clothes and classroom focus were things to be afraid of. Especially not for anyone he met in the black ops world, thanks to a little thing called plausible deniability. Nobody got chummy when assuming they'd be going home in a body bag.

It'd likely been the reason he gravitated toward kink and the Dominant/submissive world. Dungeon playtime could be a magical hour or two of intense meaning, without any of the messy aftermath. Everything with Jayd, back in Paris, was supposed to be the same thing. Lots of meaning, plenty of passion, *zero* extra strings.

But here they were now. Trapped in one hell of a huge yarn ball.

Fuck, fuck, *fuck*.

What was he going to do about it?

"So what are you going to do now, man?"

And there was the fifty-billion-dollar question.

Brick dragged his hand over his skull again. If he actually had all that, he'd offer every penny to Twylah and her friends for a fast face change—which would at least help with getting him off the island and back home in one piece.

But was that what he still wanted?

To break out of here as soon as he could?

Changing outwardly, even the terrain he crossed and the vistas he looked at, wouldn't alter a damn thing inside. Some of that he could live with. Had already been living with. The nightmares and the panic attacks would never be completely in his rearview.

But what about the new shit? The stuff he could no longer ignore, now packed to the rafters at the deep grooves along the edges of his psyches. Nooks he'd assumed were filled a long time ago, soldered by the crucible of therapy or permanently thrown out because of cold, hard self-discipline. But here they all were again, torn open by the tenacity and sensuality of one little pixie princess.

The woman who knew none of this.

The princess who, right now, was probably feeling like *his* tossed doxy—important enough to be his submissive in Paris but barely worth his civility now, back in *her* fucking kingdom.

"Christ on French toast," he mumbled. With a dagger in the butter, to boot. A dagger that felt plunged between his ribs and twisted through his heart.

"Whoa. What gives?" his friend demanded. "Don't tell me you're worried about the club, because you know we'll handle the basics until you get back."

"Right." He hauled his head out of his ass long enough to refocus. "Thanks, man. I mean it, Z."

Zeke chuffed. "You mean it . . . because you're sticking around them-there Arcadian parts for a mite longer, eh?"

Brick closed his eyes and jiggled his head. It was no use. His thoughts were all still in the same place—namely the ones still doggy paddling in astonishment because of hearing it spoken aloud. But Z was right. As in, on the damn money. He was electing to stay, at least until the Cimarron boys booted him off this pretty rock.

"I know it makes no sense, man—"

"Why?" Zeke countered.

"I'm getting to that. You want to let me fin—"

"No," the guy persisted. "I mean, *why* does it *not* make sense?" He gave that one a long rumble of punctuation. "Buddy, the way I see it, you're finally making all the sense in the world."

Brick released a low roll of thunder from his chest. "*Finally?*"

"Eh. For as long as I've known you, at least."

"Which means what?"

Was that now a full chuckle from his friend? "That it's really damn nice to hear you getting bewildered for once. Not having your next nine moves in your back pocket. Hell, maybe not even the next one. But better than that, knowing you're that lost and flustered because of a girl—excuse me, a *woman*—who's gotten all the way under that armor of yours and managed to find your one ticklish spot."

"My fucking *what*?" Forget the frown. He replaced it with a fume and wasn't sorry. "And excuse me, *lost*? And *flustered*?"

The dickwad waited a second before humming—humming!—in his ear. "I know exactly what I said and how I said it. The question now is, what are you going to do about it?"

Brick pulled away and glared at the device in his hand. Fat chance of Z getting the force of his long-distance aggravation, but he had to try. "You think I know that fucking answer?"

Another puke-worthy snicker across the line. "Ahhh, maybe you do. But damn it, Brickster, I really hope you don't."

"Do I dare ask why, or just start concocting the retaliation plan now?"

"Bring your empire and strike it back any time, pretty Palpatine. Won't change anything about what you'll have to go through now. The decisions only you can make."

"Which will only land me on the dark side, anyway?" he retorted. "Is that what you're saying?"

"Throttle back that TIE fighter, man. Haven't we been championing the dark side for quite a few years now?"

"Goddammit, I hate it when you're right."

"Hmm. About most things," the guy drawled. "But not all. And maybe I'm wrong about this too . . ."

"But?" Brick supplied the word that was clearly coming anyway.

"But I *can* say, even from the jumpy footage they're showing on the news feeds, that I've never seen you look at any other female like you do at Jayd Cimarron."

A scowl set in. "Which I'm supposed to do *what* with? Aren't they showing the shit from that pub in Paris? In which I'm supposably gunning down a stranger in cold blood?"

"Not all of it," Z qualified. "There's the twenty to thirty

seconds *before* everything goes to hell."

"In which I'm doing what?" he volleyed. "Just... being *different*?"

"If I could explain it better than that, I would. But I *can* tell you about what *I've* learned over the last few years—most notably about fate and the fun little schemes she spins to wake us up when we most need it."

Funny how easily a scowl could turn into a groan. "Crap on crackers, Hayes. Are you getting quixotic on me?"

"Maybe a dose of quixotic is exactly what you need right now, brother." His answer came with is Hisscary swiftness. "And maybe you also need to hear that I never thought any of that shit had a place in my life either. That I was fine being a big bad Dom, trying to flog and fuck my way through every willing submissive in Seattle without attachment or connection—until the day *connection* kicked me in my massive, arrogant ass. Until the one night, and the one woman, I least expected to be wielding that cosmic boot."

"Okay," Brick groused. "I got it. I got it." The main gist, at least. Nobody knew Zeke long before getting an earful of his adoration for his wife, who'd also been the most surprising submissive of his life. "But not everyone gets the kinky fantasy and then the rosy sunset too," he persisted. "You and Rayna are the exception, not the rule. A lot of us came to the D/s lifestyle because of some piece that went missing, some ending that never got written. We're lucky if we can reclaim some of those pieces in the dungeon, but few of us will get the chance to really cross the finish line."

He paused, slowly shaking his head, once more holding the phone away as if Z could somehow see him.

"You land the bonus points for believing, man—because I

know you really do. But most of us have accepted that the fairy tale doesn't happen for every lifestyle dreamer."

"Yeah," his friend agreed—once more with too much serenity. "Unless they happen to wake up in a palace, with a princess down the hall."

"Christ. Come on, Z."

"And oh yeah . . . a princess who was also caught on security cam footage, glancing up at said dreamer like he'd just hung the moon *and* the stars."

Brick grunted. It was a good substitute for his first inclination: to call utter bullshit on the bastard. Glitches galore there, topped by one important detail. Z wasn't shooting frothy blanks. He already heard it in the steady surety of the guy's voice.

That left only one viable option for what to say now.

"Fuck."

"Well." Z softened the figurative blow with a rough chuff. "You kind of walked into it, man."

Smart ass. "Fine. All right. I did."

Z joined him in a contemplative grunt. "Beats tumbling over a cliff, yeah?"

"Speak for yourself."

Because right now, tumbling off a cliff seemed a whole lot safer than the ledge he was nearing, step by precarious step. A scarp where the wind was strong yet sweet, the vista dizzying but stunning—leading to an abyss that made his heart thunder up his throat and his skin crawl with panic-driven fire ants.

As an aqua-eyed princess led him closer and closer to the edge.

CHAPTER FIVE

Strange times called for strange measures. And since this was, hands down, the strangest week of her life, Jayd refused to feel guilty about giving into her matching measures.

All right, perhaps *strange* was only the start of it. There were other descriptors too—expressions she had always heard back at Stanford but never quite understood. Expressions like "thrown down the shit pipe," "picking up the pieces," and "my favorite mistake."

Except that Maximillian Brickham had *not* been a mistake. Yes, even during those last awful moments a couple of days ago, in his room still so cruelly close to her suite—it still felt nothing close to a mistake. Every stressed muscle in her body confirmed it. Every brutally exposed nerve ending was on the exact same page.

They had an expression about that at Stanford too, right? More specifically, about the best way to fix it?

A hair of the dog that bit you.

Yes! That was it.

Except . . . that it was not.

Because unless the Creator had fashioned a dog that could make her ache like this without seeing him for three days, Maximillian Brickham had nothing in common with any dog she knew. Except for the possessive growls that vibrated his whole chest. And the way he gripped her body, his hands like brutal paws, when his desire manifested as full arousal.

And the bestial look on his face as he plunged his body into hers, before taking her to another plane of existence…

And there she went again. Right back down that hideous hole of memories. A pit she *had* to stay out of, no matter how ruthless the gouge in her belly or the ache in her heart.

She *had* to forget the Force of Nature.

And had come up with a brilliant plan for doing so.

Not even Requiemme's twisted expression, wielded via the big bathroom mirror in Jayd's suite, could sway her from the determination. If anything, her friend's wary frown was perfect for solidifying her resolve. Perhaps, at last, she had found a diversion that would work longer than an hour, without exacting a hangover in return.

She waited, calmly and patiently, for her maid to totter over, her steps ginger because of her knee-to-ankle cast. If Emme noticed Jayd's obscenely bright grin, the woman ignored it. Jayd simply waited for the woman to fully stop before the long marble vanity counter.

Once she was there, Emme frowned. Deeply.

Jayd harbored no delusions as to why. Her maid was scowling at the items already lined up on the marble counter. There were some pretty hair combs, a small paint brush, squares of foil, and a plastic bowl filled with bright blue liquid.

After a hesitant second, Emme picked up the brush. But instead of dipping it into the bowl, she caught Jayd's stare again. "*Tupulai.* Are you absolutely sure about th—"

"Emme. I love you to the end of each sunset and back, but if you ask me that one more time, I shall be forced to sing nothing but 'What's New Pussycat' for the next few hours."

Emme scandalized gasp was only half a jibe. "Merciless wench!"

"But you love that about me."

"I love many things about you," came the affectionate retort. "But *not* the mind behind a threat like that. And this?" She scooped up the bowl and grimaced again. "Probably a close second place."

"Bah." Jayd hissed from between her teeth. "I predict you will actually like it better than me."

"I would *really* like it if you went to the palais salon to do this. They are only one level below us—"

"And they are all nearly as antwacky as my mother." She huffed. "Their version of 'daring' is parting my hair in the middle instead of the side."

A small smile wisped Emme's lips. Jayd returned a similar smile while thanking the Creator for keeping her friend safe during their time in Paris. All odds considered, they both should have come out of the adventure in worse shape. Fortunately, her maid had only left behind some mental peace and a lot of skin off her left leg.

And Jayd had left behind her virginity.

Swoop.

Right away, she was back down the rabbit hole. But also like before, there were no twitchy-nosed lapins waiting in the darkness. Only Brickham's blues, brilliantly burning into her bloodstream. And his lips, knowing all the places to kiss and caress and possess her. And the voice that came from those lips, so lush and commanding…

"All right." Creator be praised again for the woman who could yank her from a reverie with two snorted words. "I cannot deny you the point. But that also means *you* cannot deny *me* the leeway to botch this up."

"Bah." Jayd stomped harder on the repetition. "You are

not a botcher."

"Says the three glasses of wine in your system."

"Says *me*, the botchery expert."

"Oh? Is that so, now?"

The woman's tease was as comforting as the way she separated some strands of Jayd's hair and began painting them with the blue paste from the bowl. Jayd had snuck a roll of tin foil out of the kitchen earlier, then cut out square pieces from it as coloring foils. It was far from a professional salon treatment, but better than what she originally expected. At least she had gotten something right this week—a defeat that seeped heavily into her answering murmur.

"Oh, yes. That is very much so."

"Hmm. Since you have had such extensive experience in botchery, now?" The query, decidedly different than the first, came with an equally jarring glance. "And perhaps, in light of certain events in Paris, a little *debauchery*, as well?"

At once, she wondered if she had mixed the hair color improperly. Either it was going too dark or she had paled by at least five shades. "All right. Which of my brothers put you up to that little incision?"

"Hmm?" Emme only looked up once, well-practiced about her casualness. "I do not underst—"

Jayd grabbed the woman by the wrist. "*Which one*, Requiemme Farre? You will tell me now." But she dropped her grip as quickly, suddenly needing to stand. "Wait. I can hazard a good guess. It was Shiraz, yes? Ev is too diplomatic. Syn is too truculent. But 'Raz is just sneaky enough. And let me guess, he asked you to do it after showing you all the extra videos."

Emme went still from shoulder to toe. Her gaze flared. "All the extra *what*?"

Emme flared her gaze.

"The camera footage," she snapped. "That they obtained from Paris."

"Footage?" Another wide stare, making the woman resemble a possessed doll. "Good stars. Of what?"

"You know what." Though now she began to wonder if Emme truly did or not. She took a deep breath, forcing herself to be more patient. "The shots of Brickham and me, from the center of Place Blanche. We were truly only pretending the groping, to throw off Trystan and his *soldasks*. And the break-in at the cemetery was necessary. It was only because of—"

"Break-in?" Emme broke in. "Oh, blessed saints and stars."

"How do you think we made it into the cemetery in the first place?" she returned. "It was close to midnight. Perhaps after."

"And the police were all over the place like bugs after cake." The woman gasped. "Oh, *my*. Are you saying *they* went in through the window as well?"

"And are you really asking that of one of the cake crumbs?"

Emme plopped the brush into the goo bowl. Ample amounts of the dye spattered up, freckling Jayd's exposed arms and cleavage in turquoise blue. *Fantastic*. Now she had a case of artificial pox.

"*Rahmie Creacu*," Emme mumbled. "Next you will be confessing to mounting the man in some awful crypt while the rats applauded."

"Nonsense."

There were certainly no cheering rats.

She looked down, blotting blithely at the dye dots with some tissue, but there were already stains in her skin—likely just as apparent as the tell she had given Emme on a shiny behavioral platter. Still, she murmured, "What makes you say that? Even as a joke? Are there rumors, Emme? Even now?" They had been back on Arcadia for less than a week!

"*Calmay, bonami.*" Emme's soothe was as gentle as her knuckles across Jayd's cheek. "My intention is not an accusation, nor an investigation. Nor have your brothers approached me about either."

Her maid had no cause to lie, but the discord in Jayd's nerves went on. "So why are you saying things like this? Alluding to Brickham and I . . . and debauchery, and crypts, and groping in Place Blanche—"

"Sweet girl, *you* brought up the groping."

"Uhhh . . ." She bowed her head to hide her sudden flush. "Yes, of course I did. As an example of the ridiculous conclusions that my brothers are leaping t—"

"You mean the same impressions to which *I* sprang, right outside the *cimetiere*? And that I am certain Ozias and Jagger reached as well?"

"Creator's bloody-stumped toes." She lost every battle against her senses, which now screamed in humiliated horror. "Emme! Why did you not *say something*? Or at least give me a look or a glance that would have—"

"Done what, exactly?" her maid returned. "Blithely noted that most people being hunted by half of Paris's police force do not do so with shaky knees, swollen lips, and blatant beard burn? That the soldier-spies helping them rarely follow their every move with such ardent interest or are fine with having a crown princess call them Sir."

"*Former* crown princess," Jayd interjected.

"Not part of the world's reality yet," Emme debated.

"Regardless, the point is the point."

And a damn solid one too.

Neither of them voiced it. Neither of them had to. A fast look toward her maid, as serene and humble as before, was verification enough. Whatever the outside world chose to infer or invent, the jig was up.

But instead of more dread, the realization brought Jayd . . . relief. A flood of it. A cleansing so complete, she was not even tempted to laugh about it. She was ready to cry.

"Highness?" The woman's sweet sough provided another tug toward the tears. "Do you . . . want to talk about it?"

Jayd turned and sagged against the vanity. "Yes. *No.* Oh, I do not know." She folded her arms and dropped her head. "Things are so confusing right now," she rasped, ending with a gulp. She knew not why she still battled the tears, except to admit that once she pulled out the stops on the spillways, the deluge was likely not to stop for a while. As in, *well* after her new color had to be washed out.

"Confusing," Emme reiterated. "Because you did not expect to be bringing Brickham home with you?"

The heat behind her eyes became a tormenting sting. "To begin with, yes."

"And that is not a comfortable circumstance for him? Or maybe for you?"

Jayd sniffed. Hard. "How about box number one *and* two?"

Her friend nodded. "And because everything you shared in Paris was never supposed to last longer than Paris. And now that it has—"

"No." As she swung a hand up high, more agony thudded the opposite direction, low in her gullet. "It has *not.* Which is exactly what I must accept here."

"Why?"

Because Maximillian Brickham refuses to see it any other way.

Because even though we are here, *he clearly cannot wait to get back* there. *As far away from me as he can get. As far away from what we had…*

For the thousandth time, she fought to justify that somehow. To sympathize with why he looked like they had flown to Alcatraz, not Arcadia. Like his room, the most opulent in the palais infirmary, was actually his locked cell and not a gift from the cosmos, part of the conspiracy to keep them together a little while longer.

Why?

Because Samsyn had gotten to him before she had? Perhaps said something? Made a caveman-style threat? But Syn had not been in there long. He'd beat her by a few minutes at the most. And though he was the most physically daunting of her brothers, Brickham's dimensions were nearly identical. Moreover, they spoke the same language of tiger snarls, tidal waves, and testosterone. No way could Syn have unnerved him that easily.

Which meant he was already spooked for another reason.

What?

Was there someone waiting for him back in Seattle? Maybe a *number* of someones? Did he have certain agreements with them when he was traveling for his missions?

At once, she doubted that. In so many ways, she sensed it was about… more. Or, depending on how one approached the subject, less. Not a female who waited for him at home. One who was somehow… with him… already. Pounding through his head. *And his heart?*

Was she haunting him from another realm, perhaps? Or maybe relentless with him from *this* one?

Or maybe . . .

That woman was *her*.

Maybe she was enough for one night but nothing beyond that. Or maybe she was too *much* to handle beyond that.

But in the end—the one he had basically presented to her on a glaring silver platter three nights ago—did any of it really matter?

Because in the end, he did not want her anymore.

It mattered not that his body was ignoring that memo. She would not have taken advantage of the technicality then, and she would not do so now. Brickham was a virile male—that was a surety—but she refused to settle for the incursion of his body without the fullness of his spirit.

"Can we just . . . change the subject?" she blurted, lifting her head until her gaze again locked with Requiemme's, courtesy of the long mirror. "Besides, we are only halfway finished here."

"We are?" Requiemme drawled, repositioning herself with the freshly loaded dye brush. "And here I was, thinking you were looking to start the indecisive peacock trend."

A giggle spilled before she could help it. "Only the males are called peacocks, you know."

"Then it shall *really* be a trend."

A new giggle, buying herself a few seconds to come up with a properly cunning comeback, until the sound suddenly clutched in her throat—as a reflected movement in the mirror snagged her gaze. And a hint of cedar zinged her nostrils. And a jolt of awareness blasted her chest. And at once, zipped lower . . .

"*Creator*," she choked out, just as that heat bore in on the most intimate triangle of her body. Too late to do anything about her psyche, compelled at once by the primal pull of the new visitor to her suite.

The force of nature who took over the archway between her bedroom and bathroom.

"Oh, my stars!" Emme's reaction followed hers by but a few seconds, coinciding with her physical start. The brush popped out of her grip, splatting the wall before clattering to the floor. "Mr. Brickham," she stammered. "What a… distinctive surprise."

"Hello, Requiemme." His stance was as determined and tall as ever despite his new accessory—an aluminum walking cane, centered sturdily in front of his crotch. "How's the leg?"

"Healing swiftly," Emme supplied. "*Merderim* for your inquiry. And yours? I mean, not just your leg, of course. All of it… Should you even be out of bed?"

It was the very query stuck between Jayd's brain and lips—not that it was going to penetrate far with the human thundercloud before them.

"I've been encouraged to take short walks," he said. "Get everything flowing again. Hunt down chances to hear pretty girls call me distinctive."

Even before he flicked a bantering wink at her friend, Jayd deep-breathed against the new nettles in her bloodstream. "It is hardly a *short walk* between here and the infirmary," she stated.

"A truth, to be sure," Emme concurred. "Nor exactly a path one would be taking if they did go too far and began exploring the palais."

"Nor an entrance door that would automatically open

for said explorer," Jayd amended, carefully gauging his composure—which, predictably and maddeningly, did not falter.

Including the stare he honed directly in on her.

That unbending, unrepentant, all-seeing scrutiny...

He kept at it for several more minutes, letting her squirm beneath his ruthless regard, before murmuring, "Good explorers know how to enlist good allies."

Jagger.

There were other options for the answer, of course, but none that made more sense to her. But even if that was not the case and someone else had keyed in the entrance code to her suite, what good would such an accusation do? Brickham was an exceptional operative. He knew the value of keeping confidences.

More importantly, being irritated at Jag meant an extra shot of boldness for her. All the better for getting through this face-off. Or whatever it was.

"What on earth are you doing here?"

Thank the Creator for Requiemme, who was able to voice the query aloud. In return, Brickham nodded as if she had gotten a script cue right—in a play *he'd* written. Undoubtedly, the scene also contained a hero in borrowed medical scrubs and a faded black T-shirt, still looking like a take-charge super spy despite the cane keeping him upright.

"I came to speak with the princess." More of him channeling the James Bond thing, which Jayd feigned not to care about. Surely the man could not know she had watched the films a dozen times each. Yes, even *A View to a Kill.*

But maybe he and Jagger had bonded *that* tightly.

A musing for another day. She could not entertain, even

with fleeting attention, the idea of Brickham forging new friendships across the island. What was she going to do if *everyone* around here got morose when he had to leave?

The imagining lasted long enough to push irritation into her tone. "Obviously your timing is not convenient," she commented, keeping her lips tight. "Requiemme was just helping me with a proj—"

"I can see that," he inserted, smoother than a chef slicing into butter cake. "And I won't be long. Perhaps I can even help?"

He finished that off by scooping the dye brush off the floor. The whole time, her maid pinned him with an indicting look. Neither Mother Abbess or Ceresi Lannister had anything on the woman.

"Let us just agree you will not take long."

Ohhh, goodness. Perhaps Captain Von Trapp and Jon Snow needed to worry too. Emme's protective claws were out in force, but Jayd could not do much to shove them back in. The woman was feeding off *her* tension, which had already razed her cocktail buzz like a blow torch through a cotton field. *Where* was the Stanford how-to guide for the moment when one was no longer toasting to their dismissive douchebag, but confronting him in the all-too-real, all-too-close, all-too-magnificent flesh?

Flesh that looked even better as soon as Emme departed the room.

And Brickham moved in closer.

Angels and demons have mercy.

How had she so easily forgotten what his proximity did to her? How small yet sheltered she felt when he loomed over her? How glaringly spotlighted but infinitely special, feeling like the man erased the rest of the world when studying her like this? Impaling her, heart and soul, with the power of his twin blues…

Oh, dear heavens!

His devastating, decadent eyes. Were they why she had gravitated toward the similar color for her hair?

Impulsively, she snapped a hand up to her head. "Damn it," she mumbled at her turquoise-tinted fingertips. The bright color would be muted after her wash-out, despite how the box touted the process as an all-in-one deal. She might have less hair now, but it was still the stubbornly dark stuff of her Cimarron genes, not her LaBarre side.

Juuust lovely.

Out of all the mental prompts she needed right now, a reminder that her illegitimate rump should not even be in this chair was *not* one. But processing that, on top of all the synapses Brickham had charged by merely entering the suite, had her more winded than a sprint on the beach against the wind. At this moment, she was even ready to lace up her runners and go for *that* option…

Oh, especially now.

As a clean wad of tissue, offered by a huge, firm hand, appeared before her downcast eyes.

As she grabbed it with her clean hand but let her nerves take over her other one—just in time to drive her shaking fingers to her forehead.

"Oh fff…" She saved herself from spewing the world's favorite F-word, but not from replacing it with equal ire. "Almighty on shit toast!"

"Well." To his credit, her intruder did not opt for an obvious gloat. His tone was gruff but kind, caressing her in much the same way that he took over wiping her goop-covered fingers. “As long as it’s blue shit, I think you’re okay.”

“That would make me an alien tree frog or a Smurf,” she countered. “And since both sound just fine compared to my own skin . . .”

Skin she was blisteringly aware of now, as the man began dabbing the tissue at the splotches on her face.

Her pores had no defense against the heat that flowed out from him, decimating the paper swifter than his gaze had gone through her initial defenses. Against every protest in her head, Jayd replied with a shivering sigh. Surely that would have the man indulging a small crow, but when she dared a glance up, his expression was just as earnest as before.

Earnest—and all-too authoritative.

She could not look away. Suddenly and terrifyingly, she did not want to.

“You’d be a pretty adorable Smurf, sweet girl.”

Maybe she could look away, after all. That was only because of the tightness up and down in her throat, oxygen battling feelings for control, until she was force-feeding gulps just to keep everything working right. Whatever *right* was anymore . . .

What it was *not,* was ongoing silence. So she gritted her teeth, pushing words to her lips. Hard, determined, get-to-the-point-before-I-jump-you-like-an-alien-tree-frog words.

“What are you doing here, Brickham?”

His features tautened. As she watched the readjustments of muscle and skin against his prominent bones, he also angled his backside more fully along the vanity counter. Somewhere in those moments, he also got rid of the soiled tissue wad, since his fingers were laced when he refocused fully on her.

Making her sit through more of the unnerving silence. And his unblinking scrutiny.

Finally, thank the Creator, he drew significant breath to speak.

"I didn't like the way we ended things. A few days ago," he qualified. "When you came to visit me."

"Yes, sir." In her mind it was no longer capitalized, though she could not tell if he discerned as much. "I am fully aware of when it occurred. And also of what ending things means."

He grimaced. "I didn't mean to imply that you don't."

"So that's why you crept across the palais and found a way in here? To imply something else?"

"No," he bit back. "No implications, okay? I just think that some things didn't get communicated right. They weren't... clarified."

"Oh, they were perfectly clear." She folded her arms, leaning as far back in the chair as she could get. "And so were you."

"*No,* damn it. I wasn't. And—*fuck.*"

That part was tangled deep in his larynx, muffled even more when he dipped his head and scraped a hand across the top. Some of her aqua dye had somehow gotten onto his palm, which wound up in his self-created mohawk. She said nothing because she liked it. If nothing else still bound them, at least they could be blue-topped twins for a little while.

The thought should not have given her so much comfort, but it did. Apologizing for the fact would have to happen later too.

"Look. What I wanted to say is... I'm sorry."

So the maddening man went and dragged in the remorse theme anyway. With all his figurative guns blazing.

"When you walked into my room, I was still trying to process the fact that I was actually here, not some French hospital with guards outside the door. I'd just woken up from a three-day nap but felt like a wall of the Alamo, post showdown, with Santa Anna still cackling over my carcass."

The metaphor pushed reluctant humor to Jayd's lips. "Only he looked like my brother Samsyn. And he was *not* cackling."

Brick parked his hands on his thighs and slanted her a matching smirk. "Oh, I'm sure he was inside. I mean, somewhere."

"Mmmph." She snorted. "He is an ass. I doubt they know how to cackle."

"Well, he's an ass who cares about you."

"Is that so?" As she pushed back to her feet, the makeshift dye foils crinkled in strange harmony. She was aware that at this point, her new look would be more an ombre than monochrome, but she cared not. It felt too good to get to this part of the confrontation. "Well, spare me any more *brutans* in the names of care and concern."

His dark brows bunched. "*Brutans?*"

"The literal translation is *beast*," she explained. "It can be said with affection . . . or other things."

"Ah." He nodded. "Other things. Like ire at your brother . . . or a soundly chapped hide at the guy who turned down your delicious body in his infirmary bed."

And he was really taking things there, as well.

She should have been glad for it. She should have stopped right there, after taking two and a half steps between the vanity and her soaking tub and turned to give him a look that at least thanked him for the concession. Because that is exactly where it would end. She had to resign herself to that. She would have to stay content with five-margarita lunches, rainbow hair experimentations, and peering at the same ocean, off the same balcony, every day. The docile princess in her tower realm, not wanted by anyone now…

Except…that was not true anymore. At least she theorized. On top of her hopeful praying, of course.

But Brickham had come to *her*, not the other way around. He had coordinated with Jagger—or someone—to get access to her suite and then gimped his way over on that cane, even with three bullet wounds and a body littered in bruises. Had he gone through all that just to apologize? Just to leave her like this, frustrated and rejected?

Perhaps.

All right, probably.

She was not intimate with every gear in his heart and soul, but the code of his personal honor *was* a key priority for him. She knew that part with more clarity than anything else.

So maybe she did need to stop, turn, and accept his effort at a friendzone framed in that integrity.

But that single stab of doubt kept twisting at her brain, digging at her heart…gnawing at her certainty.

She let the discomfort lift her head. She also let it push a rejoinder to her lips.

"If it had only been about my body, do you think my hide would be that chapped?"

Not a flinch of surprise from him, though she expected none. But nor did he let fly with the comeback *she* expected, which had her yearning to jump into the tub and take cover on the spot.

Why had she just said that? Exposed so much of herself

to him? Let him see all the parts in which he was clearly not interested, nor had any obligation to care about? Their moments in Paris were just an escape. A transition. A means of getting somewhere else.

Trouble was, she still had no idea where she was going. Not a damn clue.

"It wasn't simply about my body either, Pixie."

And damn it, with statements like that, he was not helping things. "Of course not," she snipped. "There are the other things. How could I forget? A checklist of them, right? You can officially fill in the bubble for fucking a princess now. And for safe-house sex too." She tapped a finger to her chin. "Though does it count when it is only a safe-house *apartment*? And remember, you also get the points for taking my V card. That certainly counted for a few punchholes in *your* card . . . ?"

"No!" His growl was immediate and violent. "I mean—damn it, every second with you was amazing, all right? No. Not amazing. Beyond that. Far beyond."

He huffed before chucking his cane, using the same *whoosh* of motion to raise a fisted hand. But not for long. As he drove it against the vanity counter, her cosmetics jumped and the frame bulbs flickered. But his voice plummeted to a serrated murmur.

"You don't believe me," he growled. "And frankly, I don't blame you. I handled things like a box of rocks back in the infirmary. I'm probably *still* a goddamned box of rocks, but hopefully you'll let me paint them a prettier for you now."

Jayd scoffed. "Rocks are still rocks, Brickham. They hurt when you throw them."

One side of his mouth quirked. "But pain can be a good thing, Pixie."

She worked for another scoff. Instead, wild and ravenous heat flowed up her body. Between the meaning in his murmur and the intensity across his face, she knew exactly what he was thinking about—the same place to which he compelled *her* imagination now. All the moments from Paris, in which he had proved that statement so true. And in which she had eagerly let him . . .

You're really liking this, aren't you, gorgeous?

Right here, right now, you're my clay, sweetheart . . . to be molded, painted, and then incinerated . . .

Are you close now? Because I'm fucking you? Hurting you?

Memories.

All of it was only memories.

And he was only bringing it up to dislodge her. To soften her. Deflect her heart against the blows he already had inflicted on it.

But no way was he coaxing her away from the edge that easily. Not even with a whole crate of painted rocks at his disposal.

Unless . . .

The man was willing to join her on the precipice. Ohhh yes, on the edge with his toes all the way over, sucking the cliff face for dear life.

"You truly want me to look at your pretty new stones, Maximilian Brickham?"

He relaxed his fist. Threaded his extended fingers with those of his messy blue hand and folded them in his lap.

"I truly do, Jayd Dawne Cimarron."

She hiked up her chin. Squared her shoulders.

"Then start by using the ones that really matter." She hiked her chin higher and set her shoulders. "Tell me about Asha."

He went rigid again. She was ready for that but held firm. His flared nostrils, terse lips, and tempestuous gaze were also solid dots on her radar of readiness. None of them diminished her determination.

Until he pulled in a breath that shuddered as if his throat had been fileted.

Then another, like the same cosmic demons had started dicing him up.

As he released the air, he grimaced deeply. She did too, feeling like the dirty *salpu* who had wielded the merciless knife. But not enough to let him out of this. Not enough to retreat from this path, feeling more important now that it was illuminated by his openly clonky response.

"Asha? What does she have to do with—"

"Anything?" Jayd cut in. "Or perhaps you meant *everything*?"

"Jayd—"

"Because when your mind decided to disappear in the middle of the Montmartre Cemetery, you called out for *her*. Then again, at least a dozen times, during your fever dreams as we flew here. And then on the second day I visited you in the infirmary, and *Twylah* asked me who she was . . ."

"*Jayd*."

"*Brickham*." She unclenched her teeth long enough to amend, "Do you truly want me to believe I was more than a convenient crotch for you? To see past your ugly rocks? Then pull a few out of your damn walls and talk to me. Have you not learned by now that I am not a delicate teacup? That I will not shatter if you tell me there is someone back at home, waiting—"

"Whoa." He whisked up a hand. "There's nobody waiting for me, okay?" He stabbed out a brutal stare. "Least of all Asha."

"All right," she replied quietly. "So she is someone from your past, then? And you still harbor feelings for—"

"No. *No.*" He jostled everything on her vanity again. His fist was rigid, all his veins nearly popping from the knuckles. "I mean yes. *Fuck.*" His inhalation swelled through his chest, tightening the T-shirt's fit around his bulging muscles. "She's from my past. *Far* in my past. But she was never—" He hitched short, taking another of those unnervingly distracting breaths. "She and I were *never*—well, we didn't share things like you and I did."

She slunk to the lip of the tub, weighted by her troubled curiosity. "But . . . you wanted to be, yes?" She ignored the new rise of his tension. Maybe he had to confront all this as much as she did. "Brickham. Nobody cries out for someone in so much pain and need unless they are yearning for some kind of a relationship or connec—"

"Or unless that person's dead."

Well, there was a new kind of fist. Only his statement didn't rock the vanity. It shook the air itself. And all her nerve endings. Every inch of the new crack in her heart. Jayd's mouth opened but no sound came out. Her mind yielded nothing but mental lint. A useless blank.

"And for the record, I don't yearn for relationships," he finally bit out. "Because I don't do them. Period."

"Because of her?" Jayd rasped. "Asha?"

"Jesus wept," he muttered, clawing both hands to his thighs. "No. Because of *me*."

She shook her head, hoping to line up the point she was obviously missing. "You? Why?"

"Damn it." His shoulders hunched, joining the clench of his knuckles. "I simply don't go the distance, sweetheart. I'm not that guy. You don't want me to *be* that guy. Don't tell me you haven't gotten that part yet."

Jayd surrendered to a scowl, matching his own. "Sure," she retorted. "I have completely gotten it, Brickham. That is why I went ahead and asked my silly question anyway. Just to irk you, right?"

The sarcasm was thicker than gourmet peanut butter but did the job for which it was intended. It stuck to him with stubborn tenacity—to the point she almost prepared for another of his hoarse apologies.

Almost.

Instead, he stretched the very threads of his shirt while hauling in a new breath. He slid his hands higher up his thighs, dragging with such force that Jayd was compelled to follow along with her gaze—until she could not. Well, not without confronting the prominent bulge between his legs. The medical scrubs were a sad substitute for his dark jeans in terms of hiding the dimensions of his body. Especially right... there...

"You do a lot of things to me, Pixie, but irking me isn't one of them." He had the sense to refrain from asking why she had not gotten that yet either. "Do you test my sanity sometimes? Well, yeah. But do you also surprise me, enchant me, and occasionally turn every cell in my brain upside down? Oh, *hell* yeah. That too."

He tilted his head to one side as the opposite end of his mouth notched higher. Jayd liked the warmth that spread through her chest, rising to make her own lips twitch.

"*Every* brain cell?" she jibed. "But only occasionally?"

He chuffed with low sensuality. "Gotta spare me a few for stuff like breathing, walking, and shitting."

The smoky tendrils in her chest became floating sparks through her body. Her lips twitched again. "That sounds doable." But then she gave in to a small smile. "Maybe even go-the-distance-able."

So much for the smile. Or anything like it that might have been coming from Brickham.

She had counted on a change in his demeanor. She just didn't know how huge. The darkness that took over his features was like night clouds across the moon. His subtle push away was just as gutting. If he wasn't still clinging to his thighs, which kept her connected to him in some odd way, she likely would have gotten up and given up, no more questions asked.

They passed the better part of a minute, locked in that tense hell, before he broke the air with his serrated rasp.

"I'm sorry, Pixie. You're mistaken about that. I mean it."

Jayd drew in air on painful lungs. Well, now *she* was irked—in all the violent senses of the word.

"Says who?" she jabbed. "You and that grand jury behind you, my friend?"

"Don't need a jury." He channeled his darkness into a strange and troubling ease. "Life handed down my verdict a long time ago. I'll be in solitary for the rest of my life. You know a lot of that origin story already."

Her breaths were still acts of agony. She showed him just how much by letting the sting behind her eyes turn liquid.

"A lot of the story is not all of it," she sobbed out. "If Asha hurt you that badly—"

"Christ," he muttered. "I'll only say this one more time, okay? It wasn't her. It's never *been* her."

She compressed her lips, holding back a string of frustrated profanity. "Respectfully speaking, that still tells me nothing."

One of his brows cocked. While lowering it, he hauled in a labored breath. "Tell me . . . Did you like everything we did in Paris, princess?"

Princess. There it was again, more awful and despicable than before. "I believe you already know the answer to that, Sir."

Sir. Capital *S* this time, communicated by her hard emphasis. Though the man's features hardly shifted, she sensed she had gotten past his thick skull this time.

"Adept answer," he stated. "Registered and accepted."

She nodded, unable to dim a subtle preen. "*Merderim*."

"But if we were having this conversation in my normal world, in my real life, it would've gotten your ass reddened."

It was a nice preen while it lasted. "Pardon me?"

"All of that . . . in Paris . . . was only wood shavings on my normal playing board." His answer was more brutal to bear because he changed not a millimeter of his stance. If anything, he seemed huger now. Crueler. "Hard lives spit out hard men, sweetheart. You have to know by now that I'm one of them. And goddammit, how I wish that were some trite excuse to save your feelings, but it's not. It's my truth, and it's not going to change."

He finally did move, but only to fold his arms across the expanse of his chest. His gaze intensified to a sharp cobalt shade.

"At some point, I thought there might have been hope for me," he went on. "To get . . . gentler, I suppose. Once there weren't so many pressures on all my edges, maybe they'd get rounded off, and I'd be okay for a woman to hold for longer than a few moments in time."

He blinked. In that single second, everything about him

changed again. His shoulders sagged. The thunderheads had returned to his eyes. "But when those chances came, I turned them all down. I ran from the bevels. I ran *toward* the knives and the axes. My edges became my definition, my security . . ."

"Your identity," Jayd filled in, nodding softly. "Like your very namesake."

His nod was more a harsh tic of his head. "I didn't want to redefine myself. I liked it where I was, despite knowing what I'd be giving up to do it." He hitched his shoulders with the same gruff brevity. "This is me, Jayd. I'm a hard man. On myself *and* on others."

"Others." Her echo was quiet but threaded with new understanding. "Including your lovers."

"*Not* my lovers," he bit out. "My fuck toys, Jayd. You getting a bit of meaning now? They're my submissives. My servants, there to obey me no matter what I ask them to give or to do."

More comprehension hit. "Like the people—the submissives—in that place we went to," she said. "The dungeon."

Which had been just that, in so many senses. More than what she might have fully understood . . . until now.

"Yes," Brickham replied. "Like that place."

"Which was why you knew exactly what to do when we got there," she returned. "And why they almost seemed to know you. To respect you."

He hauled in another long breath. "It was more than just kinky cordiality. Bastille—the name on the card I showed the other Master in Paris—isn't just a dungeon I belong to. It's the club I own, Jayd."

Her reaction to that was instantaneous—but not unexpected. The sprint of her heartbeat was not one of shock.

The new knowledge in her mind was revelatory, not revolting. The expression *he* was clearly dreading, of her scandal and horror, was not going to happen. Instead, she faced what she had been so ardently begging from him.

The honesty of her heart.

Every insatiably curious dirty corner of it.

"All right. So you are a prince with a fortress instead of a castle. You rule from a throne of pleasure instead of policy. How does that make you less deserving of long-term love than anyone else?"

A stunned stare finally did fly across the room. His.

"And how the hell did you swing this discussion around to *that*?"

She frowned, genuinely perplexed. "Does any of it *not* make sense?"

Brickham shifted his weight from one foot to the other. "Not . . . entirely."

"Then, respectfully speaking, answer my question, Sir."

The man ditched his shock like a fleck of rust on his precious machine. "You going to keep taking the name of respect in vain, girl? Because if so . . ."

"Then what?" It tumbled out before she could help it. Or maybe not. Maybe she *was* being a royal priss, purposely calling out the man on his evasion. Or maybe she was diving headlong into this game because she already saw through his.

So. Clearly.

Did he think he could scare her off that easily? That she would crumble and cower just because of the dark things he liked doing to women? That she would think about the steps they had already danced of that tango and now want to tear up her dance card?

Then maybe he was the one who did not know *her* at all.

Two seconds' worth of the thought led to one second's worth of her upward lurch. She popped out a hip and mirrored his tough-guy stance, complete with pretzel-twisted arms.

"Another question you do not wish to answer, Mr. Brickham?" She tilted her head. "Respectfully speaking, of course."

His composure went even more rigid. Though he dropped his arms, his muscles were still balls with pronounced veins. His thighs strained against his scrubs. His cheekbones fought with his flesh. His gaze crackled with silent but potent energy.

Oh... wow.

Her force of nature was back.

Her bloodstream responded with a thrill of desire.

Her insides churned with wild waves of trepidation.

"You seriously really want to go there, young lady?"

"I seriously really believe I do, Sir."

"All right, then. Take off every thread of your clothes."

She did not spare half a thought about it. She just moved, with trembling fingers and flimsy breaths, to obey his calm command. She had no idea what to expect. What plans he had for her. The feeling was like nothing she had ever experienced. She had no idea pure lust and raw fear were such an addicting amalgam.

Inwardly, she vowed to savor every precious second of it.

CHAPTER SIX

"*Move*," Brick growled when Jayd paused to close her eyes and pull in a long breath. Part of him was pissed, impatient that she might be considering a back-down at this point. The other part was desperately afraid of the same. If so, he'd have to honor her dissent—no matter how hellish it would be for the Dom she'd flickered in every cell of his blood.

Flickered? Oh, no.

She'd given him a full lick of the fire.

Now, goddammit, he wanted more. And intended to take it.

"Pixie, that was *not* a sweet little ask."

"Okay, okay!" she blurted. "I—I am trying—"

"No trying. No *talking*." Fuck, this felt good. "Just obedience. That's all you exist for right now. Empty your gorgeous little head of everything else but that."

He tossed her an approving rumble as she finally unhooked her bra and peeled away her plain T-shirt. The act knocked loose some of the foil square things piled on her head, forming cute little blue splotches across her delectable skin.

He'd never taken such delight in connect-the-dots before.

Mentally, he did just that—starting with the curious, jagged line between the light spray surrounding her left nipple, to the sizable blob coating her right. He imagined how her skin would pebble if he decided to smear that dye. How her pert nipples would become strained, erect nubs. How he could pinch them until the hard red points showed through the blue stain, both colors contrasted by the dark cream of her firm breasts. Fuck, he'd never been more stricken by a creative interpretation of his country's colors, even if it was still in his head.

Oh, say can you see . . .

"Perfect. You're so goddamned perfect, Pixie."

By the dawn's early light . . .

"Thank you, Sir."

"No. Talking. Only obeying, little girl. Now shuck those shorts for me."

And sweet damn, she *was* light. Early, late, and in-between—the entire glorious spectrum of the stuff. So much of it flowing from her desire-filled gaze. Even more shimmering across the dark curls at her intimate apex. It even reached to her toes, ten flawless points that were coated in red polish. A devilish color for his divine pixie angel.

The comparison got better as she rose from pushing her shorts to the floor. Her expression blended seraphic honesty with diabolic desire. Brick vacillated between adoring her and cursing her for it. But she couldn't be blamed for the open ogle, considering the state to which his dick was rapidly rising. What had made him think a pair of borrowed scrubs were a wise idea for this?

Because he hadn't, in his wildest imaginings, predicted things happening like this. By this point, he was supposed to be ejected on his figurative ass and halfway back to the infirmary, enduring the world's most knotted gut because he hadn't apologized decently to her. In every single scenario he'd concocted, nothing came close to standing here in shameless reverence of her total nudity. They certainly didn't include how he'd be contemplating her next nasty act. Hopefully, something fun for him too.

God*damn*, the possibilities. The choices were so beautifully boundless, but their time was so cruelly limited.

But luckily, he'd dealt with cruelty before. He also knew how to spit back at it—especially if kink was involved.

Especially with a subbie who had told him not to take it easy on her.

"Stand all the way up now, sweetheart. Shoulders proud. Tits forward." While he used the order to buy himself time for inspiration, the visual reward was an extra bonus. She was his stunning little soldier, at full attention even with more blue blobs dripping over her neck, collarbones, and breasts.

Fuck him so hard. Her *breasts*.

In Paris, Fate hadn't allowed him the chance to soak up their full glory. At the safehouse, he'd been concerned about making her first fuck one of her best. And during their dry hump in the cemetery, it'd been a good thing to even see her face.

Now, he couldn't get enough of ogling her. Marveling at her red dart points, seeming to strain for him despite her formal stance. Delighting at how her areolas puckered and hardened, becoming the ideal bull's-eyes for those perfect nipples.

"So gorgeous," he said softly. "But I think we can do better."

He said it because his improvisation genius had finally decided to come to the party. He indulged it with a fleeting smirk and a steady sweep of his hand toward her vanity top. When he turned back around and approached Jayd with steady intent, it was damn fun to read the confusion on her petite features. Clearly, she was ready to question what he was all about, though she obeyed his upheld finger and waited in dutiful silence.

He'd never had such a good time reducing a submissive to shivers.

The tremors that intensified as he lifted his hands, each bearing a bright-red hair clip.

They were the smaller kind of hair fixtures, used for shit like holding back bangs, able to bend and snap in the middle. Brick had no idea what they were technically called. He only knew he was going to have some fun with them.

"Yes, my little pixie. *Now* we're going to have some fun."

She was still being good. She responded only with a deep inhalation and the dawning awareness in her wide gaze. Holy crap, he loved these small but supreme moments. When a woman read his intent, knew exactly what it meant for her, but persevered with full compliance, he was that much closer to the sanctum of his Dom space.

That much closer to owning a new part of this female.

"Reach behind, sweetheart. Lock your hands behind your back." He caught the full force of her wordless challenge to that and explained, "It'll be easier for you to resist reaching up."

She gave him another questioning look.

Right before he snapped the first clip tight around her nipple.

"Ahhh! What on ear—*ahhh*!"

Her second outcry coincided with his sharp smack across her ass.

"Oh, Pixie," he gently berated. "What did I say about talking?"

"That was yelling, Brickham, not talk—ahhh!"

As he delivered another spank, he almost wished she'd

keep up the rants. Sweet God, her backside was so pert and pretty. Now, it was warm too. He got even harder, dreaming of how it would feel at the point of full heat.

Her scream hit the air another time as soon as he finished clamping the clip to her other breast. Regrettably, she took the pain without babbling this time. Brick substituted the spanking high with listening to her sharp, incensed breaths. Just as intoxicating as before. Just as beautiful as the visual he drank in now.

"Fuck me to Paris and back, Pixie." He didn't hide a note of his hoarse appreciation. "You're already ripe for the bite."

Again, no words from her—though her tiny, terrified whimper possessed his libido in deeper ways. All the ways that told him to go ahead and do it. To dip in his head, slide a clip back, and close his teeth over the decadent, dark red candy that he'd exposed.

"*Ohhh!*" she yelped. "Brickham! By the Creator, ple—"

Smack.

"Damn it! Oh, by the saints—"

Smack.

She was a wordless mass of moans as he bit into her other nipple.

She was a collection of tearful sighs as he took both the clips off.

"There you go," he soothed, circling her angry peaks in order to spread the heat from her pain. "There you go, sweet girl. Let it all burn. Let it all tingle."

Jayd pressed into him, letting him hold her close while shivers racked her little frame. Brick let the moment drench his senses too, especially as he dropped his touch to her ass cheeks and reveled in the fire that streaked over her tender flesh.

Unbelievably, as hot as he'd gotten her, he wanted more. What would it feel like to actually take her higher into that realm? To mark her sienna silk skin with welts from her Master? To deliver those brands while feeling her asshole stretch to take his cock?

Good Christ.

She wasn't going to have *any* glory from his erection, in any naughty *or* acceptable orifices, unless he turned that fantasy the fuck off.

No coming in the cotton scrubs, dickhead.

The order worked, helping him to release her ass. Jayd seemed grateful for it too, returning to her at-attention posture from before. Brick allowed himself a shit-eating smirk when noticing she kept her hands at her sides. All right, then. No more tormenting the tits for today.

To be fair, her lovely swells did look properly punished. "Damn," he said, taking just one more moment to properly triumph. "Your breasts were made for hard worship, Pixie. You may say thank you, Sir."

She darted up a peeved glance. "In your wildest dreams, Sir."

A laugh spilled out—quite possibly the best one of his life. "But I'm gazing at my wildest dream already, sweetheart."

As punctuation, he pressed closer to her again . . . with two fingers aimed toward the center of her pussy. Both his digits glided in without effort, instantly drenched by the lusty liquid that coated her walls.

"Oh, yes," he grated, twisting and thrusting even deeper. "The wildest dreams I've ever had."

At once, his darling pixie shifted her position too. With one hand, she gripped the ball of his shoulder. With the other, she clung to his flexed forearm.

"Mmm," she whined. "Mmm . . . hmmm!"

"Gorgeous woman," Brick drawled, caressing his breath across her forehead. "You like that, don't you? Knowing your cunt is prepared for me. Knowing you're so hot and soaked and craving me." She nodded into his kiss, and a wider smile breached his mouth. "That's what the pain did to you, Pixie. The flowing blood. The racing endorphins. And now, your sweet, tight channel . . ."

She flowed another groan out. It pitched to a little shriek as soon as he jabbed a third finger into her precious tunnel. When the fourth went in, she hissed sharply.

"Relax," Brick exhorted. "Just relax, little girl. I told you I wasn't going to be easy this time, and we're only getting started."

Well, that had her sufficiently riled again. One sweeping jerk of her head and he had an eyeful of her vitally curious stare.

"Oh, you heard me right," he replied to her silent demand. "Just letting you breathe now. And getting you prepared."

Prepared for what?

Again, she only shouted it with her eyes. Good thing her aquas were so huge and easy to read. Like a thousand poems he'd never get tired of devouring . . .

And that was more than enough of that. He wasn't here to spout Byron and Yeats at her. She'd asked for Prince and Beyonce and AC/DC. She wanted raw and rough and uncensored. He was more than happy to be her go-to guy.

In more than a few ways, maybe this was what they both needed anyway. Maybe this would put the final, satisfying scratch on their electric itch. Once she experienced the true depravity of his dark side, she'd be ready to flip off her switch for him and then fry all the wires. And once he knew the full force of her disgust, it'd be easier to think about getting off this island.

It had to be this way.

It was *better* this way.

So what the hell? He might as well enjoy the freefall.

"You'll find out when you find out," he finally said, addressing her question with deceiving ease. She didn't hold back on telling him what she thought of the purposeful enigma, narrowing her glower and pursing her lips. Dear fucking God, she was adorable at the height of her feist. "But I guarantee it'll all be fun . . . at least for one of us."

Her reaction was better than what he'd fantasized. Her eyebrows leapt back up, her mouth popped open, her breaths quickened to the point that her breasts bobbed with an alluring new cadence.

He was hypnotized by the sight—but only for a handful of seconds. He hadn't been lying. They were only getting started. He had some lofty, nasty ideas for this woman's gorgeous body, and new waves of creative inspiration were hitting by the minute.

But first, one more moment of beholding her face.

How brave she was trying to keep it, despite all the new quirks of fear his promise had brought on. A subtle but palpable flush crawled its way up from her chest, mixing with the bright blue dye dots from the foils still hanging out on her head. Her new color was going to be seventeen kinds of messed-up, especially after the new adventure he was concocting next, but he was beyond caring. A painfully hard dick could do that to a man, especially with an extraordinary woman who forced him to accept every drop of his testosterone.

The hormones that had him wrapping a hand to her nape and hauling her flush to him again.

That had him squeezing hard and jerking on the dry strands at the back of her head, silently ordering her to look up at him.

That had him falling into her beauty all over again, plunging his mouth solidly over hers.

At once, she opened for him. Like he was giving her any choice about it. Nevertheless, he reveled in the willing greed of her dancing tongue. All the gorgeous moans that came with it. All the passion he needed so badly, in every inch of his body and soul.

He *needed*...

And was going to take.

Until the ache persisted too hard. Or he straight-up died.

But damn it, what a way to go. This was good. So fucking good. *She was so fucking perfect.*

He necked with her like that much longer than he'd intended, but she tasted so much better than he remembered. Her natural jasmine and roses were sweetened by something else. Something with...caramel? Coffee? Tea? Candy? He didn't care. The odd combination was his new crack.

But even junkies had to come down if they wanted their highs to be better.

He groaned, forcing his brain to accept that. Though he abhorred even the few inches between them now, he concentrated on the good shit to come.

The things he was about to command of her.

The erotic places he was going to take her to.

The *no* he prayed she'd banned as much as him.

★ ★ ★

"Checking in, sweetheart. You still okay?"

Finally, an easy request the man asked of her. As she answered him with a silent, steady nod, Jayd hoped the orders from here would be just as simple to heed.

But in so many ways, she didn't.

Aside from the last week and a half, she had led a fairly charmed life. She was the first to admit that—and, concurrently, to hate it. Even her latest push at the boundaries, which had taken her all the way to Paris, hadn't felt like a trial as much as an adventure.

Now that she wasn't actually a princess, she still knew not if she even had the mettle of one. The courage to persevere through pain. The willingness to face her own fear and overcome it.

Granted, this was not like going into battle—but maybe, in many warped ways, it would help her with some of those blank pages.

Best of all, she would be doing it for Brickham. For his pleasure and approval. Right now, they both felt like everything.

"Good," the man himself crooned, leaning over to buss her forehead. "That's so good to know, because here we go."

She was getting good at conveying questions with her gaze. *Go? To where?*

"As I said before, you'll find out when you find out. But the first place you'll travel is to your knees. Right here."

Thank the Creator, another simple one. He made the moment even better by stripping off his shirt while she lowered to the tile. No way could she resist gazing up his massive body to admire the sculpted male triangle of his upper body.

So many hard hills and etched valleys. There wasn't a single soft spot on the man—a description that also applied to the part of him that supported the sharp tent in his cotton pants.

The part she also could not ignore. Oh no, not at all.

"You like looking at that, Pixie?" His soft snarl was tinged with rough pleasure now. He liked it when she gawked at him. Somehow she truly knew that. He teased her more, working the green fabric around his bulge. He tautened the fabric until it outlined its hard, heated girth.

"You like knowing what you've done to me there? How every inch of my cock clamors because of you?"

As Jayd watched, he kept working at the material against his erection. The rest of the world fell away. All she wanted, all she needed, was right there, pulsing with power and hardening with lust. All for her. All because of her. The thoughts made her dizzy. Fuzzy. Set her on fire with equally bright yearnings . . .

"You want a better look?" he husked at last—but she had no more nodded with eagerness before he said, "Well, you'll get it soon."

She rocked back on her haunches with a groan. The sexy *bonsun* before her responded with a similar sound. This could not be any easier for him, yet he was holding back—somehow, in some superhuman way—to give her all this. To show her his darkness. It was the bed she'd made, so now she would lie in it, though she prayed that took the form of her giant bed in the next room over, with Brickham pounding her into the mattress.

As if the man had also gained the ability to read her mind, he said then, "First things first, little pixie. If your hair dye was mud, we'd already have a filthy barnyard in here." He gestured toward the bathtub with an elegance that was new for her. Gods of goodness, the force of nature could move like a summer breeze. If his goal was not to spoil her for any other man, he was miserably failing.

"Ready? Good."

He stacked the words like splintered pallets, though that was less jarring than the action that accompanied them. His hand at the back of her head, anchoring into her scalp so he could guide her over to the tub. Yes, that forcibly. Yes, even with the three-day-old bullet wounds in his body.

"On your hands and knees is fine, sweetheart. I'm enjoying the view of my handiwork."

Thank the Creator it was not too late to reconsider the *spoiling her* part.

The distance to the tub seemed twice as far with unusual parts of her slapping the tiles. She took no measure to hide her angry and embarrassed grunts, timed with every degrading moment of the ordeal. But between her peeved bursts, she became aware of another sound. Brickham's bestial hums. The recognition that her servitude was bringing *his* pleasure.

Again, she was processing feelings she had never known. Purpose in her pain. A strange victory in her ignominy.

What was happening to her?

Was this man of the shadows dragging her to even darker places? Forbidden acts she should be running from? Or was he simply awakening what had been inside her all the time? And what did either answer mean?

There was only one way to find out.

To keep doing as he ordered.

"All right. In with you, girl. But no water yet. Lie on your back, facing sideways, with your legs toward me."

Even if it was trusting him about bizarre instructions like that.

"Good. Very good. Now scoot a little closer. Hook your knees over this lip."

And like that.

"Good girl."

He had that mysterious tone of voice again. The kind that reminded her of a wicked narrator in a haunted house. Sure, he knew what was coming next—but it was his secret and nobody else's.

"Hands up, flat to the spaces next to your head." He gave her that addicting hum again, watching her comply. At the same time, he grabbed a pair of towels from the rack and pressed them over her palms. "If either of these moves, there *will* be swats," he stated. "Exactly like this one."

She had been so obedient about noises for so long, her startled shriek was a foreign sound. And a frightening one.

Had Brickham just paddled her . . . *right there*?

"Hell yes, I just did." Once more, her Dominant had become her mind reader. "I don't have access to your ass, sweetheart—and discipline is sacred in my play spaces."

Jayd was too busy inhaling much-needed air to be irked by his cocky air. She knew his jesting demeanor would not last long, and she was validated the very next moment. At once, the shadows took over him again, so fierce and focused. If his wounds were giving him pain by returning to his wide X of a stance, he exposed no outward signs of it. Once more, he was all steel and sinew, coal and command . . . desire and dominion.

Thankfully, he gave her a moment to process the sight of him like that. She needed a million more, but she would make do with what he granted. These precious seconds to marvel at his rippling grandeur. To tremble at his unblinking scrutiny. To acknowledge exactly what all of it was doing to her mind, her spirit, her body.

She belonged to him.

Maybe not forever, but the heady reality of now was good enough.

And now, more than ever before, she longed for him to prove it. To stamp himself on her, *inside* her, so the indentations lasted forever.

She wanted every drop of his desire. Every corner of his shadows. Every slice of his pain . . .

And yes, even the jolt of his next unexpected words.

"Checking in again, Pixie. Where are you at, sweet girl? You may speak to answer me."

She drew careful breath. "I . . . am fine, Sir," she whispered. "Truly. I am . . . It is just all so . . ."

His brows drew together. "So . . . what?"

She could do nothing but frantically shake her head and close her eyes. "Please," she rasped. "Just . . . pull me under again. Tell me what you want."

Though tension took over more of his formidable features, his reply was wrapped in velvet sensuality. "Why don't you show me what I want, Pixie?"

Before his gaze slipped lower, Jayd became *his* clairvoyant. She felt his need like the beat of her own heart . . . the pulse that thrummed throughout the triangle she exposed to him by slowly spreading her legs.

"Beautiful," Brickham grated. "Yes. Thank you, my little toy. That's very good." He grunted while reaching down, giving his crotch a ruthless squeeze. "I want to come just looking at you. *Fuck*."

Jayd gave in to a soft smile. His burly sough suddenly made all her awkward feelings and aching muscles worth it.

But just when she thought he would grant a reprieve from the uneasy position, he stepped forward and grabbed her beneath the knees. With that extra leverage, he hauled her forward until her backside was braced against the tub's lip and her thighs were open like wings.

"Oh, dear heavens!" she exclaimed, robbed of the chance to think clearly—or the opportunity to make ready for the stinging spank on her mons. "Ohhh, *fuck*! Please, Brickham, not ag—owww!"

At least the man had yanked her forward so fast, the towels moved with her. And at least he did not leave her trembling and hurting. He remained right there, circling his long fingers through her curls and the quivering folds beneath. He peered down at her with quiet authority—and breath-robbing beauty.

"Want to tell me what's sacred in our space, little pixie?"

She gulped hard before stammering, "D-Discipline."

"Correct," he returned. "Good girl. Because without discipline, there's no understanding of the rules or the roles. And the roles are what?"

A fast lick of her lips, buying time as she struggled to remember the answer. She *knew* it, but the man robbed her of more and more recall with every knowing swipe of his fingers. Stroking closer and closer to the little crest of her desire . . .

"They . . . are . . . ummm . . ."

"Yes?"

Closer . . .

Please . . .

"They . . . You are the Dominant." It left in an exultant rush. Thank the Creator and all his angels!

"And you are . . ."

"The submissive."

Surely *now* he would rub her where she most needed it . . .

"Which means you are here to do what?"

"Please you," she blurted. "By obeying you. Which I *am* doing, yes? Brickham, by all that's holy—*ahhh*!"

Her arousal plummeted by significant notches. Being spanked soundly on one's intimates probably had something to do with it.

"What the hell was that for?"

"Speaking out of turn, sweet subbie," he admonished. "And now, yet again . . ." He bent over, parking his hands wide on the tub lip while pushing his shoulders against her inner thighs. "Have you grown tired of pussy swats already? Do I just need to get more creative here?"

Something in his suggestion had her stare bugging. The way he emphasized *creative* . . . By the stars, how could he be more imaginative than this? The possibilities boggled her mind as Brickham took a step back and started looking around the bathroom, even peering over into the vanity area.

"If we were at Bastille, I'd have a dozen clear-cut solutions for this," he murmured. "So many awesome punishments for you right at my fingertips. Maybe some clamps or wax. Perhaps a dildo or an electric wand . . ."

An electric *what*?

She was on the brink of yelling it out, consequences be damned, when the man snapped his fingers as if the perfect solution had magically materialized from thin air.

What on earth had him so entranced?

As soon as Jayd followed the trajectory of his gaze, snapping that answer into place, her horrified shriek did burst out.

CHAPTER SEVEN

Officially, Brick couldn't tack on extra discipline for his Pixie's sharp scream. She'd taken care—or was perhaps too shocked—to not add words to it, and he doubted it had carried that far beyond this cavern of a bathroom.

Besides . . . it was goddamned sexy.

Especially when it tumbled out of her again—the very second he walked to the cabinet beside the vanity and pried the brand-new curling wand out of its pristine plastic package nest.

"Now look at this," he said, purposely exaggerating his amazement. "A new toy for your new look, sweetheart? I think it's just begging us to break it in properly."

Jayd only whimpered a reply, though her legs visibly trembled. Holy shit. If her thighs were doing that, Brick could only imagine the party along her inner walls too. He was certain she wasn't viewing things that way, but the woman wasn't officially restrained. If she wasn't jiving with his wild turn of freaky, she had the freedom to bolt.

When he turned fully back with the iron in hand, dragging the unplugged cord behind him, she still didn't move.

And in the process blew his mind to smithereens.

Never had he encountered an untried, unbound subbie like this before. So brave, even knowing what he wanted to try with her. So ready to keep pleasing him despite the crazy position into which he'd pretzeled her. Still holding her thighs wide, her ass up, and her arms in place despite the blue goo spackled across them. Still not uttering a word, even as Brick repositioned himself between her legs.

"My God, you dazzle me," he confessed in a low growl. "How you make me want to hurl this thing away and fuck you until we're a pair of screaming Smurfs… But discipline has to happen here, sweetheart. You'll take it for me, right? You'll make me proud?"

She only gave him her hard, deliberating breaths. Brick braced himself to watch her delectable ass as she scrambled from the room, desperate to be away from him forever. Though it wouldn't be his first experience with a mortified subbie who'd claimed she could take the hard stuff, he had a feeling this would sting the deepest. Too deep for comfort.

But then she nodded up at him.

She was a little wan and a lot shaky, but those tiny jerks were definitely nods of concession.

And fuck him if her gorgeous orifice, spread for him like a decadent dessert, didn't weep with some thicker tears of blatant arousal.

"Damn me to the best chambers of hell," he grated. "This might be a little fun, after all."

★ ★ ★

Jayd's heart was in her throat. Her mind—at least the sane part—was gone. Her arms trembled, and her legs were naught but collections of wild tingles. At least she knew the reason for that. All the blood between her toes and hips was a massive pool of sensation between her legs.

The part of her subjected to every degree of Brickham's hot cobalt stare.

The part of her that became a matching broiler of arousal.

The part of her that sent a harsh gasp up to her mouth as soon as he slid the cold steel into her pussy.

Oh, dear heavens.

It was an instant invasion. A slow, sinister thrust wielded by a wickedly smiling god. It was strange and ruthless and persistent, and yet she choked harder as her tender tissues flexed to welcome it. She was stunned to hear the soft slicks, generated by her own body, as Brickham started some gentle pumps of the steel shaft.

Stars and saints!

Was she really doing this?

Was she really letting him do this?

Was she really *liking* it?

No. That was not the right word. Or was it? How *did* she feel about this? It was not sheer bliss, of that she was certain. But there were parts of her that called out for more. That begged her to endure, to continue . . . to persevere. It was a new and fascinating feeling. A place where she was wide open, fully bare . . . utterly free.

"That's it. What a good girl you are."

Brickham's voice was strong in her mind but fuzzy in her senses. Even so, she had never felt more connected to him. More sewn into his shadows. The darkness was cruel and illicit as he had warned her—but she did not want to leave.

She wanted more.

So much more.

"My God. You're drenching this thing, sweetheart. What a naughty Pixie you are, getting so wet even in your punishment." With his free hand, the man started stroking circles through the drenched curls of her mons, once more taunting close to her engorged little button. So close . . . but not close enough. "I think your cunt wants more of this big fuck stick. And I think I'm going to grant its wish."

She was certain she drew blood from biting her lower lip. It was her only defense against spewing with a wry comeback. What that retort would have been, she would never know—because the next moment, he took complete control of her mind as well as her senses.

The penetration was overwhelming. Overpowering. Deep and painful.

And perfect.

Everything in the world went away. Her worries. Her stresses. Her identity and all her confusion about it. Right now, she had only one persona. One purpose. To please her Master with the gift of her body.

It was enough. *She* was enough.

"*Breathe*, Pixie."

She heard his exhortation at the edges of her awareness, and she obeyed. The focus opened more than her lungs. In the depths of her channel, the rod plunged farther.

"Good girl. Such a good little fuck toy. You can take more, Jayd. Do it for me."

She took another huge breath.

More slides of wet friction in the air.

More pushes of the steel cock inside her body.

"Jesus Christ." Brickham's voice grew thick with a new intent. Something that had woven a strange softness into his gruffness. "I've been a hundred places on this planet and never seen anything so . . ." He stopped on a tight cough. "You take my breath away, Pixie. You just—"

When he interrupted himself again, this time to pull the

rod all the way out and cast it aside, she knew not whether to worry or rejoice. Had she inadvertently done something wrong? Moved or cried out against his wishes?

But as the iron clattered to the floor and he ripped at the drawstring on his scrubs, she had her answer—and it was good.

So. Very. Good.

"Goddammit." Brickham fisted the gleaming, glorious length of his penis. "Fuck it." He lined it up with her gaping entrance. "Oh, fuck *me*."

And then, in one long lunge, impaled himself inside her.

"*Ohhh!*"

Holding back rain would have been easier than controlling her scream. She just prayed, as a matching torrent welled up from her chest and burst from her eyes, that Brickham was no longer in disciplinary mode.

"Yes," he snarled, locking his cobalts on her with an array of clear intents. None of them were penalization, but they were also far from praising warmth. He was still her captivating overlord. Her magnificent tyrant. Her roiling, unforgiving beast of lust. "Don't hide a drop of those tears from me, sweetheart. Not a note of your screams either. I'll have it all from you, little subbie—the same way I'm taking every inch of this."

His context needed no explanation, but he gave it anyway. With barely a grunt of strain, the man wrapped his hands around her thighs from the outside in. His grip was massive and strong, taking on most of her weight—as well as full control of how their bodies grinded into each other. *Oh yes,* including the pressure of his pelvis against a wider swath of her pussy. *Oh yes,* including the harder drive of his shaft into the darkest reaches of her body. *Oh yes,* including how the smacks of their flesh hit the tiled walls like the most stunning symphony she had ever heard.

Ohhh... yesss...

Jayd had never congratulated herself more for surrendering to him.

For all of two seconds.

The second he ramped his pace to fuck her like an ax cleaving a log, she had no mind left for the private celebration. For that matter, keeping *anything* confidential from him. Brickham had declared it so, and she would obey. She was his helpless servant. His eager plaything. And now, his tremoring submissive... so ready to give him her vibrant orgasm.

If only he would take it.

Damn it, *damn it*, why would he not take it?

The absence of that answer had her crying harder. With every new pound of his cock, every cell of her blood soared with hope, only to be quashed with frustration. Her moans became desperate. Her sex was on fire. Her thighs were clenched, her clit was nearly her enemy.

"Yes, Pixie."

Finally, *finally*, his affirmation held what she had waited for. Like a storm on approach to a shore, he growled with confidence... and impaled her without mercy.

"Come on. You've got it for me, don't you?" he grated. "I feel it, sweetheart. I feel it trembling, so deep in this pretty cunt."

"Yes, Sir." She was out of breath and full of sensation. So much urgent pressure and hot need. "Oh, yes, Sir!"

"Not your words," he snarled. "You know what I want more, naughty pixie." He rolled his hips while his cock was still entrenched inside her. His feral moan joined her strident cry.

"Give it to me, Jayd. Give it all to—"

She cut him off with the new pitch of her scream.

With the wild spasms of her sex.

With the orgasm that painted her blood in light and lust and freedom. That rocked her body in violence and splendor. That brought a blissful, biblical dystopia to the reaches of her mind, filling it with explosions as bright as the sun.

By the Creator's equally blinding balls.

Was she dead? If so, she never wished to be resuscitated.

Unless, perhaps, if it was Brickham who brought the new air. And, like he did right now, the new pain. The sweet agony of her screaming tissues, stretching to take even more of his glorious penis. Still, he grinded deeper into her. Harder...

"Jesus... fuck me raw," he stammered. "This is so..."

"Brickham," she panted back but had no idea how. It had to be the Creator's intervention. Nothing in her mind was making sense otherwise. Nothing in her *body* was making sense. Every wire was cut. Or reversed. Or pumped with too much current. *So much. Too much!* But somehow, in some insane way, not enough. "Please," she begged. "Do not stop. Do... not..."

"Fuck, sweetheart." His baritone voice blended into her tile-pounding aria. "You've got another one, don't you?"

She could only answer him with a stuttering scream. It ruptured from her lips in time to the gushes of climaxing heat from inside. She could feel it all now, drenching Brickham anew, turning his lunges into wild, slippery bliss.

"Goddammit," he croaked. "Oh, god*damm*it, what have you done to me?"

It took several seconds for her to be fully confused by that. Most specifically, by the pique that underlined it.

"Sir?" she stammered, unsure of what else to do. "Are you all r—"

Well, that was silly. And stupid. He was definitely all right. As all right as her. The man showed her himself while slowly pulling free from her.

His cock was shiny—coated so splendidly with her cream. And dripping so profusely with his come.

"Oh."

Like before, her mental circuits could only produce one clear word at a time.

"Oh. My."

Also like before, comprehending everything from Brickham was a fuzzy chore. But the man was hardly helping. Most of his words were muttered profanity as he reached and seized one of the towels from over her hands. He returned to terse silence while rubbing out the rest of his orgasm into the plush cotton, though his jaw stayed clenched for many long moments after.

Jayd gently pushed herself backward, lowering all the way into the bathtub with deliberate care—for herself as well as Brickham. She used the second towel to wipe herself off as much as possible, though she already knew how tender her sex and its surroundings would be for the next few days. Perhaps, if she was lucky, for at least the next week.

The thought alone made her smile, even if her Dominant was intent on hanging on to every harsh ridge of his grimace. At least those edges seemed to soften once he canted his gaze toward hers again.

"Come here," he bade quietly, extending his hand. There was a heavy sigh lurking in his voice. It rushed out as soon as he lifted her into his towel-covered lap. "Fuck," he muttered while gently pulling free the few dye foils that remained in her hair. "I'm... so sorry, Pixie."

Jayd twisted her head, burrowing into the center of his chest. "I am not."

She meant every word and hoped he heard the vulnerable truth she had just exposed, as well. The full honesty of her heart. He did not get any surlier, which was a very good sign that he'd heard. Her joy brightened as he pulled on her hand and pressed a soft kiss into her palm.

"That's never happened to me before," he murmured.

Jayd stroked along his jaw, into the stubble that was rapidly becoming a beard. "Pixie says, me neither."

He made a weak effort at a chuckle. "Pixie *should* be saying she should've told her Sir that her second orgasm would feel even better than the first, so he could properly prepare his cock."

She smirked. "Perhaps Pixie should be punished for that."

"Not if Pixie doesn't want her maid suspecting that Sir has escaped through a trap door with her."

It felt magnificent to rock her head back on a full giggle. "Oh, why did we not think of that before?"

Though Brickham did not mirror her mirth, the depths of his gaze remained as cloudless as an April sky. "You're that sure we can find a trap door around here?"

She widened her grin. "Three, to be precise."

"Excuse me?"

"In my suite alone," she said. "Remember, the Arcadians are descendants of the French. The original designers of the palais enjoyed bringing their *secrets architecturaux* with them."

At last, a hint of handsome humor from him. "Now she tells me."

"Well, if you had told me you were hobbling over for some

playtime in the shadows . . ."

He reached around and lightly smacked her thigh. "Wasn't the case and you know it."

Jayd squirmed a little. Dear stars, what the man and his swats did to her. Even the playful taps. "Yes, Sir," she whispered. "I do."

He tempered his rebuke with a tender kiss to her mouth. "But for tempting me in a fully lighted bathroom, you sure know where all my shadows are, woman."

"Because they're the part of you I adore the most."

She was resigned that Brickham would take that as one more line in their new lightheartedness. She should have known he would not.

She should have known that he would hear every syllable that had emanated from the farthest reaches of her spirit, the most vulnerable edges of her heart.

She should have known that in hearing all of it, he would see her darkness too.

And that he would prove it to her now, leaning down to take her mouth with the most brutal passion of his. The most painful slam of his lips. The most primal force of his groan. She tangled her own desire with it, savagely sighing into his hot, wet mouth. She dug her fingernails into his shoulder and then along his head, until she gripped him with ferocity that spurred him into pained grunts.

Oh, no!

"Creator's mercy," she blurted, pulling away. "We have to think about getting you back to the infirmary. You should not be up and about this much. Do *not* comment on that."

She added a stern stare and a wagging finger, ignoring the fact that less than fifteen minutes ago, she would have paraded naked on the balcony at his command. Clearly, Brickham had not forgotten either. It was a secret thrill to watch his gaze narrow, wondering what discipline he was deliberating for her this time. But she was determined to stay firm. They could not strain his wounds any further. Maybe she could talk him into a little more of this heavenly snuggle time instead . . .

"*Rahmie Creacu.*"

And there, in the space of the stunned gasp that sliced across the room, went heaven.

"Jayd Dawne!" Requiemme's burst wobbled a lot like her stance. While the latter was no mystery, especially as the woman grabbed at the door frame for better balance in her cast, Jayd could not decipher the intent of the former. No, not correct either. She saw and heard Emme's halting little laugh.

"Whatever it is I have halted, *desonnum tres sorlik.*" The woman rushed forward until realizing Brickham was only draped in a towel. Or perhaps that every last dye foil was everywhere but on Jayd's head. "Believe me, no soul is happier you two have kissed—or variations thereof—and made up. But we have higher concerns at the moment."

Jayd was also on her way to a smile, stirred by the happy high from her friend's support. Until she absolutely was not. "Higher?" she demanded. "In what way?"

"At the moment?" Emme returned. "The worst." Locating Jayd's clothes on the floor, she swept them up and tossed them over with brusque efficiency. "Something has happened. Something significant. I know only that it involves Carris—and that your brothers are on their way up here to talk about it right now."

CHAPTER EIGHT

If looks could be torture devices, Brick was damn sure he was being racked, dog-roped, and waterboarded at the same time. The old-fashioned rack would definitely be Evrest Cimarron's preference, while Prince Shiraz would select waterboarding for its straightforward ease—or maybe just because he knew Samsyn had dibs on the dog roping. The most hulking of the three brothers had already channeled two Rottweilers and a Mastiff into his nonstop glower at Brick, and the mental kennel wasn't closing anytime soon.

And they call it puppy love...

How he wished it was only a piece of inner snark. But he already knew how everything must appear to Jayd's siblings, who'd burst into her suite just seconds after he'd followed her out of the bathroom. If he'd been one of them, he'd be pulling out the figurative torture options too. He and Jayd were covered in blue dye splotches, and that didn't cover the chaos of her new hair color. Her T-shirt was also inside out, and there was a massive damp spot on the crotch of his borrowed scrubs.

Under any other circumstances, he'd be getting acquainted with a holding cell in the bowels of this place by now.

But this wasn't a normal circumstance. Not in the remotest sense of the word.

The flatscreen that dominated most of one wall in Jayd's suite was tuned to BFM, France's 24/7 news carrier. The reason was obvious: a live press conference from the main

Prefecture de Police in Paris, where the soaring Florentine architecture was enhanced by a wall of stiff officers, a cluster of stern politicians, and a sizable podium that was lit up with glaring spotlights.

In the center of all that, clearly savoring every second in his massive pulpit, was Trystan fucking Carris.

Ass. Wipe.

Making it a mental mantra didn't help Brick's burning desire to plow his fist into the screen. But all that would get him was the grand escort to the dungeon, tromping through plops of his own blood along with the lingering hair dye.

But already, Carris was edging closer and closer to his carotid.

The disjointed feed wasn't helping a damn thing. Most of the reporters were accommodating Trystan by asking questions in English, which was translated at once into French for the feed. Since Brick understood both, his synapses were jumping like a round of linguistic *Assassin's Creed.*

"Once again, I shall be very clear about this," Carris said to a skeptical-looking brunette who'd elbowed her way to the front of the media mob. "I *was* in that pub on Sunday night. I *did* witness everything that happened to that poor man at the heartless hand of Maximillian Brickham."

At once, Jayd hissed. "Lying *soldask*!"

"*Calmay.*" Shiraz, definitely the prettiest of the three brothers, leaned over and tucked his sister close. "He is doing it for spin. We all know that, sister."

The glance he speared over her head spoke differently, but Brick easily absorbed the animosity. Though the man's sister was safely returned, it hadn't been by a peaceful path. They had to blame someone for that, and he was the closest target.

For now.

Jayd drew breath for a fresh rant, but the intense reporter saved them all with her aggressive lean at Carris. "*Pourquoi?*" she demanded. "But why? To be blunt, monsieur, you have not sung us any new tune. We have all seen the footage. We all know exactly what happened, moment by moment, and precisely who was involved. What you have promised yet not delivered is *why*."

"Irianna is right," another journalist interjected. "There are too many blank spaces in this narrative. Why that dingy little pub, all the way in Montmartre, when Monsieur Brickham had a room at the Ritz? Why did the man drag her *there*—and why did you wait several hours to follow them there, if you were so eager to get Princess Jayd away from the lunatic? There is footage of them a half hour before that, getting cozy on the Place Blanche. Where were you and your men then?"

"*Lunatic?*"

Jayd squirmed away from Shiraz, looking ready to hurl her own fist into the screen. Brick bit the inside of his cheek to hide a proud as fuck grin. He couldn't remember the last time someone had stuck up for him with such vehemence. It was weirdly cool. It was scarily arousing.

"*Fembla—*"

"Do *not* right now, 'Raz," she spat. "Do not expect me to be calm about seeing an honorable man—a natural protector and hero, just like all three of you—being painted as a freak predator. Those are major outlet journalists! They should be ashamed. Have they not done their homework about some of this? Have they not realized that—"

"Pixie." He dove in, knowing the arched brows he'd get from the king and both princes for his deliberate slip. The payoff, getting Jayd's attention for longer than three seconds, was worth it. Hopefully. "I think they probably did do that footwork but ran into a few chunks of... redacted material."

He didn't know how else to phrase it, especially because Shiraz came through with a confirming glance. When he was joined by a meaningful side-eye from Evrest, the truth locked solidly into place.

They might be touting him as a whack job and a murderer, but at least he wasn't that "monster" from Seattle battling chronic panic disorder on top of running a hardcore kink club. He owed them, big fucking time, for getting all that crap suppressed. Whatever it took, he'd gladly repay the favor—especially because they'd wrapped the third mystery into the package too. The most important secret to them as well as him.

"You are all familiar with the expression timing is everything, *n'est-ce pas*?" Carris leveled at the throng up in Paris. "Well, we had a deliberate reason for waiting out Brickham as we did."

A violent snort spewed from Jayd. "Because you are the *degan kimfuks* who set the trap for us?"

Samsyn whipped over a glare. "*Fembla!*"

She glowered back. "What?"

"Watch your fucking language!"

"*Silence.*"

It was the first word King Evrest had uttered since they arrived, but it was already in a language Brick supported. Clear leadership was like a magic spell in a pit of chaos, especially if one's unofficial enemy was on TV making statements that sounded all too official.

"Maximillian Brickham took Jayd Cimarron to Montmartre because he was getting ready to confront her with a devastating truth," Trystan declared. "A specific truth about her past."

"Shit." Brick was joined by Samsyn and Shiraz in the gritted growl. Requiemme got busy with a rasping plea to her Creator, but Evrest and Jayd were silent.

Too damn silent.

But there was no time to dissect all that. Like them, Brick was morbidly riveted on the screen. Carris was a ringmaster in the hot light of stardom, not about to jump off his trick elephant of momentum.

"A truth," he added then, "that will change not only her, but the fabric of our nation."

Fate gave them a split second of relief, as Irianna the Intense released a scathing chuckle. "You are speaking about a twenty-four-year-old princess, monsieur, not her elder brother."

"Ahhh." Carris was ready with his own scoff. "A princess. But do you *really* mean . . . a *princess*?"

"And here it comes," Shiraz snarled.

"Scum of my sweaty scrotum," Samsyn spat. Since it bested anything Brick had in mind, he gave the guy nodding props.

"And that means exactly what?" another reporter demanded, already inciting Carris's act of "sincere concern."

In a matching tone of laughable sobriety, Trystan declared, "The man who died by Brickham's hand on Sunday, in front of Jayd Cimarron's eyes, was a quiet local artist—"

"Named Louis LaBarre." Irianna was back to her brutal impatience. "We know all that as well, Monsieur."

"Of course you do," Carris conceded with urbane ease. "Every one of you has done your due diligence, researching every detail you can, yes? That means you also know that LaBarre lived in Paris for just over twenty-five years—but that you hit sizable walls about learning anything about him before that."

Before he was done, Irianna and her trenchant scowl were in widespread company. Every reporter in the throng was outright flushed with impatience. After savoring their frustration for another moment, Carris continued.

"That is because all his public records have been purposely sealed. And *that* is because, twenty-five years ago, Louis LaBarre was living on the island of Arcadia. More specifically, he had moved into the royal palais as a sponsored artist for various island beautification projects. He was hand-selected by the queen to help with the refurbishment of the palais itself."

Well, that livened up the sweaty horde. "Hand-selected by the queen . . . in what way?" came a demand from the crowd. "Are you alluding to something more?"

Carris clicked up a confident smirk. "Not an allusion," he asserted. "Because there is actual proof. For a number of months during that project, Louis LaBarre had a passionate and secret affair with Queen Xaria Cimarron."

More energy blasted the horde. Contemplative scowls became prurient gapes. Fascination flared into astonishment.

And then bedlam.

"Are you saying that Princess Jayd was the product of that affair?"

"Do you have solid scientific proof of the claim?"

"Who knew about this? How high in the Arcadian palais did the cover-up go?"

"What does this mean about the succession of the

Arcadian crown?"

"Did Jayd know about this already? If not, when was she told?"

"Was *that* why she was on an off-grid trip to Paris?"

After those questions were yelled in fifteen ways apiece, Carris settled the storm with a dramatic inhalation.

"Saints' shriveled balls," Samsyn grumbled. "What the hell is he scheming now?"

"I firmly believe that the princess had no prior knowledge of this information," Trystan stated, "and that she only learned it because of Mr. Brickham, who was seemingly in concert with Mr. LaBarre to extort money from Jayd and her family."

In Paris, more gasps from the crowd. In Jayd's living room, more rounds of hissed profanities. The only one abstaining from the cussing party was Evrest, though Brick wasn't sure how long he'd resist.

"Since we strongly suspected that was the case, my team and I decided to lie low and follow the man. Let me tell you, it was rough going to keep our silence, especially as Brickham began to compel and constrain the princess."

"Compel?" was no Intense Irianna, but she was also no slouch about tenacity. "And constrain? That is not the story *we* have gathered, monsieur. The additional footage of the two implies they were close and affectionate. Perhaps even intimate."

Brick was relieved to watch Carris swipe the air as if erasing a chalkboard. That was only half as fun at witnessing an insane rush of jealous color to his face. "If they were, I am certain he forced her."

"*Forced?*" Jayd exclaimed. "Is he fucking kid—"

"Language!" Samsyn barked.

"But the *bonsun* lies like pond scum!" she exclaimed. "Who does he think I am? *What* does he think I am? Some helpless marsh reed, snapped in half by the first alligator who approaches and wants to bite?"

Brick swung his head around, notching his own glance to that of her oldest brother's. Had the seething little sprite just compared him to a swamp gator? Exactly how mad was he? Jesus on a river reed, she was too gorgeous for her own good in ranty mode.

Thank God for Shiraz again, moving in with a firm hand on her shoulder. "Ssshhh. We know this, all right?"

But for all the glass waters of the guy's reassurance to his sister, he swung a hell of a stormy glare back at Brick. But could he be blamed? Jayd's outburst had delivered one hell of an informational boat into the brothers' protective harbor. Whether Brick would sail or sink in those waters, he had yet to know.

"We were hoping to catch LaBarre and Brickham in the act of their blatant corruption and carefully selected our time to uncloak our presence," Carris continued. "But before I could move my men in close enough to capture audio on their exchange in the pub, Brickham got wise to our intentions. As you are aware, he is retired from one of the most elite special forces teams in the world. We knew it would be a delicate feat to pull off."

The tenacious woman who'd prompted him to accuse Brick of rape was at it again. "So he spotted your men closing in? How and when did you know that?"

"When he shot LaBarre in the face."

"Goddammit," Brick muttered. It was odd but comforting when Samsyn added a non-translatable Arcadian profanity.

"*Bonsun* was waiting for that one," Shiraz added.

Just like Carris waited for the reporters to regroup themselves, preparing follow-up queries. But it was a fake-out. They weren't going to get any. With the lofty hike of his chin and the stiffer set of his stance, the asshole was clearly winding up to start his second act.

And fuck, did he ever.

"As you all know, Brickham eluded us by rendezvousing with a squad of accomplices that included an Australian named Ozias Demos, his lover Jagger Fox, and a full private jet crew at Bourget. Though my men and I assisted French law enforcement personnel in chasing them all the way to Bourget, they successfully boarded the plane, keeping both Princess Jayd and her ladies maid assistant in their captivity."

The mob rustled again. Noisy as they were, Jayd and her girl growls were louder. "Captivity, my plush island backside."

"Captivity," came Irianna the Intense's interruption, minus the irate princess embellishments. "That is a weighted word, Monsieur Carris. Are you standing firm on that allegation? That Jayd Cimarron is being held hostage on her own island? Perhaps in her own home?"

Carris narrowed his gaze. "Are you standing firm that she is not?"

Irianna huffed and backed off. Obviously, the palais press office had taken some time off since their princess's return. Undoubtedly, that directive had come straight from His Majesty Evrest. Trouble was, it hadn't kept them ahead of the media wolves—who were all about to go rabid on their asses.

"Regardless of either answer, the facts of this situation remain very much the same," Trystan persisted. "One: Maximillian Brickham and his ruffians took advantage of an artless young woman in the throes of shock about her true ancestry, perhaps her entire future. Two: just as she might have gotten some peace about that revelation, that man put a bullet through her father's head as she looked on. Three: if everyone in the Palais Arcadia is not being held at gunpoint by that gang, that means they are harboring wanted criminals." He spread out his arms and gripped the podium hard enough to lean up and over it. "And that means that something must be done about it."

Like tentacles of a psychic octopus, Carris's menace twisted through the crowd. Though it was good to observe skeptical sneers on some faces, there were few too many of those compared to the reporters who still chomped on Carris's bullshit, lured by melodrama in the name of jumping ratings.

Fortunately, Irianna seemed part of the saner segment. She jabbed her microphone at Carris, prequeling the question on everyone's minds. "Something done like what, monsieur?"

The podium again became as the guy's dance partner, succumbing to his smooth swivel back toward the journalist. "I am most happy you asked that, mademoiselle."

"Certainly bet he was," Shiraz growled.

Evrest slid his eyes shut before muttering, "Creator help us."

"This morning, I personally expressed the urgency of the situation to your nation's magnificent president," Carris relayed. "He has been most supportive in his concern about everything—the security of not just our princess but our entire country."

"Which means what?" Irianna asked again.

"That I shall be returning with my team at once to Arcadia, backed by a troop of France's most highly trained special operations personnel. Our gratitude is boundless for this gesture—"

"Which is *what,* exactly?" demanded a square-jawed, dark-skinned guy at the rear of the throng. "You are a member of Arcadia's Pura faction, *oui*? So do you intend to storm the infidels' castle now? Has the French government just pledged supporting you in a military coup?"

"Oh, my word!" Requiemme rasped.

"Creator have mercy." Jayd's gasp erupted at the same second.

"Is he fucking serious?" Samsyn roared. "How many operatives did they give him?"

"*Rerda,*" Evrest snapped. "*Calmay!*"

"What he said," Brick inserted. "Cool the jets, kids. That throng has throttled all the way past eleven, and Carris is dancing in the jet fuel with a lighted match."

"He is right," Evrest asserted, even as his brothers gave disgruntled side-eyes. Brick was a few degrees more forgiving. Probably wasn't a stellar idea to refer to them as kids, but they'd have to wait on his apology muffins until later. Clearly, Carris still had a few soundbites up his sleeve.

"Come now," the bastard chastised to the lanky reporter. "*Coup* is such an ugly word for our beautiful kingdom. At this time, my only concern is keeping Arcadia's denizens safe through whatever means might be necessary. We are hoping the campaign will be brief and peaceful, but—"

Mercifully, they were all saved from the rest of the loon's antics. Evrest punched the remote with a white-knuckled thumb. "Brief and peaceful?" he gritted. "While already referring to it as a campaign?"

"I am not inclined to suggest a royal motorcade at the

airport and a formal greeting in the rotunda," Shiraz stated.

The king returned the remote to its holder with a decisive slam. "If that *bonsun* and his horde get anywhere near the palais, we have something to worry about."

"Which he already knows we are thinking," Shiraz countered.

"Which means he will attempt an unexpected entry point," Samsyn put in.

"Which means we have to be ready for him anywhere," Evrest insisted—only to be quickly negated by the other two men.

"We have not the adequate numbers," Samsyn declared. "You know this, Majesty." With his respectful nod and the deliberate use of the title, he numbed some of the rebuke's sting. "The battalions at Saqique and Minos, as well as the more remote banks of the Mousselyn and into Sauvage, have been downsized and redistributed. There has simply been no need for lots of personnel in those regions."

Evrest paid back the deferential nod, murmuring, "Of course. And that will probably still hold true for the more secluded villages, so we shall focus on the probable access points along the coast."

Shiraz nodded. "Wise."

"Wise but not infallible," Samsyn inserted. "Even if I beef up the coastal watches with the citizens' guard and some of my sharper training recruits, they will be like clumps of farmers with pitchforks compared to the French operatives on loan to that clown."

"That pathologically *lying* clown." Jayd yanked off every ribbon of propriety between her voice and the words, once more convincing Brick that she had to be more enchanted elf than actual human, while balling her hands by her sides. "Except for the one truth he swore he would stay silent about. *Damn it.*"

She rattled the floorboards with her furious stomp, but Emme braved the tremors to step over and cup her princess's shoulder. "Anger is just another way of letting him win, Highness."

"*Highness?*" she flung. "You just watched and heard what I did, yes? You know that means I am no longer Your Highness, right?" She circled her stare around. "That I should no longer even be living *here*—"

Evrest swooped up a hand. "A matter we are going to shelve for later, *fembla*. You *are* still my little sister, even if by half. And at the moment, I claim dominion over the half that agrees to obey me."

Brick should've anticipated what her retort of a pout would do to everything inside him. The look was doubly devastating because she only meant it by half. In the thorough thrust of her beguiling lips, she was fighting Evrest tooth and nail. But in the depths of her gorgeous aquas, she was still adoring him. No. Beyond that. There was a bond there, between the princess and her king, that went beyond their mutual affection and trust. A union that Brick would never know but always be fascinated by.

"All right, all right," Jayd groused. "I shall follow your lead, Majesty."

Evrest's exhalation was a different sound, though relatable in more ways. Brick wasn't going to crow about the unique thrill of bending the Cimarron princess, having already done it in vastly separate circumstances, but he indulged a silent fist bump with the guy.

"*Merderim mahaleur*, sister," the man offered with gruff sincerity.

"You are welcome, brother." She relaxed her stance, rocking back on one foot. "I really do trust you, after all."

Evrest pulled her into a gentle hug. "For which I am grateful."

She broke their embrace first, seeming impatient. She worked the balls of her feet now, softly bouncing up and down. "So, I am at your service." She turned, including Samsyn and Shiraz in her sweet enthusiasm. "Where can I help the most? I imagine there will be a central command set up as soon as possible. Does it make sense to have it downstairs near the commissary, where we set up storm shelters and community events? But if I can lend better insight out on patrol with Syn or Jagger—"

"No."

Their objection, in the same triplicate of violent baritones, was no surprise to Brick. Regrettably, it was to Jayd, who didn't see the urgent protectiveness that had manifested as clueless testosterone.

"No . . . what?" she asked, blinking as if they were part of an optical illusion that she'd unravel any second. "You do not want me out in the field? That is fine. Emme and I shall coordinate support for the command center with Camellia and Lucy. I assume you will be needing Brooke with one of your units, Syn? Though perhaps Cam would feel safer watching the child care center, close to Leo and the other childr—"

"*Fembla*." Samsyn, who'd apparently drawn the short straw on talking to his sister this time, grabbed Jayd's hands in his. "Heed the Creator's wisdom and listen to us this time."

She crunched a full frown. "I *am*. And I understand if you

do not want me outside—"

"Of this suite."

So much for the short straw. Clearly, Samsyn had been picked this duty because of his talent for getting to a point like an Olympic high diver. Minimal splash. Nonexistent tact.

Jayd tilted her head so fast, she was almost kittenish. With the splayed claws to match. "Excuse. Me?"

"*Desonnum*, sister. But—"

"The hell you are sorry," she snapped. "And the *hell* you are going to start trilling about how it is for my own good—"

Samsyn dropped his grip and folded his arms. "I do not have time to *trill* right now, little one. There will be no argument. This is for your vital *protection.*"

"Ohhh, no." She balled her fists, turning the kitten into a lioness. "Dare you not, brother. Dare you *not* with your stupid nobility about this!"

"*Damn it,* Jayd." It was Shiraz's first fierce burst of this encounter, and he came out with figurative guns blazing. "Nobility has nothing to do with this."

Jayd straightened and nodded. "And finally someone with the testicles to say it."

"That does not make Syn wrong." The guy nodded with firm finality. If Lisbeth Salander had been a dude, Brick imagined he'd look and act like 'Raz Cimarron. He'd even bet his left nut that the dark and restrained prince was hiding some illicit tattoos and piercings. "As the man himself has stated, Trystan is launching this campaign with several goals in mind. But let us be obvious, if not completely clear. Even if every other box on his list was soundly filled in, the *bonsun* would still burn this place down to get to you."

Jayd visibly paled—as she should have. Brick had to

concede to the instability of his own composure. As long as he was on this island, *nobody* was *getting* to Jayd unless he knew about it, present company excepted. Maybe not even then. They could make up new rules after he left—

Oh, hell no.

Now wasn't the time to tromp that bed of nails, especially as Jayd's color returned to normal, mere seconds before her obvious preparation for laying into her siblings again.

"So let me get this straight." She slammed hands on her hips and pivoted with purpose. Here came the deliberate pace that would one day strike mortal fear into her offspring. "Trystan Carris will be inward bound within the hour, determined to take over the palais and possibly the throne itself, with the help of his troops as well as a well-trained special ops team. We, on the other hand, are on the defensive and low on capable operatives—which means every able-bodied Arcadian is needed for this effort. Except, it seems, me."

When she stopped, an arched stained-glass window framed her small posture. As her brothers looked on with rigid scowls, Brick almost succumbed to a smile. Since the stained glass depicted the entwined dove and hawk of their family's crest, he was damn near sure she'd purposely stopped in that spot.

"Instead, it seems I am to be stowed away in an ivory tower, embroidering kerchiefs for our soldiers to dab up their own blood from the battles. Unless I am not able-bodied for even that?"

Once more, the brothers were eerie matches to their torture machines. Samsyn growled like a foaming dog. Shiraz rolled his eyes like he'd gulped too much water. Evrest was again the frowning statesman, ramming his hands at his back with taut tension.

"*Fembla,*" the king murmured. "Do you think, after all we have seen you accomplish, we would insinuate that?"

"No." Jayd dropped her head between her slumping shoulders. "So that means you are insinuating the other choice. That I am no longer Arcadian."

"Fuck," Samsyn rumbled.

"Are you serious?" Shiraz leveled.

"And are *you* questioning why?" Brick interceded. His query was equally sincere. As much as he already respected these guys, it seemed they needed to hear a few things. Truths that their little sister was all but screaming at them.

"I do not recall your opinion being solicited," Shiraz bit out.

"Well, perhaps it should've been," Brick countered. "Forest through the trees here, guys?"

"Says the *bonsun* who helped our sister paint the forest blue?" Samsyn erupted. "With some fucking sketchy brushes?"

Brick smirked. "Sorry, honey. Euphemisms won't get you anywhere."

"But they might land *your* swiss cheese ass in the middle of the Misere Swamp!"

"Oh no you will *not.*" Jayd was all bared teeth and clawed hands, punctuating herself with a *thwunk* of hands into Samsyn's chest. "What, in every speck of hell there is, has lodged itself up *your* stubborn ass?"

Samsyn's nostrils billowed. "Besides the fact that he is not denying—"

"What?" she spat. "What might or might not have happened between us? How does that factor into anything right now, except if my virginity is still a bargaining chip for you all?"

"The saints wept." The warrior yanked a handful of his long hair free from its queue and pulled hard. "Jayd Dawne, for fuck's sake. You know that was never an important factor—"

"Until now? Because if you mean that, I fail to see what Brickham still has to prove to you. He saved my life, Syn. He did it on *several* occasions. He put up his whole body as collateral for mine—"

"So now he has come to collect repayment from *your* body?"

"Whoa." Brick threw up his hands. "First, I don't roll that way, buddy. Not now, not ever. Second, last time I checked, your sister was a grown woman with a damn good head on her shoulders and the ability to use it. Perhaps it's time you gave her a little credit for that. *I* have, which is why number three is so easy here." He tucked in his thumbs and pinkies, fanning out the proper count on both hands. "Your sister's definitely onto something here. Maybe you really haven't bothered to check for logs up your ass because you're talking out of both sides of it."

Shiraz stomped up with a ferocious glare. "How dare you!"

"No. How dare *you*," Brick countered.

"Once again, I do not recall your opinion—"

"Being solicited. Got that part, man—but sometimes, nasty medicine is the best thing for you." He curled in all his fingers except his pointers, just in time for Samsyn's furious fume. "Simmer the fuck down. I see your side of things too, gentlemen. And I get it. I really do. She's your little sister, but she's more than that. She's something unique and extraordinary. Losing her in any way is likely a terrifying idea for you."

He waited a moment, letting that one sink in—but not just for the guys. He wanted Jayd to see their faces tighten, confirming his truth. He wanted her to feel the change in the air and to know without a doubt how much she truly meant to them.

His cause got a boost, surprising but satisfying, from the king himself. "Terrifying does not begin to describe it," Evrest muttered with grim force.

"It probably doesn't," Brick concurred. "But trying to prevent it by boxing her back up . . . that's like trying to rewrite a bad book by switching the ink color in your pen. It's not going to help things. Not really." He dared a glance over at Shiraz. "You said it yourself five minutes ago. Carris won't stop until all his special boxes are checked off, even if it takes destroying this place. So consider that scenario. Even if you dress Jayd up as a bell clapper and hide her beneath the biggest bowl in the highest tower, he'll still find her—and probably take out some innocents along the way. People like Requiemme here—"

"No!" Jayd cried.

"Or maybe he'll hit the childcare center first. Did I hear things correctly? That Queen Camellia and Prince Leo might be sequestered there?"

"Oh, *hell* no," Evrest snarled.

"But the reality of the situation, all the same." Brick steadied his voice as if conveying they simply couldn't get hummus with their falafel today. "In short, everyone's hearts are in the right place here, but execution is already a mess."

The air thickened to the texture of—*voila*—fresh hummus. Luckily, Brick had logged in lots of hours with worse sludge. It'd take a few minutes for all of them to click shit back together...

"He is right."

Or less than a few, if one of them was Samsyn Cimarron.

Though Brick was certain he still hadn't won a popularity contest with the big guy, Syn gave a terse nod while scrubbing a hand along his beard.

"About *this* particular point *only*, he is very right," the big prince admitted. "This time, I am not squabbling with both of my ass cheeks either." He knotted his long hair at the nape and secured it with a floral stick from the arrangement on Jayd's writing desk. "If Carris gets this far and does breach the palais, hiding will not be an option. We must only be concerned with a viable escape plan."

Brick didn't give himself permission to chuckle, even inwardly, at the warrior's mangle of the idiom. Samsyn's intensity already overrode the temptation. Undoubtedly, the guy was flashing back by a few years, when the Pura sneaked into this place using the laundry chutes as access points. They'd slipped out with equal ease, along with their high value hostage: Syn's new bride, Princess Brooke.

Holy shit.

The story, with which Brick was pretty familiar since it had made its rounds of the spec ops community, was nonetheless a fresh strike to his solar plexus at this point. How would it have just an hour ago, if he'd come up to this suite and found Jayd gone—only to learn she'd been taken hostage by those Pura pissants?

No wonder the memories turned the giant Arcadian into a haunted man.

"Very well, then." Evrest's directive, everything short of a royal mandate, effectively ended everyone's morose musings.

"We all have some priority lists now, yes?" He dipped his head toward Samsyn. "Re-org and deploy your battalions, security chief." And then reapproached Jayd, extending firm grips to her shoulders. "And you, little dynamo, please change into some clothes that do not look like you lost a Muppets wrestling match, so the team in the commissary will take you seriously."

During the few seconds it took for Jayd to process what her brother had said, Brick cocked his head with admiring contemplation. "Muppets. Damn. *So* much better than Smurfs."

Evrest managed half a curious glance before being tackle-hugged by the pixie between them. "Of course, Your Majesty," she damn near squealed. "I will not let you down, I vow it."

"You mean *we* will not let him down."

Jayd whipped her upper body back around, using her brother's formal lapel for purchase like Spider-Gwen. "Huh?"

Brick smirked. "You think I'm leaving your side anytime soon, Pixie? Plan or no plan, if there's a possibility of that bastard making it here and getting his hands on you . . ."

"Brickham."

Her grateful gush took over the air he suddenly couldn't get in, just thinking about Carris's intent if he took possession of her again. Because that was how the thug would view it. She'd be his property and nothing more. Not fucking acceptable.

"Thank you," she rasped, swinging her embrace to him. "This means so much."

Just like that, he was able to breathe again. "I'm all yours for the whole fight," he pledged with a huge grin. "Put me to work, boss babe."

She wrapped her arms all the way around his neck, even more sweetly effusive.

Her brothers weren't exactly doing the same. Literally *or* figuratively.

"Boss babe?" Shiraz gritted.

"*Pixie?*" Samsyn spat at the same time.

"Loosen your corsets," Evrest decreed. "Or would you rather stand here and bicker instead of making the most of the gift Carris laid in our laps?"

Once more, Brick nodded in deference to the man. There was a wise mind beneath the highest crown of this kingdom. Trystan's need to boast about his campaign was a secret weapon for them all, and pointless squabbling wasn't the key to optimizing it.

Thankfully, the other brothers didn't take too long to realize that. But as they fell in line behind Jayd, preparing to leave the suite, Evrest hooked a hand around Brick's bicep.

"Mr. Brickham? A moment of your time?"

"Ermmm . . . sure."

He uttered it out of confusion more than trepidation, but Jayd whipped around a stare that clearly flipped the fraction around. Still, he sent her another reassuring smirk. Just as her phone buzzed in the charger on her desk. "Forward into the fray, Highness," he said. "I'll be hobbling by your side in no time."

A smile grabbed the outer corners of her lips before lighting up his whole chest. "Promise?" she volleyed.

"I promise."

"You shall be all right, then?"

She dotted that one with a warning glare toward Evrest. He dipped an auspicious stare in return.

"Now *I* promise," he assured.

Jayd pressed her lips together. Her glower hardened.

Clearly, his little pixie didn't entirely believe her brother.

Brick wasn't sure he could blame her.

CHAPTER NINE

She was not sure which stress jabbed harder at her belly. Not knowing what Ev had in mind to chat with Brick about, or not knowing exactly what *Maimanne* had to talk over with *her*.

Oh, yes. As in right now. To the tune of being summoned to her mother's suite with three consecutive text messages on her phone.

At least she had a decent excuse to flop against a wall and groan with as much petulance as she liked. While it felt as wonderful as getting to belch after being in a corset too long, she already realized her mistake in the indulgence.

She hadn't waited until Syn and 'Raz stomped fully away.

Sure enough, both of them stopped so fast that their boots chirped against the polished hallway tiles. Samsyn, with his wider strides, got to her side first.

"Bad or worse?" he murmured right away. It was a well-loved part of their family shorthand, used for everything from taking a bad tumble to dealing with a particularly pesky journalist—or fifty. It stood in for idiotic generalities instead getting directly to the subject at hand.

And in this case, it was perfect.

Jayd, all too happy to cut to the chase, held up her phone with the text messages screen on bright. At once, Syn proved why a brotherly growl was sometimes better than a belch outside the throne room.

"Bloody fuck toast," he rumbled.

"Hmm. Good one," Jayd muttered. "You would have even been thanked for it, but I have made up my mind to be rankled with you until Bayrami."

Shiraz, having caught up to Syn, scowled. "What, so you can kill him then? And ruin my favorite holiday of the year?"

Syn chuckled. "But then you would all have to honor me too."

'Raz rolled his eyes. "As I said, do *not* ruin it."

Samsyn let the comment roll by. With his attention reengaged by the screen Jayd had yet to switch off, he again channeled his inner hound dog.

"What do you think dearest *Maimanne* wants?"

A trilling laugh escaped. "Perhaps to explain why she kept such a massive secret from me?"

"And to apologize for it?" Requiemme looked happy for the chance to poke that in.

Jayd was certain she joined her siblings in an obvious eye roll of response.

"You are referring to Xaria Cimarron, yes? The queen mother of *this* island, who thinks the Creator owes *her* for so much as a hangnail?"

"Hmm. Good one." Samsyn threw over a fast wink. "I would thank you for it, but seeing as how you volunteered to be my murderer..."

Shiraz wheeled around and yanked her into a tight, sheltering hug. "Whatever it is, just know we have your back, yes?"

"Agreed." Syn's rumble was the reassuring lining on his hold too, sealing her in from behind. "Whatever asshole antics the rest of the world deals you, nothing changes this, *fembla*.

Nothing changes *us*."

It was another family-close expression, though it was buried deeper in the past than his earlier one. Back to a simpler time, in special places. During those precious summers in which she and her brothers were just kids with stick swords and treehouse castles. When the boys proudly wore the flower crowns she had made for them while they sat in a "ceremonial circle" and made that vow to each other over an "official" cup of pomegranate juice.

Nothing changes us.

Damn it. *Oh, damn it!*

She pushed out the words aloud, past the salty drops that had done the same to her eyes. "Mushy *soldask*," she rasped, trying to elbow Samsyn. "I have not thought of that in so long."

'Raz's laugh was a gruff burst into her hair. "Me neither."

Syn's grunt was low but good-natured vibration in their huddle. "And I have never forgotten it."

"All right, then," she declared, reluctantly pushing free from the sibling sandwich. "Enough goofing off. Get on with it, you giant dorks. Go save the kingdom."

"You mean giant *badass* dorks." Syn swept up a hand, fingers poised in horns like a rock star. "Get on with it yourself, shrimp dip. Go appease the queen."

"Can I not just help save the kingdom instead?"

Syn's grin softened, giving away his commiseration for her agony. He leaned back over to peck the top of her head. "Everybody helps in their own way, little one."

She snorted. "Is this the part where I tell you to fuck off?"

Shiraz chuckled. "Oh, *my*. The interesting lessons someone learned in Paris."

Jayd was robbed of her comeback by another vibration

of her phone. She groaned but glanced at the screen anyway, hoping it was a check-in from Brickham. Never mind that they had been apart for all of five minutes, or that he had come to her suite with nothing but the clothes on his back and the cane in his hand. In the last seven days, she had seen him accomplish things more impossible than manifesting a phone from thin air.

Damn it. The text was not his.

But nor was it another summons from *Maimanne.*

Little jewel, are you almost here?

Her breath hitched, but it stopped her not from doubling her pace. *Little jewel.* Only one person had claim to that nickname for her. The outside world knew him as Ardent Cimarron. But to her, he was . . .

"*Paipanne?*"

It rushed out while she crossed the transom between her mother's formal receiving room and the more casual tearoom beyond. Once there, she swiveled in place with a confused frown. She stopped once Requiemme walked in, also peering around with curiosity.

"Where are they?"

Emme shook her head and swept out her hands, palms up. "Hrmmm . . . *they*?"

Jayd jerked a fast nod. "I think *Paipanne* is with her."

"But where? Your mother always greets you in here." She gingerly laid her fingertips on the gold teapot that took center stage on the ornate mahogany sideboard. "Nor, it seems, is she planning to. It's cold."

Jayd twisted her lips. "Something is off."

Emme's eyes widened. "Should I call for guards?"

"No." Fully aware she might be cursing herself a fool for it soon, Jayd did not renege the call. "It is not that kind of *off.*" At least she did not think so.

Emme squirmed. "You also did not think we had to worry about Gervais and Remy."

"Fair enough. But I promise I will scream right away if there is something you need to know." She held up a pacifying hand as soon as her maid broke out a worse glare. "*Please,*" she entreatied. "Just stay here, okay? I have no idea what is going on, and you know my parents and their pride."

She almost slipped and said *stupid* pride. Worse yet, with an addendum like *chronic vanity* or *pompous paranoia.* But there was something else about the way *Maimanne*—and now *Paipanne* too—had summoned her. Something that did not help her frayed nerves as she pivoted and pushed against the big oak door that led to her mother's most private sanctum.

The wires in her psyche sparked madly again.

The portal was not supposed to give way so easily to her touch. Nor was its small creak supposed to be so obvious in the thick, still air beyond. The air that did not feel or smell or even taste the way it should. No smoky French ballads from the old turntable in the corner. No jonquil and jasmine perfume mixed with almond cookies and milky tea. There were traces, of course, of those familiarities—but they were swiftly overtaken by other elements. Old dust and dead flowers. Spicy cigarettes and sweet wine.

She almost wondered if she had stepped through a portal to land back in Paris—in the middle of a brothel. But then her father stepped into the foyer, snapping her back to this strange reality.

Well, not as strange as before.

At least not at first sight.

The man had seemingly woken up about his overly needy

text and was back to being cordial but cool. He reached to embrace her, but the clinch was barely more than that. His pecks on her cheeks were as perfunctory as ever. He gave tiny squeezes to her shoulders.

Ah, merderim *times a million, Father. Nothing says you desperately missed me like a couple of shoulder squashes.*

And nothing made her want to abolish the thought than the moment he stepped back.

As if his feet were cement blocks.

As if his exhalation contained droplets of acid.

As if the drops in his eyes were formed of the same.

"Daughter." He swept one hand from her upper arm to the corner of her jaw. His fingertips trembled against her skin. "Merciful Creator. You are safe."

"I . . . am."

Stars and saints, now *she* was yearning for the regal masks again. How she suddenly realized she could do with a lot of their safe decorum, their predictable parameters. But nothing about this situation was predictable. Clearly, *Paipanne* needed her as much as she did him. He was trusting her just as fully. Showing her his fear with as much nervous faith.

This was, she suddenly realized, what she had asked for. Life without a safety net.

"*Paipanne?*" she uttered after too much of his edgy silence. "What is it? What is happening?"

In the middle of his gray-tinged beard, his lips compressed. He lowered his hand in order to scoop up one of hers. He followed suit with the other hand. "In light of Trystan Carris's newest stunt, your mother insisted that you two speak."

She fought the urge to wrench away. "Because my own stunt was not worth the response?"

He pulled in a stiff breath. "Jewel, I do not think she was aware of your—well, your little trip." His grip tightened around hers. "But I was," he croaked, shaking his head. "I *was*, Jayd—and I prayed like a medieval friar through every second of it."

Confusion formed a painful crunch across her forehead. "Why?"

An equal amount of the stuff invaded *Paipanne*'s face. "Because I could not sleep. Or eat. Or think of anything else." He hunched in, peering more closely at her. "Because I am your father, Jayd Dawne." He cut her eye roll short by jerking at her hands. "*I* am your father, damn it."

She ceased on doling out the reactions on that. Already it was clear they would not hold water to the man's determination. No. Beyond that. He was pledging the words to her like a scrap of his DNA was in her blood—a reality she was not about to talk him out of now. Perhaps not never. If Trystan was successful with any part of his wild scheme, it was doubtful she would ever get to see or talk to her family again.

Which meant they all needed to pitch in and help.

Which meant her parents—well, her mother and her stepfather—could not have picked a worse time for this bizarre reunion.

Or, perhaps, had not picked a better time.

Either way, they needed to get on with it. Despite how every bone in her body screamed in strange dread of exactly that.

"Where is *Maimanne*?" she asked, unsure of any smoother way to phrase it. "The original messages were from her, so—"

"Yes," he interjected, fully grimacing with it. "I know. After we turned off Carris's press conference, I got up to get more gauze and bandages. When I heard your mother's phone buzzing, I figured out what she had done. I must admit, we had some immediate words about it… But then I realized, in light of the *bonsun* and his treachery, she might actually be thinking clearer than I about the whole thing."

"About *what* whole thing?" Jayd demanded. "Gauze… and bandages? Why?" She huffed. "*Paipanne*, what on earth is—"

"Jayd?"

Though the interruption was coarse and frail, she automatically corrected her posture. Because that was what she always did when her mother was in the room. Because she recognized it all as the self-comfort it needed to be now, especially as *Paipanne* winced as if a sword had gouged him straight through.

"Jayd Dawne?" came *Maimanne*'s new call, containing a strange wince of its own—discernible enough to make Jayd throw a matching look toward her father. "Ardent, where is she? My *chér-kik*. My beautiful little girl."

It had become a soft but desperate keen, intensifying Jayd's scrutiny at her father. He reacted by re-donning his armor—the figurative version of the stuff that she remembered so vividly from her formative years. No. Her whole life.

She had seen chinks in those shields on only three occasions. Once, when he and Evrest had fought bitterly over her college selection. The second time was during his formal abdication of the kingdom's crown to Ev. The third time was thirty seconds ago.

She was damn glad it was over now.

"Eyes up, *bijheur*."

She complied, but not because he had uttered her nickname in Arcadian. Again, it was the urgency in his tone.

The implication that he needed her to really hear him. He proved that with the fervent look on his strong, noble face.

"I know you were hurt, Jayd... not being called up here sooner." He took her hand again, and she wondered when he had switched out his bones for iron rods. But while his grip was glacial, his words were soft and warm. "I am sorry about that. But there are reasons. Good ones."

"All right." Jayd reinforced her hold too.

"Like the rest of us, your *maimanne* was not prepared for the information Carris and Santelle brought to Evrest last week. But *unlike* everyone, she endured a deeper cut from that blade."

"Of course," Jayd concurred. "It finally exposed her mistake."

She was unprepared for his reaction, which came on a vehement surge. "*Not* her mistake. "Do not say that again! You were not, have not, nor ever will be a mistake. Do you hear me?"

"Yes," she rasped, bowing her head and drilling her resentful glare into the Turkish-carpeted floor. "I hear you."

He huffed hard but then inhaled slow, visibly restraining himself. "That is a start, I suppose."

"A start?" She jerked her head back up. "Of what?"

"To you *believing* me."

She reared back a little, unsure what was more unsettling: the plea in his voice, or the truth he so accurately nailed with it.

"Yes," she finally said. "A 'start' is an excellent way of looking at things."

Right now, she could give him no more than that. And was grateful he did not demand it.

"You already know that the Pura were tipped off about all

this from a former aide of your mother's," *Paipanne* went on. "An individual Xaria, as well as myself, considered to be a close and dear friend."

Jayd did not miss the pained creases at the corners of his tight gaze. "You both knew her? This person?" She had no idea why that caused a subtle change in her view of the situation, but it did.

"Yes," he admitted. "She was a member of our inner circle, so to speak. One of the people we could both rely on to keep our confidences." The confession led to a new contortion across his face. "There are many skeletons in both our closets. You have probably discerned all that by now. While neither of us are proud of that fact, we have also been aware of the trusted individuals who helped keep those closets closed."

"Until one of them did not."

He tipped a small nod. "Until one of them did not."

Jayd fumed into silence. There was the key to the shift in her perception. Her parents had certainly not been right or smart about their indiscretions, but lately she had learned that sometimes—so many times—the right thing was not the most obvious choice. Everything worsened when things were dragged into the court of public perception, with the media as self-appointed judges and barristers.

The dismal result? Not a damn thing was clear anymore. Not the truths that had always defined her reality, not the perceptions that had always bound her heart. Definitely not the people who had always set the boundaries of her future.

Would they ever be again?

But did she even want them to be?

"So you are afraid this . . . person"—it was impossible to label the nameless woman as a friend—"will go public with even more information? That she will sell *your* secrets too?"

Paipanne rolled his eyes. "I do not give two steaming piles of *bokau* about what that little traitor says about me. I wear no official crown in this land anymore. But I still have friends in places that could make her life a living hell." He twisted his lips. "Which will be exactly the case once we find the filthy *salpu*."

Jayd frowned. "What? She has gone missing?"

His gaze darkened. "'Twas not unexpected. Regrettably, we got to the point of realizing that when it was too late—a good hour after Santelle and Carris left Evrest's office last week."

"So the *bonsuns* tipped her off."

"Likely," he muttered, nearly back to his normal aplomb about it. But she knew when her father was acting for the sake of optics, and he was giving himself away like an LED bulb in cellophane. Sure enough, his voice roughened as he added, "But we have not stopped watching the ports or the road rest areas since you disappeared, so we will know right away when she reappears."

"Which might be sooner than later once Trystan returns." She pushed herself to voice it aloud. Right now, every ugly possibility had to be brought up and considered. "If she was more than just an information broker to them . . ."

"Yes," *Paipanne* returned. "We are aware. Though we hope it was only a convenient transaction for both parties."

Jayd could not nod emphatically enough. It had been difficult enough to think about her truth being sold for a price, but considering it all in a new light—that *Maimanne*'s betrayal had been rendered in the name of the Pura cause—jumped her to a new level of stress and rage that was hellish to hide.

And yet, as *Maimanne* rustled again, selective cloaking was exactly what her psyche demanded.

Something *was* off-kilter in here. This time, Jayd realized it was about more than just the strange scents and sounds—well, lack of them—on the air. The strangeness went deeper. Beyond her mother's strained scufflings. Beyond the clean but cloying smell that emanated even out here.

"Jayd? *Jayd?*"

Creator's mercy. It was plain, painfully so, in the tearful urgency of *Maimanne's* begging voice.

"Ardent? Why are you dawdling?" A moment, strangely wonderful, of the woman's typically imperious tone, before she descended back into a weak croak. "Did she get here or not? Is she—"

"Here, *Maimanne.*" She almost faltered on the simple words. While somehow knowing they would soothe her mother, she already saw their opposite effect on *Paipanne.* She narrowed her eyes, but he did not relinquish his dark resignation. "I am . . . right here," she called out, still hoping she would magically read his face.

But while that had just been an easy feat, it was a pipe dream now. And so it went, being in Ardent Cimarron's universe sometimes.

She just wished it had not been this time.

If she had gotten a clearer bead from him, she would have been prepared.

She would have known *this* was what waited for her in *Maimanne*'s inner suite.

The sight of Arcadia's queen mother, positioned on a chaise next to one of the huge arched windows, with posture so rigid and regal.

But beneath that proud poise, all the vivid tremblings.

All the useless efforts at self-control.

All the twitches of the woman's nervous lips, stretching her gaunt face.

All the tiny twists of her fingertips into each other, over and over in some strange, self-comforting rhythm.

All the heartbreaking truth of what Father was trying to prepare her for.

All the incredible, awful ways this whole drama had taken its toll on her mother.

There was more to notice. More that she saw as she carefully crossed the room, wondering if she was about to trip some hidden security laser beam. Things that had nothing to do with her mother's cosmetics-less face and housecoat-clad form. Though she could not remember ever seeing the woman in either form, it was not about that. Not anything on the *outside*...

Oh!

Damn it!

Just in time, she clamped a brutal hand over her gasping mouth. Fortunately, *Paipanne* moved up and lent much-needed support around her opposite elbow. Without it, she would have likely collapsed to the floor in a tearful clump instead of being able to lower to it on trembling knees.

"*Maimanne.*" She whispered it this time, yearning to eviscerate herself for the testy impatience of her previous shouts. So long before this moment, as she gaped at the sharp gashes surrounding her mother's eyes. The marks, so painful to look at, were eerily similar to the scarred gashes across the woman's wrists. "Mother. It is me. Truly. I... I am here. I..."

She faltered, not knowing what else to say. She also

learned, with scorching swiftness, that words were impossible when the air felt like glass. *Paipanne* seemed to commiserate, his eyes soft but his chest pumping hard. Jayd watched, oddly transfixed, as he stepped behind the chaise's headboard. *Maimanne* tracked her head toward his movement.

Tracked it.

But not *seeing* it.

She gulped. It felt like a pier piling shoved down her throat. She looked harder, wondering if she had just been observing a trick of the light across *Maimanne*'s gaze. No such fortune. Her mother was truly this messed up—and her most horrifying instincts, supported by *Paipanne*'s tension, kept conveying it had been self-inflicted.

"Yes, Xaria," her father murmured. "She is right here, my *raismette*. Try to look at her, darling. Just for a moment."

Maimanne gingerly turned her head. Jayd slid her hand down and wrapped it with her mother's. She tried but failed to ignore the fresher marks across *Maimanne*'s closer wrist.

Holy Creator on high.

No wonder she had never been summoned that night. And that *Maimanne* had failed to reach out at all.

She had been fighting for her life.

More clearly, someone *else* had fought to preserve it first.

When she looked up once more, she was certain who that person was.

Thank you, Paipanne. *Thank you so much.*

His gaze glistened, indicating he received and treasured her tacit message. She dropped her own teary gaze back down. But the haze of her emotion was only a part of the new filter through which she now beheld her mother.

In her heart, the woman had always held a place of special

awe. Xaria Cimarron carried herself like Elizabeth Windsor, groomed herself like Grace Kelly, and owned every room into which she walked like a combination of Beyonce, Aretha, and Gaga at once. Jayd constantly struggled to believe the woman's DNA ran in her veins—yes, even in this moment, when so much had changed. When the woman returned Jayd's hold as if it were her last purchase before tumbling over a cliff. When she forced her gaze open with a small wince, clearly straining to see past the healing ointments that fogged her eyes.

"My beautiful girl," she rasped, stretching out her other hand to feel along the side of Jayd's face. "It *is* you. What on earth did you do to your hair?"

The demand was as beautiful as a ballad from any of the divas she had just evoked. "Oh, it is still here." With a nervous laugh, she tugged at her damp ends. "Just . . . less of it."

Maimanne fingered the spikes too. They were probably the color of peacock quills by now. Just as swiftly, the woman jerked her head in an unintelligible way. Jayd braced herself for the ensuing critique.

"I . . . like it."

Jayd fought whiplash. "You—ermmm—do?"

"Yes," *Maimanne* said. "But not half as much as I love you."

And now whiplash was the least of her concerns. She had no idea what this reactive feeling was, bringing on the strange wrench of her stomach and the dizzying heat to her cheeks. It was certainly not *un*pleasant.

"You—um—uh, all right," she finally managed in a strained sough.

"I should have told you so before now," *Maimanne* blurted. "So many times, Jayd Dawne . . . I should have told you!"

"Ssshhh now." *Paipanne* stroked the side of her neck with a massive thumb. "You are telling her now, Xaria. And she hears you."

"I do." Jayd pressed a kiss into a puddle of her own tears along the back of her mother's hand. "Every syllable. *Maimanne*, please do not—"

"But if I had said them sooner, you never would have doubted their truth. You never would have run away to look for that wretch who gave you nothing. Who gave *me* nothing, save the gift of you." She switched her touch from Jayd's face to her own, only now her fingers were self-punishing claws. "I never should have looked at him. Not even once. I never should have bought his despicable illusion. I *never* could have believed his beauty was as thin as his morality!"

"*Maimanne!* Stop! Please!" Jayd joined her father in fighting *Maimanne*'s shocking strength, but the woman kept plucking at her eye socket as if needing to yank the organ all the way out. "He is not worth your grief by half! By even less!"

She almost plowed on to relay how Louis LaBarre had matured past the point of anything close to it, but what solace would that bring? *Maimanne*'s mind had seemingly stop-framed on her seducer from twenty-five years ago, not the skeletal addict she and Brickham had met back in Paris. Worse, even those distant memories had brought Arcadia's queen mother to today's present mess—where she loathed the *concept* of LaBarre so much, she had tried gouging out her eyes because of it.

The eyes that now flowed with milky mixtures of ointment and tears as *Maimanne* reached again for her.

The eyes that squeezed tight before her mother tucked her close, an embrace she had stopped dreaming about a long time ago.

The eyes that quickly turned her shoulder into a pool of wet, as *Maimanne* wept quietly for long minutes on end. Each and every one was a treasure to Jayd. All the messy magnificence of them. Every inch of the wet. Every aching drop of the emotions. Every sloppy sob she gave in return to her mother.

This force of nature . . . who now *felt* like a mother.

Force of nature, indeed.

At once, she could not wait for the chance to have her parents meet Brickham. As soon as humanly possible. Yes, there was still that small, nagging warning that it would likely be just once, but did that mean it could not happen at all? That she was forbidden from looking forward to the magic of it? Not so long ago, she had never thought a moment like *this* would ever be possible with *Maimanne* and *Paipanne.*

Miracles did happen. All the time.

This one got even better too. It was enough to make Jayd laugh aloud, from the moment *Paipanne* shifted around and gathered *Maimanne* and her in his massive embrace.

And now, there was complete warmth.

Absolute acceptance.

Consummate perfection.

Yes. A miracle.

"Your *maimanne* started from our union because *I* wandered first, Jayd. Your conception is what started pulling us back together."

And now, those astounding words.

"My beautiful little girl. You brought so much back to my life before you were even born."

And then those.

"This still does not mean we are perfect," *Paipanne*

injected. "It simply means that you showed us that we have to *try*. For each other, and for all of you kids, we promise you that we will always *try*."

Even more joy.

Then a thousand more sublime sensations, overflowing every lane and curb of her heart, until they drenched her soul as well. Until she was a buoy of elation on those waves of happiness, to the point that she was not aware of her fresh sobs until she had to suck in a glob of snot.

Thankfully, her parents were ready with indulgent laughter and thick tissues. After Jayd evacuated her nose as politely as possible, she sat back and stared at her parents. And then stared some more. It was the only option she could grasp. The only way to properly wrap her mind around this moment. She could only keep taking it in, over and over. Force-feeding its incredible reality into her psyche.

After the better part of a long minute, *Paipanne* spoke up again. "Do you believe me now, *bijeur*? Do you feel all of this, from both of us?" Once more, he folded one of her hands between both of his. "You were our ultimate blessing, Jayd Dawne. Never, ever our mistake."

"Our *what*?" *Maimanne* stiffened, reparking her backside on the chaise. "Who said that?" She squinted Jayd's way. "Did *you* say that? Why?"

Jayd consoled her with a new pat on the hand. "I was only the first to utter it, Mother. No doubt the kingdom is already afizz with a thousand other expressions for it. Some kinder, and certainly some crueler . . ."

"Well, fuck those *imbezaks*."

Before Jayd could scrape her jaw off the floor, *Paipanne* gave his wife a roguish chuckle. "Darling, the side effects of your medications have certainly been an adventure."

"Fuck the medications too," *Maimanne* grumbled. "Nobody calls my daughter a mistake and gets away with it."

She started to fuss, even pulling her hand free from Jayd's grip and starting to wave it around as if attempting a lewd finger gesture or a boxing ring punch. Jayd was clueless as to which, since *Maimanne* was miserably failing at both. Or perhaps reinventing both. Yes, that fit her mother better.

Thankfully, *Paipanne*'s smile said that he agreed. Still, he suggested, "Perhaps it is time for you to consider a small rest, *raismette*."

"I can rest when I am dead. And I do not plan on *that* anytime soon."

Jayd let herself have a light laugh. "Thank the Creator."

"Just a small one," *Paipanne* insisted, already spreading out a burgundy chenille throw. "You want to be awake to monitor how the boys are doing at corralling Carris, right?"

Maimanne tossed a cute side-eye. "I hate you when you are right, you know."

"Not any more than you want to climb me like a hussy and have your wicked way with me."

Jayd needed no other incentive to bolt upright. "On that disgusting note, I am *very much* out of here."

She did not disguise her happiness when her father followed her back out into the foyer. There, she could give him the heartfelt hug that had been brewing for several joyous minutes.

"*Merderim, Paipanne*," she husked into his neck, inhaling a lungful of the tobacco and tarragon scent that was distinctly his. "*Merderim, merderim*. This was all . . ."

Nothing I ever expected. Everything I ever wanted.

Before that part could blast past the moguls in her throat, *Paipanne* rumbled out, “I know, *bijeur*.” He tightened his hold with rough emotion. “I know. And I hate that it came to this before your *maimanne* and I told you all of it. That was wrong, and I am so damn sorry.”

Jayd pulled away far enough for their gazes to meet. “You said it best yourself, yes?” she offered. “Sometimes you will not get it right. You can only promise that you will try.”

He affectionately chucked her chin. “Why yes, I *did* say that.” And then sobered just as fast. “Just as I said them to your *maimanne,* twenty-five years ago, when I returned from the campaign against Gaddafi and beheld her condition.”

Curiosity already got the best of her. “You could tell? Were you gone that long?”

“I was away but a few months,” he explained. “Yet as soon as I set eyes on her, I knew.” His gaze turned to velvet as his lips inched into a smile. “Your *maimanne* is always a stunning woman, but pregnancy illuminates her like sunshine through stained glass.”

“Despite knowing that she was carrying another man’s child?”

She brutally bit her lip to avoid ending it with a sob. *Maimanne* really needed her rest, which would not be helped by a bawling daughter in the foyer. Thank the Creator for *Paipanne,* who saw her conflict at once. His hand was strong against her hair, stroking in a reassuring rhythm.

“Your mother was lonely long before I left for the battlefront with my men. Nobody was more responsible for her misery than me.” He inhaled heavily while closing his eyes in remorseful squeezes. “I had grown so full of myself. Drunk on my pride of our accomplishments as a country, floating high on the arrogance that had blown my head to thrice its size. And naturally, I assumed the size of the *other* head had grown in proportion."

"*Aggghhh.*" Jayd pushed back, whipping her head back and forth. "*Paipanne,* really?"

"You asked for the truth."

"And am seriously regretting it now."

"Regret is not worth the invitation into your head, *bijeur.* Or your heart." His humor faded beneath more somber intent. "Remorse is a wicked wraith who will show you no rest or mercy. He will steal the things that matter most. Love and loyalty, connection and devotion... In his hold, they will become naught but anger and fear and..." He shook his own head, as if every thread of silver through his loosely tied hair had become a snake. "Just believe me, all right? Accept the word of a man who waited far too long to break free from the scourge."

"All right, *Paipanne.*" She meant it, every syllable's worth, and fought to push that meaning into her voice. Still, her father seized her hand and tugged hard.

"No, sweet girl. Not just *all right.* You want to truly honor your *maimanne* and me? Then learn from this. Learn from *us.* Do not settle, daughter. Do not tell yourself that *all right* is livable. Do not be so afraid of looking at the dark that you deny yourself the light as well. One cannot exist without the other. Banish one and you have banished the other. And Jayd..." He resettled his weight until he was consuming the space in front of her, dipping his head in order to bore all his focus into her. "You deserve the light."

Another gulp thudded down her throat. Once again, it was painful—but sweetly so. She had to take several moments to wrap her mind around the beautiful words in her ears. But in doing that, she had to accept the rest of her thoughts. The hovering insecurities. The incessant doubts.

"Even if the whole island concludes that I do not?"

"To quote a wise woman, fuck those *imbezaks*." His brows tightened into a deep V. "If the Arcadian people want to rip the crown from your head because of a few different chromosomes, then we cannot stop them. But nothing—*nothing*—changes your place in my heart, or in your brothers' hearts, as a daughter, a sister, and an irreplaceable member of this family." He tapped a spot high on her sternum. "And nothing—*nothing*—changes the perfect princess you have become in *here*."

Well, forget gulping. It was impossible to do so now. Every ounce of tension in Jayd's frame, including a huge chunk she had not even been aware of, flowed the other way instead. "Oh, *Paipanne*..."

The torrential tears and the messy sobs took over. She was a blubbering fool as she pushed her forehead against his chest. Her feelings intensified once *Paipanne* folded his arms around her. As he wrapped her in his irrefutable strength, all the waves of his love surrounded her... dragging her into a happy undertow of assurance and warmth and hope.

Hope.

Such a small word. Such a powerful force.

The ferocity she welcomed in all its bold bounty, searing her mind and heart with so many awesome images.

One of them flared noticeably brighter than the rest.

A vision that grew more intense from the blaze of a cobalt stare. Then the brilliance of an easy but sexy grin. Then the blinding sheen of light, playing along enormous, elegant muscles. Then a thousand more things that turned her blood to kerosene whirlpools and her mind a helpless buoy on those waves.

She rendered not a word of complaint.

Because the foam on those waves sparkled with so much hope. And she was ready to drown.

Maybe...

Just maybe...

She told herself not to care about finishing that. She reminded herself that hope had betrayed her before. That she was never going to be the progressive princess for her people that she had dreamed of, and trying to resolve that disappointment ended up in witnessing her father's murder from two feet away.

No.

Not her *father*.

Louis LaBarre had not been a fraction of the father that *Paipanne* had always been—and still was being, up to this very moment. Guiding her with his conviction. Brightening her with his humor. Comforting her with his care.

Loving her unconditionally, despite that she possessed not a drop of his DNA.

Loving her mother with just as much devotion.

Showing her that if two people were truly dedicated to the challenge, life was not a daunting mountain. It was a triumph waiting to be scaled. Even through the dark parts. Even through the uncertainties. Even when hope itself was determined to kick them down.

But right now, after wiping her tears and thanking *Paipanne* with a fervent kiss on the cheek, she tucked hope as close as she could. She clung to every bright point of its star, guiding her steps down every flight of stairs to the commissary—and her heart back to the side of the man she was determined not to give up on.

CHAPTER TEN

"I am grateful for the gift of your time, Mr. Brickham. Especially in light of these . . . odd . . . circumstances."

Evrest Cimarron's stance, as diplomatic as his statement, was silhouetted by the gold sunbeams reflecting off the sea beyond Jayd's balcony. Brick had no actual idea of what time it was, but it'd been at least a couple of hours since Twylah took away his lunch tray and urged him to fill the afternoon by getting some rest.

Factoring in the half hour he'd waited for the hives to abate from hearing "rest" for the hundredth time in three days—or less sarcastically speaking, to make sure Twylah had truly left him alone for a while—plus everything that had happened since he got here, it had to be nearing late afternoon.

Which didn't give anyone a lot of time before nightfall.

When Carris and his shiny wonder force would probably get here.

Goddammit, he hoped the monarch made this quick. But also that the guy opted for the I-am-king-hear-me-roar mode for this instead of the what-exactly-are-you-doing-with-my-sister approach. Brick had much more experience with the former. As in having zilch knowledge of the latter. Subbies rarely showed up at the club with their siblings along for interview duty.

"Not a problem, though I think I still have you beat in the gratitude arena," he responded. "Without the care of your medical team, I'd likely be a prime snack for the rainforest beasts by now."

He deliberately didn't mention the scalding hot waters of the foreign relations bath in which Arcadia was currently swimming. Good chance that recognition was occupying every other thought in the man's head.

Brick only wished he wasn't stressing about what occupied the other thoughts.

"I am glad they put you on the mend so quickly," the man answered. "You *are* feeling better, I trust? To have found your way this far across the palais?"

A chuckle rumbled out of him. It felt as fake as it sounded. Goddammit, he was actually that nervous—and a dozen kicks into berating himself for the stupidity. Which was *also* wasted energy.

Brakes. Reverse gear. Now, *motherfucker.*

Spinning up some panic wasn't an option right now. Good chance the Arcadians knew nothing about his not-so-elegant secret, since there was a good chance their medical systems couldn't talk to any databases back home.

That was just dandy by him.

He'd be gone soon enough, and nobody here had to be the wiser. But that also meant keeping his shit together for the moment. Taking advantage of the benefit it presented: to show Evrest he'd been worth the risk. To prove to the man that he hadn't gambled the integrity of his country on a senseless murderer.

Trouble was, he'd imagined this encounter differently. To exponential sums of the word.

In his mental planning sessions, he and Evrest were somewhere like a palais office or his room in the infirmary, not a few steps from where he'd dominated the man's sister to mind-bending degrees. The blue dye streaks along his skull and neck were never part of the equation. Nor were the fingernail scratches now mingled with them. Certainly not the countless wrinkles in his clothes, or the distinctive scent with which they were still tinged. That blend of sea spray and spice unique to one person alone. The smell that surely Evrest detected too.

"I have it on good authority that the forest beasts are vegetarian. On the other hand, I cannot speak for certain palais pixies."

Oh, yeah. The king had picked up on things. Unnervingly so.

"Though now I am wondering... do said pixies nibble all they want, or only bite with permission?"

And what the fuck came after unnerving?

He was damn sure it was aggravating. Maybe even infuriating. Yeah, probably that.

King or no king, he told the guy so with a pronounced flare of his nostrils. He was damn sure his gaze got fired up to match. "That's a chunk of mighty bold assumption. Respectfully submitted, Your Majesty."

"Respectfully accepted, Mr. Brickham." A decisive *whomp* hit the air, courtesy of Evrest's slamming palms. "But the best assumptions are based on plausible accuracy. And that precision is grounded in solid research."

"Research." He echoed it to buy himself a few valuable seconds. A lot could be observed in that amount of time. In this case, the scrutiny earned him nothing but a tall island monarch, standing with purposeful neutrality. Too neutral. Tranquility like that reminded him of green skies before a hurricane. Good surprises weren't in the forecast. "So just what have those investigations revealed?"

He finished with a defined hike of a brow. It hardly fazed the king.

"You would have me detail it out?" Evrest volleyed. "Or shall we save valuable time by diving to the point?"

No more sardonic smirk. But damn it, Brick couldn't rein back his gruff chuckle. "Under any other circumstances, Your Majesty, I'd be offering to buy you a few beers after this shitstorm is over."

"At the bar in your Bastille club?"

So much for anticipating the hurricane. But at the same time, so much for thinking that gale was going to be terrible.

"Well, we have a few thrones in the place for you to pick from," he supplied past quirking lips. "If that's how you like to play."

"*I* am not the subject of this discussion." The man bit it out between seething looks. "And in many ways, nor are you."

"Couldn't agree with you more." He also couldn't be more sincere about it. "And while I know my opinion still isn't being solicited here . . ." He set his jaw to meet the man's stare, gleam for determined gleam. "None of this is simple lip service. I mean it. Your sister is an incredible human being. I'm lucky for the chance to have known—"

He was severed short by the similar slash of the king's hand. "'Twould not be a wise choice for us to discuss how you have *known* my sister, Mr. Brickham."

Well, that made it official. If there'd have been a sword or ax in Evrest's grip, Brick's head would be rolling toward the corner.

Weirdly but awesomely, the adrenaline from that thought was . . .

Invigorating.

Shit. Was this actually him using a jolt of anxiety as a positive? Was this his brain thriving on the spur instead of descending toward dread? Fuck right it was. And while he wasn't close to being full primeval against Evrest's Godzilla, there was a symbolic katana in *his* armory now. He wielded it because he had to. Because if he didn't, Evrest Cimarron would start twisting facts into his own sordid version of the truth.

"I didn't force her," he said with the full force of his conviction. "I did nothing of the sort, damn it. I know Carris made his point about that with some razzle-dazzle credibility, but—"

"*Fahrmay,*" the man all but snarled. "Silence your insolence." Another gash of Evrest's hand through the air. "What kind of an *imbezak* do you think I am?"

"Okay, chill out." Brick stiffened. "I didn't say that at—"

"I would believe my infant son's babbling before a single syllable from Trystan Carris."

"Got it. Loud and clear." But he held his position, needing only a second of study on the man's terse profile, before demanding, "Unless . . . I haven't? Come on, man. Will you just unload it already?"

Evrest glanced over. His scowl was blistering but bolstering, likely a look he'd perfected through the years when needing to throw adversaries off his scent. At last, he pulled in a breath and spoke again.

"Razzle dazzle." He dug into the new idiom with blatant curiosity, despite how his gaze revealed a decent comprehension of the context. "'Twould seem to me that Arcadian *bonsuns* do not have the market cornered on the stuff these days."

And that was the end of the adrenaline gravy train. It wasn't a great place to disembark.

There were prickles all over his skin. His heartbeat decided to do a four-hundred-meter sprint. A matching throb began in his head. It beat harder and harder until coalescing into the cannonball of his rebuttal.

"Fine. You want to go there again, man? I already told you I didn't force her. *Ever.* No alcohol, drugs, hypnotism, magic wands, or singing woodland creatures. What your sister has shared with me was because she wanted it. Because she clearly, freely asked for it."

Since that was enough about that, because the guy *was* right about only so many biblical details being necessary, he slowly and steadily stepped back. Evrest acknowledged the gesture, subtle as it was, by dropping his hands.

"I . . . believe you." Despite the man's short pause, his tone was sincere. He backed it with a firm nod.

"Thank you." Though Brick mirrored the nod, he pulled in a steady breath. "Maybe it's time you also believe that your sister is a grown woman, capable of making a lot of decisions on her own." He took his turn for inserting a meaningful pause. "I meant what I said earlier. Jayd *is* an extraordinary person. She's got a spirit of fire and a mind that can scale mountains."

"But a heart that can be crushed by pebbles."

Well, shit.

He kept the grumble to himself, though was too late from veiling it across his face. That was clear as soon as he beheld the I-told-you-so on the king's features.

"I have heard you, Brickham," he said with welcome commiseration. "And I also acknowledge the veracity of your testament. All of it. But now I request the same from you."

While finishing, he turned and strolled toward another part of the suite. The smaller sitting room had a wide window seat, a pair of cushy couches, and a small nook with a mini microwave and a tea preparation area.

Already, Brick figured this was one of Jayd's favorite spaces. He had all the proof he needed from the small stacks of paperback books at the corners of the seat provided his proof. They looked like a combination of motivational tomes, biographies, and Victorian classics—but all those categories were eclipsed by the number of vibrantly covered paperbacks featuring women in battle leathers, brandishing jewel-encrusted daggers, swords, and crossbows.

Sure enough, after lowering to the cushion and picking up one of the books, Brick scanned a blurb that evoked secret gorgons, a guarded curse, and a girl who battled them beside the enchanted prince of their hidden dark realm. At the same time, Evrest pulled a couple of bottled waters out of the small refrigerator beneath the tea accessories.

"As you have aptly stated, Jayd is very much a woman now," the king said, offering one of the bottles. "But as you can also see, right in your hand, there are parts of her that remain a girl."

Brick gave a defined shrug. "I still read Doc Savage novels. And comic books."

"And often pay triple digits for collector's items of them."

Half a profanity spurted beneath his breath before he muttered, "You *have* done your homework."

"To the degree that Shiraz has turned a few shades of green over your *Venom* collection," the man filled in.

"So are you saying that because my entertainment is expensive, it's more—what?—grown-up than your sister's?"

Though the monarch's beard was well-trimmed, it became a seamless field of black from the taut compression of his lips. "Of course not," he bit out. "I am only asserting that she has had a quite . . . tethered . . . existence." Swiftly he defended, "Not through anyone's fault, least of all hers. It simply is what it is, for security and necessity, and has been despite her overseas schooling and extensive traveling."

Brick didn't respond. Besides having nothing to add, he caught a new glint in the gaze that contained all the greener shades of Jayd's opalescent hue. A light that told him Evrest wasn't actually done.

"While Jayd has indeed chafed at the locks through the years, the fact remains that her . . . locks . . . have not been ever been popped off."

Ohhh, definitely not done.

Brick sputtered on the glug of water he'd finally taken. "Thanks," he croaked. "Fascinating point."

Evrest went on as if he hadn't spoken. "It did not surprise any of us to learn she had likely gravitated back toward . . . familiar situations. Toward the safety of . . . constraints."

Brick barely resisted the temptation to choke.

Thankfully, he thwarted the urge once more. "What happened to certain details getting left off the sibling chat loop?" he challenged.

"As I have already stated—"

"Yeah. Got it. Research. *Shit.*"

"You had to know everything we would look into, Mr. Brickham, before your plane was cleared to land here. And then again, to greater depths, once Jayd's . . . affections . . . became apparent."

Brick widened his nostrils, once more hauling in as much

air as he could. "Okay," he muttered. "Fair enough, all the *tethering* considered. And then once you snapped it together with a rundown of my hobbies . . ."

"Which are not simply hobbies," the man countered. "Correct or not?"

Through some twisted miracle, Brick flowed into a new shrug. It felt damn good because he meant it. "It's nothing Jayd doesn't know already."

And to mean every syllable of that confidence too? It was beyond good.

All the way up to the part when it didn't.

When it was jarring, because of the next recognition it brought.

The part where he realized that, apart from one gigantic secret of his soul, Jayd Cimarron knew every major point about the rest. Fortunately, the Cimarron Scooby Spy Gang wouldn't ever know either.

Only seven living entities on this planet knew about the darkest moments of his life. Five of them were Bamiyan cave rats. One of them was Doc Sally, bound by professional oath to keep the detail safe in her file back on base. And the other one was long since dead.

"Well, knowing it all and comprehending it all are two different things."

Evrest's retort, for all its terseness, pierced the air with perfect timing. Brick was all too happy to banish Asha's memory to the back of his brain again.

To help with the cause, he lifted his gaze and focused on the view beyond the window. There was a small tropical oasis that looked like a private garden, with a sprawling banyan that cradled a good-sized treehouse. Past that, a wider lawn was bisected by a flagstone footpath that led out to the vast white beach. No detail of it resembled Bamiyan. *Thank fuck.*

"That so?" he finally replied to the brooding monarch, who'd started projecting impatient vibes. "Exactly what part of comprehending do you believe your sister incapable of?"

It was slathered with more snark than he'd intended—but maybe that was a hidden good thing. While Evrest Cimarron deserved every ounce of his due respect as Jayd's sovereign and sibling, he wondered if anyone had ever dared call the guy on the carpet like this. To demand his figurative money be shifted to his real mouth. To ultimately hold his feet to the fire.

But now that he'd done so, what could he expect?

Evrest answered that by sweeping back around with a let's-do-this air.

"You call her Pixie, yes?" the man said, not letting another beat go by. "That probably started because of the new haircut, but you quickly realized it fit her in many ways. The way her trust level—or lack of it—shows in her eyes. That directly affects her stubborn streak, betrayed most notably by what she does with her chin and shoulders."

"Impressive." Brick gave up a steady nod. "Observant man."

"No," Evrest volleyed. "More like loving brother." He settled his stance and firmed his gaze. "The brother who also knows that her most transparent surface is her heart, and not because she wears it on her sleeve." As he stepped closer, his gaze took on laser intensity. "It is because her entire *being* is covered in it, Mr. Brickham. Do you get that? Do you truly and fully comprehend that? Do *not* answer me right away." He flung up a hand. "Do not think about handing me over some trite agreement that you think I want to hear. Think about *her.* About this woman you keep calling extraordinary. Think about what that truly means when it comes to Jayd Dawne Cimarron. She is not a princess—or a daughter, or a sister, or a friend, or an Arcadian—because it is all simply her duty. All these things are imprinted upon her because she cares that deeply and sees all of it with that depth of loyalty."

He paused, stabbing a hand through his hair like the limb suddenly weighed five hundred pounds.

"She is not just extraordinary, Mr. Brickham," he finally murmured. "She is *good*... to an existential importance of the word. That doesn't make her naïve or clueless. She understands decency and kindness and the reality of people in this world who lack it. It simply makes her—"

"Fragile."

For a long second, he couldn't believe he'd spewed the word. But then he shook his head, perplexed how he hadn't connected it sooner.

No. That wasn't true. Nobody in their right mind would ever consider using that word for Jayd—at least not first on their list. Not the twentieth, fiftieth, or hundredth either. He certainly hadn't when the woman had first blown his mind in that tiny Paris alley. Not when they'd had to go undercover by getting nearly naked at the kink club either. Definitely not when she *had* gone nude at the safe house, giving herself to him with such confidence and magnificence.

But between all those times, in her moments of revelation, she'd handed over the pebbles that Evrest had referred to.

The tiny stones that could break her glass.

The iridescence in her eyes when she spoke about her brothers. The love in her touch when she fussed over Requiemme. The kindness with which she treated everyday people like bartenders and flower sellers and even metro train conductors.

That was before his memories of the signs only he'd seen. The small tears that escaped as she shuddered after an orgasm. The deep devotion that mingled with her passion. The adoration that shined along with her submission.

Fucking Christ.

It really was all there.

He just hadn't seen it. Because he hadn't wanted to.

"Fragile."

Because of what Evrest Cimarron was about to add to his affirming echo of it.

"An oak is solid until lightning strikes it. A glacier can be melted by the smallest spark. Even granite is invincible until an earthquake splits it open."

A long beat stretched into a tense minute before Brick realized the man was really done with the poetry. That it was his turn again—to come to the right connection from it.

More importantly, to do the right thing with it.

More precisely, the things he *wouldn't* be doing.

Like looking at Jayd Cimarron and mentally stripping her. Like letting her see he was doing that. Like letting her act out on that observation with her mesmeric eyes and her tantalizing touch. Like telling her he liked it with any number of growls, groans, strokes, and stares of his own.

Not anymore.

Goddammit, he meant it this time. He wouldn't be the lightning that decimated her. Or the fire that dissolved her. Or the fault line that split her.

More than anything, he refused to be the brick that shattered her.

CHAPTER ELEVEN

A throng of palais staffers had already gathered in the commissary, working together like Kris Kringle's elves before Yule time.

Jayd entered but kept close to the wall for a long moment, besieged by conflicting emotions as she observed the scene.

Half her mind was heavy, wishing it really was December and everyone was working toward the upcoming joy of the Yule. But the other half was full of endless pride, brimming its way to her smiling lips. Even if these people decided she should never again wear an Arcadian crown on her head, they could never rip her homeland's banner from across her heart. Nothing would change her love for this island, a beautiful and bountiful reflection of its spirited, steadfast denizens. *Nothing*.

As fully as that truth consumed her, another took over with equal intensity.

From the second her gaze found Brickham once more.

A cold front hit as her heartbeat tripled. All the oxygen in her blood went to fascinating new places, eliciting a silent gurgle in her throat. Three seconds later, she was back to feverishly hot.

And she was absolutely, unequivocally, *not* sorry about it.

She watched, lips slightly parted, as he leaned on the mop that had apparently taken the place of his other stick. As he shifted, the last rays of the sunset snuck across the shipping dock where he stood with Ozias. The nectarine and mango colors made him look more formidable than ever. His wide shoulders were flexed. His jawline was high and proud. His chest was a carved masterpiece despite the tight T-shirt he had re-donned after their passion in her suite.

Perfect passion. From a magnificent man.

Nobody watching him now would think he had been half-conscious and bullet-ridden less than a week ago. Maybe he really was a magical force of nature. Or maybe he was more of what he looked like right now: a warrior, bold and audacious, staring into the mouth of a feral dragon. Well, sun beams that looked that way.

She had several more metaphors ready too, but Emme appeared from a door near the loading dock. She was carrying an office supplies storage box with a closed laptop resting on the lid. Oz greeted her warmly, though Brickham stared as if she had just shared an ice cream cone with a tuberculosis victim.

To Emme's credit, she still smiled sweetly up at him. After her unrequited diplomacy was thwarted, she pivoted and approached Jayd. "Insane idiot wanted go out on patrol with Oz, Jag, and the other battalions," she explained. "I told him it is one thing for a man to put mind over matter when orgasms are promised, but that—"

Jayd choked again. "You said what?"

"Last I checked, Highness, *orgasm* was not a forbidden word."

"By the Creator." Jayd dropped her head into a splayed hand.

"Save the exasperation for when you really need it, hmmm? Because if Trystan Carris and his band of merrymakers decide to pass Go or any of the other logical places and come right here to collect *you* instead of two hundred dollars, your stubborn Lancelot needs to *rest*." The woman's face took on careful but insightful energy. "And perhaps, if that suggestion came from you as well as me . . ."

"How about better than a suggestion?" she returned. "He and I can work on setting up the intake table together."

"Perfect!"

She did not give Emme more than a few seconds for an ovation. "But only on one condition. *You* get off *that*, as well." She gestured toward her maid's giant cast. "Looks like Ayce is getting some folks together to make up food boxes and fold blankets."

The woman's instant blush was not a shock. "Ayce? Oh . . . ermmm . . . he is here?"

Jayd giggled. "By the Creator, woman. Your act fools no one, least of all me."

Emme flapped her hand as if to smack Jayd like a fly. She brought it to rest across her auburn curls, which caught the light gorgeously in their half-up style.

"Saints and stars," the woman muttered. "I likely look like a pasty marmot. And my hair—"

"Is the cutest," Jayd interjected. "And the man is going to understand that you have had no chances for blowouts lately. Would you just go and get in some nice bonding time for once?"

"Bonding about *what*?" Emme attempted a last-minute finger-comb through the ends of her long curls. "What do I say? What do I do?"

"Well, one foot in front of the other is always a great start."

But saying it and abiding by it were two different things—as Jayd learned once more while pivoting back toward the intake area.

Sure enough, pacing closer to Brickham made her forget she even had lungs anymore. Or decent balance. Or a name.

Pixie.

Now there was a name. A name she already craved to hear on his lips again, with her sizzling senses and giddy psyche working in concert until she likely looked like a simpering *imbezak* with her head in the clouds. And why not?

In its deeply twisted way, the cosmos had conspired in Brick and hers favor—to the tune of six days and counting. And he was still here, so beyond the realm of fantasy yet so gorgeously grounded.

She saw that he was actually making friends besides Oz and Jagger. Perhaps he and Evrest had forged the start of a friendship too. Perhaps, Creator willing, they had discussed subjects *other* than what she and Brickham had been doing in her master bathroom . . .

And here came the waves of delirious hot and cold again. Was this why they compared desire to a fever? If so, she never wanted to leave the sick ward at all. Better yet, she hoped he read every delicious, salacious thought in her head.

"*Bon aksam*, beautiful Sir."

"Your Highness." He glanced up only briefly while scooping up a clipboard with a checklist clipped to it. During those two seconds, he warmly smiled.

At once, she visibly startled.

Your Highness? Even *princess* was better than that. And *now* he was into his assignment from Requiemme? And *smiling* about it?

What was this alternate universe, and what had it done with her growly Sir?

"Requiemme told me you went up to see your folks."

What. The. Hell? It was worthy of a repeat, at least internally. He made the remark like they had become a pair of cordial coworkers. He was being… conversational. No ornery crust on his vocal pizza. No seductive timbre in any note he spoke.

"I did," she managed to stammer. "They finally wanted to see me."

"And? How'd it go?"

She resisted the urge to smack the center of his chest. They were close enough for that now. She could even smell herself on him still, faint but sweet. She stood there, waiting for his nostrils to flare as acknowledgment of the same, but he still smirked as if they discussed naught but the weather.

And maybe the man was just being nice. Could it be he simply wanted that? Could he be truly interested in how things went with *Maimanne* and *Paipanne*? Why was it so hard for *her* to just believe that?

Time for that to change. To trust that the last week had started to change him too.

To think that maybe… he cared about what her parents were thinking.

That he cared about a few more things around here. The things in her world.

That maybe, just maybe… he wanted to stay in Arcadia a little longer.

"Actually, it was amazing." Just like the whole world felt now. As the elation really set in, her grin cracked wider. "They told me that they support me, no matter what. They also told me about the happiness they had together when I was born, in spite of everything. They had some very rocky times, but they made it through." She gave in to a frustrated laugh.

"I am relaying it abysmally. But I want to tell you everything. More than everything. Oh, Brickham, I want to—"

If so, what did that mean?

He cupped her shoulders hard enough to snag the words in her throat. His touch was far from gruff but also nothing like the way he had held her just an hour ago. "We'll have to back burner this for now, okay?" He eyed the checklist with a deepening frown. "There's still a lot to get done here, and if Carris is hitching a fast ride from Paris, there'll be human fallout from his touchdown point sooner than later."

"Of... course."

Jayd twisted her lips. But what to do with them then? An understanding smile felt as far away as their connection in her suite. And in some ways—all right, many ways—her heart shivered worse than the minutes after his rebuff in the infirmary.

Which, right away, she kicked herself for. Down to the last silly, selfish drop of emotion.

Damn it.

Was she truly serious about this? About him? About proving herself a worthy woman for him to take a chance on, not a girl besotted by her rampaging hormones?

"Yes." She answered it aloud because she could. Because while Brickham knew not the affirmation it truly represented, she needed him to hear it—and to know she meant it. "Of course," she said again, engraving it more firmly with her nod. "What do you need me to do first?"

Before Brickham could render an answer, Oz sauntered back over.

This time, the Aussie was wearing a Kevlar vest along with thigh armor and knee pads. A black tactical helmet was tucked beneath one of his arms, and a compact rifle was secured across his chest.

"Yippee-ki-yay," the guy quipped, readjusting one of his thigh pads. "Time to roll. So you're all apples here?" He ticked a nod in Brickham's direction, seemingly oblivious to how his friend nodded and frowned at the same time. "Beauty. Check you out on the other side, hot stuff."

"Yeah, yeah. Have fun storming the castle, asshole."

Jayd struggled to glom a little chuckle onto Oz's but never found the right internal plug for it. Was she the only one who heard the conflict past Brickham's sarcasm? That past the casual sneer, there was a conflicted warrior? That he was tapping tense fingers against his thighs because he longed to be strapping bulletproof gear onto them too?

As soon as Ozias had paced out of earshot, she pivoted to Brick with new determination. If she could lend just a sliver of empathy to his world . . . to be the person who made *his* day a little better this time . . .

"Brickham." She went all-in on the risk, pressing her hand against his. "I want you to know . . . we appreciate you being here. *Right* here."

He swooped his gaze down at her. His lips were still twisted in that conflicted scowl, but the rest of his features mellowed a little. "I know, P—" He slammed his lips together again. "I know, princess."

Princess.

It was better than *Highness*. She tried telling herself that, at least twenty times over, while gritting her teeth to maintain her diplomatic smile.

What, in the Creator's name, had Evrest said to him?

And how much bodily harm could a woman inflict on her

big brother short of assassination?

But there was not a spare moment for wallowing in that stew. She had no time for simmering, not when her frustration was nearly at a boiling point.

That left only a few viable options for going forward.

One: evaporate every shred of sustenance in the figurative pot.

Two: let the damn thing get too hot and then explode.

Three: add good intentions and turn this mess into a half-palatable soup.

"All right," she said, figuring he could interpret her heavy sigh whatever way he wished. By now, it was clear the man wished to be sailing clear of emotional waters anyhow. "Where do we need to start?"

★ ★ ★

Hell on earth.

It wasn't a term that daunted Brick anymore. He'd already been on that cruise more times than he wanted to remember. Danced until dawn with starvation, deprivation, and fear. Been to every station of the torture chamber buffet. Sang the sole song on the menu in the karaoke bar: "Just Kill Me and Get It Over With."

He didn't feel like warming up the pipes for that custom ditty just yet—but God fucking help him, he'd come damn close in the last two and a half hours.

Like every worthy stint on the persecution rack, things were easy enough at first. Every word from Evrest had still resounded in his mind, such aching reminders of how he'd already let things with Jayd go too far.

So. Damn. Far.

But he'd been determined to hold steady, being aloof but friendly to Jayd, even after Requiemme had hooked them up on the intake table preparations. And yes, even when Jayd beamed about it like a celebratory ballerina.

He'd embraced the metaphor, in turn giving back something between a brooding Baryshnikov and a polite Polunin. And it had worked—at first. All the way to the second that the perceptive Pixie collected on his number and then called him on it.

Hard.

Brutally hard.

As in the cutting diamonds in her eyes, turning every color of inquisition and hurt. As in the dismissive obelisk of her posture, her shoulder blades sharp bites through her shirt. But especially in how she went so quiet. Not *silent*. She still spoke when addressed and kindly commented to everyone who needed her, except that it hardly seemed like *her* doing the talking. But now, she was different about it. Subdued. Distant.

Defeated?

He almost shook his head in violent rejection of that idea. Coupling that descriptor to his audacious sprite was like calling Mt. Rainier a foothill.

She was the same person who'd nearly flipped him the bird when he'd given her the broke-dick mope in the infirmary. She'd also been the only lover to pull him out of a guns-blazing panic attack. In a *cemetery*. So no way was she capitalizing on the new emo hair color just because of him.

His theory was validated as the standing speakers in the room's corners suddenly crackled. His adrenaline torpedoing the stabbing pain near his wound sites, Brick surged to his feet.

"That's field radio noise," he stated.

There were fewer sounds on the planet he was more certain of. Definitely none that stirred such an urgent but bittersweet reaction. Unbelievably, even after Asha and Bamiyan, there were parts of him that still longed for the rush of the mission. The anticipation of hunting down backstabbing cocksuckers who'd just presented themselves to the world as "misunderstood victims." Yeah, that part never got old.

For now, he had to settle for listening to the scrapes and scuffs and grunts that gave away their direct connection to a soldier racing along the front somewhere. As of right now, they still had no idea where, but it was a definite sign that something was up.

There hadn't been a peep from any of the comm patches so far, which wasn't a huge surprise. As of the last tactical update, Samsyn had activated at least fifteen recon units across the island. Brick assumed they'd all been ordered to zip it on the comms until a positive sighting of Carris and his boys was made.

Was that the hot scoop now?

Brick remained in place, deciding initial caution was the better call. Sometimes radios simply got punched by accident.

During the wait, he got in a quick glance at Jayd. *Fuck.* Anxiety bristled in her eyes; tension lined her posture.

Fuck, fuck, *fuck.*

Screw it. He may have pledged not to be her Kryptonite, but he couldn't bypass on at least being the Power Stone for her Titan gauntlet.

It was as easy as crossing the room to the temporary tech station that had been set up on a small presentation area in the room. During normal circumstances, he imagined the palais staff using this as a focal area for operational meetings and parties. There was a smaller public address system off to the side, not being used for this occasion. The larger speakers provided clearer, louder sound—through which more chaotic sounds now vibrated.

"What's the twenty on this?" he asked the palais security rep who was handling this makeshift bridge. The woman, who clearly knew what she was doing, had a shoulder name patch that read *Iscah*.

"On *these*," the tech clarified, looking up through a long front lock of hair that looked freshly dyed in a red-black mixture.

Sheez. The palais salon must've had an overstock on the coif colors this week.

"There's a new hit from the unit lead at the air strip." Iscah pointed to a flashing yellow dot on a glowing green map imprinted onto a sheet of hard acrylic that measured about ten-by-ten feet. "But also over there, from your friend Demos and his team, out at the Drehd Forest."

"The Drehd Forest?" As Brick repeated it, Iscah efficiently rolled a tracking ball until the acrylic glowed with more imagery. This time, there was a topographical detail of the terrain across the island. He hummed, communicating his approval.

Damn. Samsyn Cimarron had invested in some shit-hot toys for his intel team.

Between one blink and the other, a couple of red dots flared to life in conjunction to the goldenrod ones. He assumed Iscah had inserted those to alert the rest of the frontline units that they'd gained some company on the south end of the island. Regrettably, there wasn't time to waste on commending her for the fast thinking. At the risk of being trite if just to himself, they had bigger fish to fry.

"Well, shit," he muttered to the tech instead. "That's quite a forest."

Judging from the density of the topographical feed, perhaps even a Forest, capital *F*.

"That is a large affirmative."

He whipped into a double-take. The corroboration wasn't from Iscah. The king of Arcadia himself was the one stepping up next to him.

Brick dipped a deferential nod. Seemed the best move for communicating his mix of surprise and admiration. Evrest had probably defied his closest advisors to come down here and give face-to-face motivation to his staff and sister. Was the guy checking up on *him* too? Maybe. Probably. But Brick guessed there were better reasons for the man deciding to leave his designated palais safe room, especially at this very moment.

Evrest Cimarron believed in leading, not just administrating.

In being with his people, not lording over them.

In knowing their world firsthand, not evaluating reports about it.

All recognitions that Brick acknowledged down to his marrow. But not willingly. Not remotely close, damn it.

Because all that equated to new understandings. Evrest was the real fucking deal, not just the dude in the big brother box. The man rocked the world leader box too. And the stand-up guy box. And probably a few more checkmarks beyond that.

Which clicked all the way to an irreversible conclusion.

There was no room for backsliding on the pledge he'd made to the guy. Not by an inch. Not by a *centimeter*. Not now.

Not even with Jayd looking so small and scared across the room. Not even with how every tendon in his body screamed at him to go and pull her close, squeezing away her stress one last time. To whisper assurances into her hair and press kisses against her ear.

Not. Now.

Because now, she was an expired fantasy. The pixie that shouldn't and couldn't be his.

The monarch responsible for that moroseness was the same one who jerked him out of it. He snapped his head up again as Evrest shifted forward. The man's noble features glowed electronic green as he reexamined the modern map of his kingdom.

"It surprises me not that the *bonsuns* have shown up at both places," he said. "By air, they have few options except the strip, carved out of the southern palm groves. By land, they might have done better to try sneaking in over Tahreause or Colluss, but the terrain is steep in the former and rocky in the latter."

"They're also located on your opposite shores."

"Indeed," Evrest returned, not looking impressed by Brick's quick answer. There'd be time for those gold stars later. Or not.

"So what's the hitch?" he demanded as well. "This is all manageable, right? Unless the French have brought armed warheads?"

Surely Samsyn had banked on the same probabilities as his older brother. If Carris and his entire crew had flown down here, only the fields near Faiant Township or the Sancti Airstrip were viable touchdown points. But choosing the former would've forced Carris and the boys to fly inland, exposing themselves to instant radar detection.

In short, the asshole was shitting the bed in all the places they'd anticipated—and hoped for.

So why was Evrest silently scowling as if a boogie monster lurked beneath the proverbial mattress?

"Cimarron? Yo, man?" The unconventional address earned him some side-eyes from Iscah and her palais staff friends, but he stuck to his conviction. Something told him the man needed direct, not respect, right now. "*Evrest.* Come on. What's eating your underwear?"

That garnered him a sharp intake of breath from the man. But before Evrest could issue the answer that went with it, the field radios flared again. An identifier on Hayloh's screen pegged it as Oz's comm. *Yesss.*

"Wizard to Greenbeard." His friend was whispering, which usually meant good progress on the op. Good but scary. "You copy, Greenbeard?"

Greenbeard. Not the craziest call sign, but Brick swore to God, this island and its hair color fetishes . . .

"Greenbeard copies," came a gruff, low rasp.

"You seeing this?" Oz queried.

"Affirmative," Greenbeard responded. "I count six—no, seven—fancy friends at my twelve and three. And—Creator's balls—now eight and nine."

Brick gritted his teeth and held his breath. In his periphery, Evrest did the same. He tilted his head slightly, trying to send a calming look to Jayd, but she was already chewing a fingernail and jiggling a knee. Everyone else in the room projected similar vibes. They were terse and silent, as if they were passengers in Greenbeard's vest pockets and the French, now so close they could be heard tromping the forest floor, passed too damn close for comfort.

Through another three minutes—yes, Brick kept time via Iscah's computer clock—nobody said a word. Not anyone around him. Not Oz. And definitely not Greenbeard, with the invading soldiers practically on top of him.

At last, the forest-flattening boot steps faded. Then abated.

But after that, for the better part of another minute—yes, Brick was still watching, for lack of better things to do with his nerves—there was no audible check-in from their green-whiskered friend.

But then . . .

At last . . .

"Whip out the dance card, Wizard. These pretty young things are looking ready to rock with you."

Brick audibly exhaled. It was echoed across the room. Just as fast, everyone pulled new oxygen back in. It didn't escape his notice that the biggest suck-down belonged to Evrest's lungs.

What the hell was going on with the man?

He sneaked a step closer to the guy. "Penny for your thoughts," he growled lowly. "Or would that be a dagger for your wrists?" He didn't relent his stance when the king gave up another sharp breath and nothing else. "Goddammit, Cimarron. What's in your brooding tea?"

Evrest figure-eighted his head in a cranial shrug. Brick was tempted to snarl louder. Christ, this guy and the mixed signals. The king seemed more like an annoyed CEO than a chieftain on the edge. Was it as unintentional as it seemed? Or was the guy purposely trying to give him psychological whiplash?

"They did not drop that many operatives in the middle of

Drehd for the mere game of it," he finally said with a scowl. "I only hope that Oz, Jagger, and their teams know that."

As if Ozias had long-distance hearing, his crisp accent crackled over the speakers. "Copy you on that, Greenbeard. Eyes are open. We're ready for the bastards. Roll your dice northeast as planned and commence Sub-Operation Spades and Aces. We'll put fifteen big ones on red once Tails antes up at the table."

An achingly familiar huff had Brick jerking around along with the king.

"Saints and stars." Jayd's tone was thorny, though her gaze was a cement chunk of worry. "*What* is going on? Spaces? Aces? What is a Tails?"

"It's radio code, Pix—Your Highness," he responded before wheeling his regard back to Evrest. "The kind we can be encouraged by, right?"

"Yes," Evrest returned. "And . . . no." He didn't blink when weathering the intense curiosity that Brick joined to Jayd's. "Tails is Fox's radio ID, so the direction sounds like they are rendezvousing with his team. Since each team has five men on it, the *fifteen* is likely a reference to their strength as a combined force."

"And those logistics line up with Jag's location," Iscah supplied.

"And that is another good thing . . . yes?"

As soon as Jayd concluded that with a heavy gulp, Brick hyperfocused back on her. A huge question still loomed in her gaze, but he couldn't discern its verbiage or purpose. But here was a way for *him* to have purpose, without having to get close to her again.

"So what's the not-so-good part?" he demanded at once.

Evrest responded by stepping back toward the electronic map. As soon as he swept a hand across a large black square at the edge of the heavily forested texture, Brick tightened his confused frown—in conjunction with Jayd's and Iscah's gasps.

"Creator's mercy."

"Creator's balls."

"What?" Brick prompted them before glowering Evrest's direction. "What the hell is—"

"Censhyr?"

Jayd's question was featherlight but strangled by agony.

"Censhyr." Iscah wasn't so pastel about her tone. "Of course. That is exactly where they are bound." After words beneath her breath that had to be some unique profanity, she spat, "As transparent as crows after maggots. Disgusting *bonsuns*."

"Disgusting but smart," Jayd asserted, back to a doomsday glare. "Where else are they going to access a whole army, willing and able, after a few simple key turns?"

"What the *fuck* is Censhyr?" Brick leveled again, looking to Iscah now. He wasn't sure if the royals were good for the answer, considering they looked like the revelation had confirmed a global apocalypse.

Fortunately, the tech specialist had kept her head. For the most part. "It is our high-security prison complex," she explained. "While the palais dungeons are deep enough to be soundproof and secure, they were never designed to accommodate modern-day prisoners for long. Nothing beyond basic lighting, plumbing, and alarmed egress doors have been installed down there."

"So you went ground-up on a better facility outside of town." He nodded at Evrest. "Smart move."

While the monarch accepted his compliment with a matching dip of his head, Evrest didn't surrender his tense posture and clenched jaw.

"Of course. Very smart," the man growled. "Unless a loose cannon courtier with intimate knowledge of the place has become one's sworn opponent."

All at once, the guy's behavior wasn't such a mystery.

Though damn, how Brick wished it still was.

"Just *how* intimate?" he bit out.

Even after a taut huff, Iscah beat her king on the answer. "He will certainly not have to toss pebbles at the window to get in."

"And once he does that, more doors will open." The terse addendum belonged to Jayd. "Since the Pura regard themselves above the law, many of them have landed on the other side of it."

Brick cocked his head beneath the weight of full comprehension. "And, therefore, have written their own tickets into Censhyr."

"Where shrines to Carris have become more popular than passwords to porn streams," Iscah muttered.

Brick grinded his teeth until his skull rattled. "Altars erected between hours of boredom, anger, and extensive training time."

"The ideal recipe for an insurrection," Evrest added from his own locked teeth.

"Just shake and serve," Jayd contributed. "No need to add water or stir."

"Fuck," Brick spat.

"They need to hold those *bonsuns* back," Iscah muttered. As if knowing she'd stated the obvious, or in an effort to blow off nervous energy, she rechecked her monitors with some nervous dial twists and mouse clicks. "If they step foot inside that prison—"

"We are *aware,* Iscah." Jayd twisted her fingers and compressed her lips. "*Merderim* for being concerned," she muttered. "But we—"

"Do have three units deployed against their one." Evrest's statement probably wasn't what she'd had planned, but Jayd stepped back as if relieved for the new motivation. "So the odds are looking good, I promise."

Pleasant shocker: Iscah actually grinned about that. But her impish expression only lasted a few seconds, since the guys on the front fired up the radio feed again.

"This is Tails, reporting in." Jagger Fox's hail was clipped but strong over the line. "The poker room is full. Wizard and Greenbeard are checking out the rest of the casino."

Evrest visibly eased. "They have successfully joined up," he said.

"But they can still see Carris's squad too?" Brick cut in. "Am I hearing that correctly?"

No more than two seconds of fuzz passed by before a separate radio clicked into the exchange.

"Tails, Command copies the update. Fine work from all of you." The praise sounded somewhat strange, but it didn't take Brick long to know why. While he was sure Samsyn Cimarron had a Build-a-Bear side somewhere, he'd been certain the guy's public façade was a hundred percent pissed-off grizzly. Thank God the bear himself was all-in for letting everyone process that for a second before pushing his comm button again. "Are the toolbelts still on premises in the casino? I repeat, how many tools are visible for you?"

Brick pinched a couple of fingers over his mouth, stifling the burst of his snicker. Some things were so good, they didn't need translation.

The same mild mirth permeated Jagger's calm reply. "Command, we have *all* the tools in the casino. Repeat, we have eyes on all nine tools."

"Excellent," Samsyn responded, this time with an unmistakable undertone of dark mirth. "Keep it that way."

"Roger that, Command. Down to every last man here."

Jag's confident comeback brought a swell of pride to every Arcadian in the room, but none more radiant than the glow that emanated from Jayd. But all too quickly, her effusive smirk faded. Her gaze was a fresh collision of concern.

"Brickham. Do you think—"

"They have it well in hand, *fembla*." Evrest's snap made no secret of his irritation. While Brick didn't blame the guy—after all, *he'd* likely been the one on top of the pedestal from his fun little metaphor—the move was damn near worthy of an eye roll.

Breathe in and chill out, king brother. Won't be long before you're first fiddle in little fembla*'s esteem again.*

His private fume made it doubly satisfying to watch Jayd's viewable one. "I was only wondering, if Trystan himself decided to lead that battalion—"

"I said *already* that Jagger, Ozias, and Grenier have an excellent handle on the situation." Evrest went stiff in the spine and completely coiled with his fists. "They have been trained by your own brother and seasoned in many field operations. You must trust that—"

Brick didn't enjoy chopping the guy short by jolting up a firm hand, but if he had the choice to save Evrest's or Jayd's stress level, there was no contest. "What I think he's meaning to say, princess"—*instead of press release platitudes in which you're not going to have lasting confidence*—"is that the guys aren't going to take any stupid chances. And yes, they've been trained for stuff exactly like this. So unless your boy Carris has been secretly training as an expert parajumper . . ."

"Creator's toes," Iscah interjected. "He is right."

Evrest stroked the back of a hand over his neatly trimmed beard. "Very likely, yes."

"Well, don't get excited on *my* account," Brick groused. Jayd, now at the point of pacing off her tension, barely noticed.

"So if he is not leading the advance on Censhyr, where *has* he gone?" she asked.

"Shit." Brick shook his head, fully humbled. The question should've been assaulting him already. It definitely should've been doing so in place of his time-waster of a pissing contest with Evrest.

A shrill alert from the radio patch broke through the air. "All units, this is Command. We have hit blackjack. I repeat, we have hit a perfect blackjack at the air strip. The house has won the game."

Instantly, Iscah pumped a fist.

Though Evrest looked ready to, he only lifted a small smile while Oz's and Jagger's reactions crackled over the speakers.

"Good on you!"

"Creator be praised!"

Jayd stopped short, whirling around before her next pacing lap was done. "Wh-What is it? What has happened?"

Brick was semi-lost himself. "Unsure." But as he cocked a fresh stare at Evrest, that awareness got more acute. "Cimarron? A translation, maybe?"

But Evrest was already rocketing back over to Iscah's station, extending his hand toward the tech. By the time he got to her side, Iscah had slipped off her headset. She offered to him with a tearful smile.

"Command, this is Pit Boss," he said. "*Lüt vous plait,* confirm that one more time."

Brick expected Samsyn's growl to roughen up the connection at first. But the guy sounded outright jovial, if not chest-beatingly cocky, as he responded.

"Affirmative, Pit Boss. We definitely have him. Pathetic *prispoul* was hiding next to the septic tank, beneath the plane's lavatory. As if he thought we would not look *there* for his rotten form?"

"Excellent work, brother," Evrest said. "Are you able to verify with visuals?"

"Transmitting."

Samsyn's concurrence had Brick taking the rushed route to Iscah's console as well. But once there, he chose to hang back a little. Evrest was wound tight, and this was absolutely his moment of triumph. More importantly, keeping back meant he could be in the general vicinity of where Jayd had relocated. At this point, the periphery of her presence was better than nothing at all.

Though damn it . . . depending on what they were about to view on Iscah's monitor, *nothing at all* might be his reality sooner than he thought. Or wanted.

CHAPTER TWELVE

As Jayd approached the tech station at which Ev was bent like an anxious space program engineer waiting on a shuttle from the stratosphere, she wondered if *she* was the one returning from an accidental trip to those heights. Her head felt huge. Her knees were cotton balls. She honestly had no idea if her feet were still attached to her body.

As Iscah's monitor pinged, the sensations worsened. In the next five seconds, she would know if she could breathe normally again or not.

How she wanted to reach out to Brick. To soak up his strength as the anchor it had so quickly become in her world. To feel his warmth as he squeezed her hand and to know that the connection would give her the fortitude to keep her head high, her intentions true.

But while he was so close, he seemed so far away. His sights stayed riveted on the large monitor. His hands remained at the small of his back, clasped tightly together.

Maybe, for now, it was a good idea to keep her attention focused, as well.

Besides, she still had Emme. The woman stepped up next to her and linked their elbows, lending much-needed commiseration in the seconds she needed it most.

"Dear Creator on High, we pray that you have enabled His Highness Samsyn to capture Trystan Carris by his filthy balls and drag him into the glaring light of Arcadian judgment."

Jayd was saved from having to tamp a giggle when her maid's conclusion punched the air at the same time as Iscah's click on her comm wheel.

At once, a gritty picture filled the screen.

Also at once, no one had any doubt about the identity of the prisoner in her brother's custody.

Thank every saint in the universe.

But that was not what blurted from her suddenly parted lips.

"Oh," Jayd rasped. Just that and just once. But she did not have to worry about forming anything else, with Emme taking over quite perfectly on the duties.

"Oh, Highness. Creator be truly praised. They *did* catch the awful *kimfuk*!"

It seemed merciless to quell her responding chuckle. "'Twould absolutely seem that way, *bonami*." Weirdly, she wondered less about a status update on the mission now, and more about the karmic balance that Carris's capture seemed to knocked loose. Nothing else could explain the new freedom of Emme's profanity button.

She *had* to get Brickham's input on the matter.

But when she lifted her head and turned back toward him, he was no longer there.

He was not anywhere in the vicinity either.

The cement block returned to stand in for her head once again. Jayd let it guide her in a clumsy roll as she wheeled around, searching for him. But he was nowhere in the throng that had now closed in on Iscah's monitor. She was stopped by many of them, clasping her for tearful celebratory hugs. Though she forced out pleasantries and smiles, none of the sentiments climbed from her lips to her mind. That, of course brought a new tidal wave of guilt—to this crowd, she was still their princess no matter what—but she could not spare even a corner of her mind for that consideration right now.

Where was Brickham?

And why did her senses *not* want to answer that?

How did they already pound with one sole suspicion? That Brick had only been biding his time until this moment. Waiting Trystan was finally in cuffs—which signaled the moment he could escape his.

The cuffs that might as well have her name engraved on them.

That, in some disgusting way, Evrest had locked down with resounding snicks.

Evrest.

She should have known that her *bonsun* brother, and the harmless conversation he had behested from Brickham, would be the explanation for her lover's abrupt change. It was *not* about getting the intake table ready or focusing on the looming threat at hand. It was not even about them being back in a public situation together.

It was bigger than that.

Big enough to have Brickham activating all his sneaky spy wiles and slipping out of here during the single minute that everyone was distracted. The sixty seconds in which she had not been excruciatingly aware of his every move.

Except for the agony of this one.

And then the one that followed it.

And then several more, in which she tried talking herself off her own mental ledge. Perhaps he had not actually snuck *away*. Maybe he had sought out the facilities or finally gone to grab some food from the buffet line. She knew he had not eaten for hours. She had not pushed him to do so, out of gratitude that he had not foisted the same pressure on her.

But after she observed at least six other men leaving the lavatory and confirmed the lack of his huge form in the buffet line, she reverted to assumption one. Which was not an assumption anymore.

Which was *not* the move she was letting him get away with.

And yes, she was damn sure she could follow through. Brickham had a head start, but was still the stranger in a strange palais: a building that was actually a collection of other buildings, erected at different times and then linked together as afterthoughts. Seasoned courtiers often compared the place to a stucco hedge maze.

And she knew shortcuts through it. Many, *many* detours.

She checked her instincts first. Brickham would not return to her suite even if Evrest had not stepped in when he had. Though he was alone, she sensed that made no difference. The man had not bolted from the commissary because of a need for fresh air. He wanted to get away from *her,* period.

Another presentiment had her avoiding the infirmary, as well. He had no possessions or even clothes to collect from the room, and he would obviously peg it as one of the first places on *her* search list.

Then where?

And why was *that* the query to double as the off switch on her intuition?

All right, then. She would use simple logic.

Where *would* he dash off to, if wanting to hide out from everyone because—

Of what?

All right, rationality was not helping either. Not without the key chunk of information she was missing.

"Damn it," she rasped, dropping to a low-lying balustrade in the central foyer. Though she dropped her head against her folded arms, she gritted her teeth against the sting behind her eyes. "Damn *you*, Evrest!"

"*Fembla*? What are you doing out here?"

She rushed back to her feet as the protective baritone bounced off the stone walls and marble floors. Her tears were still clenched away, but Creator only knew how long the fortitude would last. Especially if her king brother turned out to be the one dogging her every step.

It was not Ev. She whooshed out a grateful breath—but quickly questioned if Shiraz's arrival was worth the celebration.

"Well?" he demanded. "Why have you strayed?" It was not a Samsyn-level boom but nowhere close to Ev's diplomacy. 'Raz's military gear only augmented his austere demeanor. "Why are you not in the commissary with the others? And why is Emme not with you? Are you full *fougin*? You are exposed like this *alone*?"

"*Fougin?*" She rocked back and folded her arms. "Yes. Crazy. Of *course* that is what I am, for even thinking I did not have to scratch a paw at the door for permission go straying in my own home."

His brow knitted. "That is not what I meant, and you know—"

"*Do* I?" she snapped. "Know that, I mean? Because all of you are so forthcoming about conveying that to me? About communicating *anything* with me?"

"All right, all right." He held up his hands, maddening about the soothe. "I only wish to help." His furrows got deeper in response to her skeptical bark. "*Fembla,* on my honor"—he pressed his two longest fingers against the Arcadian military crest embroidered on his uniform's shoulder—"none of us knew about *Maimanne* and LaBarre until damn near the moment you did. Do you honestly think we would withhold something like that from you, even for a day?"

Jayd did not—could not—answer. His remark, even with its tender intent, was so far off the proverbial mark. Did he truly not get that?

"I did not think that for a moment, *rerda,*" she finally managed to mutter "You must know that."

"Well then, why are you ready to tear my head off with all your—" His choke of dawning recognition was as irritating as his benevolence. "Oh, Creator's balls. This is all about . . . *him,* yes? That . . . American."

She flared her nostrils. "You mean just like the American to whom you are engaged?"

He pulled in a tense breath. "Lucina is an event planner, not a spy for hire."

"And that makes a difference . . . how?" she snapped. "Unless you think that protecting me on several occasions, to the point of taking bullets to ensure my safety, does not prove his equal worth to Lucy? For that matter, to Camillia and Brooke as well?"

"I did not say that."

She laughed without mirth. "So what *are* you saying?

"Camellia is the queen of our kingdom. A damn good one. And Brooke has risked her life for Arcadia as a commendable soldier."

"Which has exactly *what* to do with Maximillian Brickham?"

Shiraz dropped his hands to his sides and rubbed his thumbs between his other fingers. Jayd instantly knew the tell. He was practically making fire with that flint-and-steel agitation.

"I am only looking out for you, *fembla.* All three of us are." He pushed a rough breath between his locked teeth. "Damn it. We were so worried when you were gone."

She jogged up her chin. "Well, I am... sorry," she said, infusing it with all the sincerity in her heart "'Twas not my intention... to string you out that hard."

"I know," 'Raz replied. "And accepted. *Merderim.*"

She waited through a long pause before lifting her head once again. She peered intensely at him before scooping down her head in a no-touch nudge. But the *imbezak* reacted as if she had not just jumped her brows to the moon and bugged her eyes until next summer.

"Well?"

"Well what?" Shiraz asked.

"This is the part where you apologize too."

Her brother shied back. "Whatever the hell for?"

"For what you insinuated about Brickham. For mincing his honor and character without even knowing him."

He went full-bore glower. "I will jump into the Tahreuse lava hole first."

"'Raz!"

"Dare not, sister," he snarled. "Dare. *Not*. Go. There."

"There being the hell where?" she countered. "You mean back to the land of consideration, kindness, truth, and granting the benefit of a doubt to the stranger who saved your *fembla*'s life?"

"After helping himself to her mind and body?" he spat.

"Now we can only pray he had no aspirations on anything else."

Jayd blinked hard though kept her head high. She did not dare give away that his prayers would already be in vain. That Brickham had already claimed more than her virginity and sanity.

He had taken her heart as well.

He had to know that by now. But did he *want* to? Did she want him—or any of them—to?

She yearned to scream for lack of an answer.

Instead, she charged with shocking composure, "Aspirations, brother? To exactly what? I am a princess stripped of her birthright, and the whole world now knows it. I might remain a figurehead but will likely not have financial gains beyond what the high council agrees to pay me. By the same stroke, neither I nor my children will have any viable claim to the throne. So what is your point again?"

Shiraz jabbed his hands into his pockets. Kicked at an invisible pebble on the shiny floor. She almost guessed that he was . . . fidgeting. But she knew better of the brother to whom she was closest, chronologically and emotionally.

"You are . . . tender . . . about him right now, *fembla*," he finally ventured. "And I understand that. But after a while, I hope that you will see things—see *him*—more accurately."

"The way *you* see him, then?" she flung. "Because—what?—you are wiser, worldlier? Because your experiences make you an expert about all men now?"

He jerked his hands out of his pockets. "I am not a seer, sister. Of course I know not everything in the way of men. But I *have* spent time around more of them than you—and I know what it looks like when a male does not merely desire a woman. I recognize it when he wants to . . ."

"What?" Jayd demanded when he trailed off for too long. Once more, her air was tight in her chest and her limbs felt slammed into high-voltage chargers. "When he wants to *what,* damn it?"

"Eviscerate her." He winced as if hating himself for spewing it. But he did not back off. If anything, the spill emboldened his commitment to the comparison. "'Tis an ugly verity, but a truth all the same. Men like Brickham—"

"You mean Dominants?"

So she *could* throw him off his game. But not for long.

He quickly recovered from his clutched choke before offering, "You are aware of more than I assumed."

"Well." She kept it smooth, cautious about overplaying the preen. "You know what they say about assumptions."

"Excellent point," he returned. "Especially because my point has nothing to do with a disposition for the lifestyle."

Thankfully, he did not go for the obvious gloat either. But Jayd could not summon any demonstrable gratitude. "So your point is about what?"

"Men—destroyers—like Brickham are everywhere."

Her spine, already a ramrod, stiffened more. Her temples throbbed, but this time she let them. Perhaps they would lend to the intensity of the glare she whipped at his watchful face.

"I am not destroyed, brother."

Could he not see that it was just the opposite? That because of Maximillian Brickham, she was a woman more aware of her power than she had ever been? More aware of what she could endure and be stronger for it? Braver about the risks she could dream of, the fears she could face—and overcome?

"Not yet, sister."

No. He did not see that at all. To the point that he did not pause before donning his boardroom scowl while maintaining his soldier stance. That he barreled on, breaking out the words she had not asked for and never wanted.

"You do not see it in him, Jayd—and by the Creator's scepter, I hope you never have to. I hope that the man has chosen to put your happiness above his hunger, and to leave you with only good memories of all that you have shared."

And there went her spine again. She was certain her discs were now dust. "His . . . hunger? For *what*?"

A similar chill seemed to take over Shiraz's spine. It was not comforting to witness. "I wish I could say it is a rarity, to witness this kind of thing—but the reason I speak of it so boldly is because I have seen it too frequently." He filled his lungs with even more weighted air. "There are men who fulfill their military service in darker places than the rest of us. Much darker. In shades of pitch black."

As he uttered that part, Jayd gulped hard. In her mind, she also saw darkness. The shadows inside a Montmartre Cemetery crypt. In those black depths, she saw Brickham's terror-stricken face. The place his mind had gone to, so far away from her . . .

"Go on," she rasped at last.

"Those men have been to places, and done certain things, that have taken things from them," he continued. "Stripped out certain parts of their souls. And when they return from those kinds of things . . ."

"They start looking for those things again," she filled in.

"Not looking," 'Raz countered. "*Hunting*. And then, when finding them, taking. Stripping like they were stripped. Obliterating, just as they were—"

“No.” Jayd flung up a hand. “*Not* taking,” she asserted. “Not if it is freely *given*.”

“But to what point?” Though he bit out every word, a strange sheen entered her brother’s eyes. He reached out to fervently cup her shoulder. “When you are depleted, will he stop taking? Will he be able to?”

Jayd breathed hard, not issuing an answer to that. Not because she had none. Because she had too many.

He will never take too much.

He will never deplete me.

Because he will never stop filling me up too.

Unlike anyone will again…

The certainty of it crashed in, sinking her like a cannonball in the sea. She stepped back from Shiraz, but her steps were clumsy and heavy… and flooded with dread.

“Jayd. Please, *tupulai*. We are just trying to make sure you do not get hurt from all this.”

Too late.

It was absolutely, definitely too damn late for that.

Because he had absolutely, definitely just confirmed the contents of Ev and Brickham’s chat.

Her stomach confirmed that by panging one awful message to her mind.

You need to get out of here. Right now.

But not overtly. Not if she did not want ’Raz ordering a full security detail for her.

“All right… fine,” she stammered out. “I—I understand.”

Thankfully, her brother bought the performance. “Good. *Merderim*.” He dipped an assuring nod, and even smiled a little. “I know it might not be so easy to do in the next few weeks, but if you need—”

"To use the facilities."

She was unsure if his hiked brows were due to her rush or her randomness, but it was still the best option she had for an easy escape. She stubbornly stuck to it.

"Fine," Shiraz said. "I will escort you."

And why did she not see that from several miles back?

"I know where they are, *rerda*. Besides, I might be a while. It's that time of the month."

"I can wait."

And why did she also not realize that her brother was the only male on earth not bolting because of that subject?

Damn it.

★ ★ ★

Fifteen minutes later, 'Raz was proving as good as his word.

Creator have mercy.

Jayd said it, interspersed with some saltier language, as she paced the bathroom's lounge area to give him the illusion of her continued bonding time with Mother Nature.

At last, she gave in and plunked down on the velvet chaise in the pretty sitting area. Maybe, in this case, doing nothing was doing something. Maybe the *bonsun* would get equally bored and finally go away. Better yet, maybe someone would call him on the radio, wondering why he was not at his assigned security station.

But there he was still, just outside the door, whistling a really bad version of "Bad Blood." When he started to insert all the song's *hey*s too, she curled her knees to her chest and screamed into them.

"Sometimes, brother, it is an act of mercy to leave Taylor Swift alone."

Shiraz kept whistling. And *hey*ing.

She followed her screech with a groan. She was no longer in the restroom. She was trapped in hell. The only missing things were brimstone and darkness.

She jabbed her chin up. Then straightened higher. Then murmured beneath her breath, "*Darkness*."

A huge grin bloomed across her lips.

Just before she dragged aside one of the velvet curtains behind the chaise.

At first, it looked like nothing more than the plain wall. But if she knew better... and had remembered some things right...

Creator be praised.

Sure enough, the panel gave in to her touch. An inch. Another. Then a few more, until there was just enough room for her to step through.

As soon as she did, the hidden alcove became a pivoting chamber, transporting her a hundred and eighty degrees.

When it stopped, she was facing a world of damp, permanent nighttime.

Thankfully, the tunnel was equipped with motion-activated wall sconces. They looked fairly modern, though in comparison to the damp and dirty walls, a prospector's lamp would be state of the art.

She smiled again, already liking the metaphor. Like a prospector, she was hoping for something better than what she had left behind. Hidden gold, only not in the form of shiny nuggets. Right now, all she wanted was an effortless escape. A way to access any part of the palais free from her brothers and their sheepdog ways. Protective love was one thing. Too much slobber was another.

She continued on, using the compass on her watch to gauge her direction. She was northbound, which meant she would soon be underneath the kitchens, administrative offices, and operational hub of the palais. Perfect. She had no intention of startling the staff members in any of those offices, but getting to the hub would likely mean more tunnels to pick from. All she needed was one that led outside . . .

Escape challenge number one rose up much sooner than she expected. Twice as formidably.

"Damn it."

The passageway was completely sealed off. A dead-end comprised of bricks as solid as the ones she had just passed through. Though these stones seemed a little fresher than the walls to her left and right, they were nonetheless bricks, and—

"Ohhh. *Damn it.*"

She let the repetition caress the air like the dawning recognition it was. She even finished it by humming a little Taylor herself—"Shake It Off" for this round—while carefully running her fingertips over every seam of mortar between the bricks.

Until the mortar was not mortar at all.

One spot, up and to the right, looked just like the rest of the hardened clay but was actually a rubberized patch that glowed beneath the heat of her touch. Exchanging "Shake It Off" for a triumphant gasp, she pushed against the plastic—

Until her gasp became a yelp, blending with the *whir* of activated gears.

Gears that pulled the entire wall into a hidden pocket in the cavern floor.

"Well," she murmured. "Jamie Bond, reporting for duty."

Her light giggle bounced around the walls as she continued on.

But all too soon, she was once more not so ready to laugh.

The passage bent several directions, even curving so much to make her think she had just made a massive loop, but never did she come across any forks or crisscrossing paths. She only had two options for her journey: forward or back. Her compass indicated she had veered slightly to the east, but not so far that she was far from her original estimation of a destination.

What was going on?

Why could she not hear at least a faint bustle from the offices and kitchens on the other side of the walls? These stones were *not* lined with soundproofing foam . . .

She scuffed to a stop. Emitted a huff to match. Technically, this might be escape challenge number two.

As her head resolved itself to the fact, her heart clenched. She could not change the layout of this tunnel. It was what it was—just like so many other things about life itself right now. About the universe that would go on turning, despite her soul's pleas that she be let off the wild ride. Better yet, that it would all spin in reverse. That she could be cast back to the night when a towering force of nature strode into a Paris alley and sucked the air from every membrane in her lungs. When that air had returned in the form of a moan from deep in her throat, as he'd pressed her body to a wall and his fingers to her clit in a secret Montmartre warehouse . . .

Never again.

As the syllables taunted her mind, desolation thrashed her soul.

And her will could no longer hold her tears at bay.

Never again.

"Stop it," she rasped at her roiling heart. Somehow, as she compelled her feet to drag her forward again, she added, "Stop trying to think it will be any different, damn it!"

Because it would not be.

Time would not rewind. Or reset.

The adventure was over.

And so were she and Brickham.

Even if she could figure out where he had absconded, she was rapidly running out of time to do anything about it. Too late for undoing the damage of Evrest's interference. Too late to beg Brickham to stay a few days more. Too late to hope that in those days, he would look at her as more than his little Paris asset.

That he would simply look at her as . . . *more.*

"Stop. It."

She bit the words onto the air in time to the way she dug her stomps into the ground. And yes, it really was that by now. Sometime in the middle of her soul's fissuring, the castle's concrete foundation had become a hard dirt path. She had not perceived the change until now, when her brain took tactile pleasure in grinding her shoes against the damp earth.

A diversion she was smart to recognize, since it did not last long.

Because the ground was now . . . emulsifying.

In less than a dozen steps, she went from tromping across packed clay to *slorp*ing through a muddy mire.

What on earth?

In the figurative *and* literal senses . . .

She would have found a better way to express that, if not for the raw shock breaking in on her brain—courtesy of some new sounds on the air.

Sounds she was *not* expecting to hear in caverns right below the palais. A resounding rush of water. A bright, foamy fizz. A soft howl of wind.

And all of it smelling like saltwater.

What. On. Earth?

She spurted it aloud, each word punctuated by a couple of her gloppy steps. But after three more turns in the tunnel, nothing changed about her view. So why did the oceanic symphony go on?

Louder.

Louder.

Until it was such a clamor, it drowned out even her stunned gasp. Which, to be honest, was probably more of an outcry. Which, to be more honest, nobody in their right mind would have denied her. Not if they were beholding the same sight that overwhelmed her now.

Jamie Bond, indeed.

This surprise was definitely shaken, not stirred.

And one of the most breathtaking vistas her island home had ever gifted to her.

In theory, she was still in the palais. Just not *in* the palais.

She was still under it—though she now stood at the edge of a small underground lake. Its sparkling swells were fed by the tides that flowed in from a small cave about thirty meters away. The full moon was high enough in the sky to illuminate the colliding waters, turning them into a liquid swirl of blue, green, silver, and gold.

That was only the beginning of the glory.

While nature had carved out this cavern to begin with, its existence was obviously ordained by the original palais designers. The support pillars built into the rock walls matched the soaring drama of the architecture upstairs, making the grotto look more like a preserved temple of Atlantis.

The effect was enhanced as she took another few steps, triggering the motion-activated lights that were rigged to the top of each column. The lamps pointed down, creating luminescent circles at their bases. Between those rings and the moon's glow, there was only one spot, directly in the lagoon's center, that was still immersed in darkness.

Naturally, her gaze was not tempted to spend a great deal of time in those shadows—until she had no choice about the matter.

When those black waters began to surge most abnormally.

When they began to rise—most alarmingly.

When they began to take shape, with heavy rivers cascading down a large form. An obelisk made of bronze, growing by every second. The ticks of time that sucked away more of her terrified breaths, until her chest pumped hard and tiny whimpers accompanied each exhalation . . .

Up to the moment her lungs refused to cooperate at all.

The instant that she recognized a jolting truth.

The tall, steely form was no manmade obelisk. But it *was* all man, surely carved by the Creator's own hand. Magnificent and muscled. Glorious and godlike.

A force of nature.

Her force of nature.

CHAPTER THIRTEEN

Holy shit.

Was he dreaming?

Brick scrambled to validate the conjecture by ruling out the other theories assaulting his mind. He hadn't swum low enough to be getting the bends, and he absolutely wasn't high. If he was having a hallucination, it was a damn good one.

A dream still made the most sense. This incredible fantasy pool deserved an equally entrancing siren on its curved rock shore.

That had to be his answer. Fantasizing was the logical coping mechanism for being carried into the cavern by an unanticipated high tide. But it wasn't like he had planned to take the swim at all, let alone check the tide charts beforehand. Dunking himself in the Mediterranean had simply seemed a better idea than getting drowned in a fresh wave of dejection. All the *feelings* that refused to set him free, even now.

The selfishness that wouldn't unchain him from this goddamned mope.

The punishment that he deserved.

He'd broken the rules. No, he'd shattered them. Gotten too damn entangled in the op to the point that he couldn't give the mission up. Yeah, despite its happy ending. Despite how he'd never have to worry about Jayd again.

But goddammit, he *wanted* to worry. About everything. About her bold, impetuous spirit. About her open, trusting heart. About her dreams and her goals, her sanity and her safety...

And yes, even now, about the fantasy he'd conjured of her. Whether that dream girl was going to stop staring at him and remember exactly where she was stepping...

And continued to step...

Until she careened right off the lagoon's edge.

And on her way into the choppy water, let out a shriek to finally shatter him. And horrify him.

"Jesus Ch—" He dove forward, breast stroking toward her like the obedient fool he was. Reality was about to hand him his soul on a plate the second he reached and watched his fantasy turn back into pixie dust. In this case, perhaps pixie drops.

But he wrapped his hand around a very real shoulder. And then around the other. A wonderfully real warmth flowed over his chest as Jayd sputtered and coughed past the soaked curtain of her hair.

"*Rahmié Creacu!*"

Holy shit. That sounded pretty real too.

Did he dare test the postulation?

"What the hell are you doing here?"

Not his smoothest reality test, but damn how he rejoiced in the results. Down to every infuriated light in her eyes and every twist of her lips.

"I live here, Sir. And *your* excuse?"

Oh, damn it. She was begging for it. Before he could resist, his most insolent smirk splayed itself into existence.

"So... you were just taking a stroll underneath the palais to get some fresh air? That it?"

Her mouth relaxed. Her body softened against his by the same degrees. *Shit.* Clearly, she hadn't gotten his abstinenceis-golden memo yet. Not even an email version.

"I shall answer your questions when you answer mine."

She tilted her head, channeling so much of her sassy sprite side that Brick started fantasizing again. This time, about what he could do to tame that wild little creature. How he could haul her out of this pool, yank down her leggings, and give her a discipline session like she'd never known. He already saw it: the wet smacks of his palm against her gleaming backside. He felt it: the heady sting of hitting her wet flesh. And oh yes, he heard it—the echoes of her high wails along all these hard walls.

Shit, shit, shit!

"After the crowd in the commissary started closing in, I needed some air." Not a lie, but not the whole truth. Slivers of panic had definitely soaked in at the outskirts of his psyche, but having Jayd nearby had taken a lot of the edges off—at least until they got too sharp. "I headed for the beach. The water was warm. Seemed a no-brainer."

She narrowed her stare. "Even with your wounds?"

He shrugged, deliberately emphasizing the shoulder with his half-dissolved sutures. "Saltwater keeps shit clean, right?" He ignored her little huff and went on. "Anyhow, I was fine until the tide decided to be a beast. Idiotic, I know. But Puget Sound isn't exactly known for its mean rips."

Jayd canted her head the other direction. Holy God, she was such a sweet sight in yeah-you-*are*-an-idiot mode. But perhaps she was getting distracted in interesting ways, just like he was. He hadn't exactly packed a swimsuit for this island detour, so their sexes were only separated by her thin yet soaked leggings. If he was feeling everything accurately, she was already hot and needy. And goddammit, his dick was already a boulder.

"Pixie?"

"Yes, Sir?"

Fuck. He'd absolutely walked into that one, and most of him wasn't sorry.

"Your turn," he prompted in a slow, meaningful growl.

In return, she first straightened her head. But just when Brick expected more kittenish stalling, she declared, "I was not just taking a stroll."

Intuition supplied him with some possible follow-ups. Maybe a sense that went beyond that. An awareness of her that nearly supplied the explanation already. Then again, he was the guy who'd first thought she was a fantasy. Maybe she still was. If so, then she wouldn't disappoint.

Who the hell was he kidding?

This woman would never dissatisfy him. She would never be anything short of dazzling for him. She'd always astound and amaze and fascinate him like few ever had.

No. Like *no one* ever had.

"If you must know, I was looking for you."

Her admission, and its threads of accusation, weren't a complete surprise. Still, deep inside, he was glowing like a kid who'd gotten a smile from the cute girl at the mall.

"It was your moment to celebrate with your brother," he mumbled, already looking away. "And with Samsyn on the way with Carris, I figured you all would want to—"

He couldn't determine how to label her sharp laugh. It wasn't a full bark, but it was better than a ladylike chirp.

"And you truly think I *want* to spend any time with my brothers . . . why? And please do *not* with that confused glare, *Sir*."

"Who says it's a prete—*ow*!"

The tracks from the woman's gouging nails were probably going to be permanent. She was clearly after the same result with the blue fire in her unrelenting gaze.

"The Creator is not merciful to liars, Brickham."

"Thanks for the post of the day, Pixie." He lowered his head, impaling their gazes tighter—and bringing their mouths an inch closer to each other. Maybe this wasn't a good idea after all . . . or the best damn move he'd made tonight. His tone dropped to a husk as he managed to follow up. "But maybe you want to clarify some of this shit now, little girl?"

At first, her answer was a leap of brows to match his. The expression exploded into a gasp once he grabbed hold of her ass and squeezed.

Holy God. He was immediately enthralled. So much so, he repeated the brutality with twice the force.

God*damn*. Her second cry was sexier than the first. When she finished it by chomping hard on her bottom lip, he had to clench his buttocks to prevent his pre-come from erupting into the lagoon's waters.

Shit. Shit. Oh, fucking *shit.*

Thank her damn Creator, the woman finally decided to comply with his command.

"What happened?" she grated, her breath brushing his mouth like airborne honey. "Between you and Evrest? What did he say, Brickham? What did he tell you?"

By the time she finished, the words were wobbly with tears.

It took closing his eyes for long moments to fend off their stabs down to his heart. "Nothing I didn't know already, Pixie."

He braced himself to receive some new ravines in his

skull, courtesy of her fingernails. What he got was a thousand times more agonizing.

Her face washing into a total blank.

Her hands splashing limply to her sides.

Her back etched beneath her soaked shirt as she turned away from him.

"Jayd."

Nothing answered but the waters around him, smacking against each other like a bowl of goddamned tears. But even the metaphor felt wrong. Undeserved. He didn't get to have this moroseness. Not when he'd pretty much brought it on himself.

"Pixie!"

But something inside him didn't listen. The same part that already bellowed like a butchered animal, miserable and incomplete, with more of its flanks sawed off every time she took another step away.

Why did it feel like this?

Why hadn't it felt like this when he'd walked out of the commissary earlier? Hadn't his spine been just as stiff, his mind been just as firm about how everything had to be now between them? Nothing had changed about that. Any of it.

"Jayd! God*damm*it."

Oh, yeah. This was really knowing better, yeah? Screeching like a peacock as his hen declared his plumage unsatisfactory. Fuming like a mongoose who craved her vicious bite. Pouting like the douchiest Dom on the planet, unable to figure out why she wasn't staying still like a good little submissive.

Because she'd never be that.

She'd always dance on the border between fiery and frustrating. Willing but questioning.

Always, *always* questioning...

Nothing he needed.

Everything her country needed.

A princess for their new age. A woman to set an example for so many others.

A female he could never call his.

A woman who affirmed exactly that as she kept walking, toward the opposite shore of the lagoon. Once there, she hoisted herself up and out of the water but stayed up on all fours.

Christ on *high*.

If this was her idea of rubbing it in about what he was giving up, she was sure as hell succeeding.

But as soon as her head dropped between her hunched shoulders, he saw things differently.

She wasn't out to one-up him.

The woman was back on dry land but clearly struggled to keep herself from drowning.

"I...cannot do it anymore, Brickham. I...cannot even try."

But she was going under anyway.

Fighting a tide of desperation, aided by an undertow of exhaustion in a night full of too much anxiety. Brick saw it all, through every strained striation of her neck and back, and hated himself for it. With every muscle in his body and synapse in his head, he longed for the chance to follow her onto that shore, grab her by the hand, and give her everything she wanted.

Except what she really wanted.

An escape from her life. A light to guide her to—what? Adventure? Romance? Sexy times abroad with the hot

American guy? A simple path out of her tunnel?

Shit.

He didn't know how to get out of his own tunnel. And the parts about light and adventure? Last time he checked, that only happened to warriors named *Wilson* and *Rogers* who carried shields with stars, or tap-dancing sailors from forties musicals. Too bad he hadn't known it years ago, when he'd tried to be that unlikely success story.

Tried. And failed.

And because of that failure—because of the mirage in his mind of being SOCOM's odds-defying Little Engine That Could—a woman had died.

A woman so much like the one before him now.

A human who gave to the world straight from her heart and deserved all of the same in return.

A person who didn't need a guy like him moving in on her, exactly like he couldn't control himself from doing now.

What the *hell* was he doing now?

Drifting nearer to her side of the water instead of attempting to swim the hell out of here? Helping himself to another push from the tide in order to lurch up to the ledge himself? Murmuring her name as a guttural plea while crawling up behind her—and then over her?

What the living crap?

No, no, no, no!

But every chamber of his mind resounded with the opposite. Every voice in his senses screamed like a different demon of the unholy possession she had over him. The unignorable bond. The connection he couldn't refuse, as long as he could reach her. Touch her. Flatten his chest along her back and form his lips against her neck…

"Do. Not." The words reverberated up her throat before forming a tangible bubble of fury around them.

"Can't. Stop," he finished with a hiss as the heat at the center of his body softened the fabric encasing the center of hers. "Can't . . . be away from you."

"Brickham." It was a cry and a breath together, a plea like none other she'd ever given him. "*Please.*"

"Can't. I'm sorry, Pixie. I can't . . ."

The appeal in his own rasp was just as strident now. Not far behind was a stronger jolt of his self-loathing. *You're not that guy, damn it.*

"I'm sorry, sweetheart. I'm so sorry. I just . . . can't . . ."

Help myself.

Because apparently, he was that guy. The pussy-whipped clown who had no idea where his cock was leading. The stricken fool now consumed by the female beneath him. She wasn't even trying. But damn it, what she was *doing*. Her smell, musky and potent. Her sounds, airy and inebriating. Her movements, small yet intense.

Stroking against him even more.

Tying him to her even tighter . . .

But not close enough.

As he reached around, finding one damp nipple and then the other, Jayd set another couple of cries loose on the air. Again, they echoed a thousand times—revealing the high pitch of arousal beneath her snarling anger.

"I'm sorry," Brick mumbled into her neck again. "I'm so sorry."

"Liar," she bit out.

"Guilty." He dug his teeth into the bottom of her ear. Another whimper from her. Heavy gasps that shoved her erect nipples back against his fingers.

"I hate you."

"I need you."

"Brickham. Please. Oh . . . please . . ." Her syllables slurred together, a cocktail of carnality that infused his blood better than any drug. But was it her rage still doing the talking? Or something else that boiled through *her* blood? It made her breathe harder. Had her fully trembling now.

And him too.

"Brickham. Damn it! Oh . . . *ah*!"

It was an insane risk. But for a fleeting second, his mind left him—and he really did shove her leggings down. He got them halfway down before having to stop, processing the reality of the sight before him.

Shit. This was really happening. She was really here again. Beneath him. Exposed to him. Offering herself to him. God, *yesss.*

He wasn't taking any of it for granted.

At once, he used a hand to pull back one of her damp ass cheeks. The other, he scooped toward the core of her sex . . .

The tightness of her pussy . . .

The perfect river of her lust . . .

"Damn," he groaned. "Pixie . . ."

Her head fell forward again. He grunted hard, savoring her blatantly submissive position. Pretending he was inside her with his cock. Celebrating how her sweet cunt squeezed his body as tightly as her fiery spirit surrounded his soul. Basking in every perfect piece of this moment. Swearing to himself that he'd remember it all. That he'd likely pump himself to a million orgasms because of it.

"I still . . . hate you."

"I know," he growled.

"And I am still . . . going to . . ."

"Oh, I know that too."

He was so close, his dick rested against her lax ass cheek. It wept with pre-come, and he pumped his length to gather up the milky drops. He used them as extra lubricant to get a second finger inside her, joining his desperate moan to the primal sound that tangled the length of her throat.

At once, her body gave in to him. Her walls eagerly sucked on his digits, vibrating in time to his steady, solid rhythm.

He leaned over to gain some leverage, pumping even deeper. The position also allowed him to scrape along her clit before re-entrance, while using the same friction to work his cockhead between their bodies. That part was hardly necessary. He was certain if the wind merely changed direction in here, he was going to blow his load across her beautiful ass cheeks.

But not before her. Damn it, not . . . before . . .

She began rocking herself on his fingers. Brick moaned in approval, determined this would be the best finger-fuck of his existence.

But suddenly, he was thrusting into nothing but air.

And was too stunned to issue anything but a harsh rasp—as he watched Jayd scramble away.

He was still speechless as she regained her feet and awkwardly hauled her leggings up. Though her knees were still shaky, she took a couple of plodding steps. Her shoulders slouched back in as she hugged herself with hands that had gone painfully pale.

Fuck. Fuck. *I'm sorry, Pixie.*

This wasn't what it seemed. None of it.

But how to blurt that and convey what it really meant?

All the things beyond it. All the things he could never just open up and confess.

Wasn't what it seemed...

Because you were beyond what I ever dreamed.

Because you still are.

"Jayd—"

"No." Her posture stiffened. At once, he yearned to be *her* obstinate underling, rushing to do whatever it took for her understanding, but he was undone when she sagged again. Her sorrow impacted him worse than before. The full weight of what her heartache was almost unbearable. "Please, Brickham... no more. Just..."

No more.

Exactly what she became then.

As soon as she jolted away as if her exit tunnel contained a monster that decided to snatch her up as a midnight snack.

But that had to be his most epic delusion of the day.

She hadn't been torn away from him. Not compelled or forced or pulled either.

She'd run because she wanted to. Because it was what *he* kept telling her she wanted. Because at last, she believed him. About everything.

So... all a good thing, right?

"Sure," he snarled beneath his breath. "Right."

No. Nothing would be right, ever again—starting with the lowlife reflected at him from the lagoon's wind-whipped waters. The medal-wearing champion for elite-level assholery. The jerk who'd told his submissive it had to be over but then nearly rutted on her like a sea lion cornering his cow on a rock.

And now, the tool who sat here on his ass instead of going after her. Not to push at her anymore. Just to ensure she got back safely to the civilized part of this joint. But he was too pathetic for that. Too mired in the anxiety he battled to quell. The nerves he fought with painful lungfuls of breath. Without all that, he likely would've been rocking his head back to laugh. As she'd already said with such vivid glory, she lived here. Once upon a time, as in a few hours ago, she'd even offered to take him on a tour of the castle tunnels.

It'd be a miracle if he found his own way out now, much less to a place where borrowable clothes could be found. Might serve him right if that wasn't the case. Begging a flight out of here with his johnson in hand was starting to sound like poetic justice.

In the end—or what felt like the agonizing equivalent—fate was merciful. After following the tunnel on the other side of the lagoon, he quickly found his way back to ground level and then onto a circular panel that rotated into a women's bathroom. By that point, he was practically past the concern about his nudity.

Fortunately, there was only one person using the place, and she giggled when he appeared. The woman pointed at his package with slurred commentary, making him vow to never again complain about drunk co-eds celebrating summer break by hunting down Bastille's address. Not even after their thirtieth plea for a hot Seattle billionaire to put them in his red "bad girl" cuffs.

Luckily, the bathroom's cleaning closet was unlocked. A pair of janitor's coveralls fit everywhere but his shoulders and crotch, but beggars sure as hell couldn't be choosers.

He hoped Evrest and Samsyn's celebratory moods matched that of his friend from the bathroom. As soon as they approved his request to catch the next available air transport, he'd be off this island for good. He didn't care where the damn thing was bound for. He was after mercy right now, for both Jayd and him.

The woman—and her pleas and her tears—were right. They couldn't keep doing this to each other. Sealing the bond tighter was only making it shittier to break.

As in next to impossible.

Funny, how every step he took back to the commissary felt the same way.

But every wince was his own damn fault. From abandoning his cane on the beach with his clothes, to toughing out the hike from the lagoon, to ensuring that every physical pain corresponded to the stabs from his spirit, he was a corporeal and cerebral mess before clearing even half of the palais's massive main foyer.

Seemed coincidence wasn't ready to let him finish the trip either.

He stopped without grace, nearly slamming to his ass when realizing he wasn't alone in this part of the building. But that alone wasn't what lit up every hair on the back of his neck.

This was a public section of the palais. Though the hour was late, there should've been some more stragglers from the celebration he'd escaped nearly an hour ago. But the footsteps, which echoed everywhere and nowhere at once, were too certain and determined for drunk Arcadian revelers.

Brick tucked behind a corner pillar, already calling himself twenty kinds of a paranoid idiot. Still, he kept the effort swift but silent—not a simple feat when one was hustling a hundred and fifteen kilos on bare feet. Still, unable to shake his strange instinct, he stayed frosty for anything to repurpose into a weapon.

Paranoid. Idiot.

But if Oz, Jag, and their green-bearded pal hadn't caught everyone back in the forest, perhaps the palais had a few unwanted visitors now. And even if they *had* contained all the French force members, nothing was stopping more Pura zealots from taking up the mission in Carris's absence—with their eyes on one prize. No, two. Recovering Carris would only be their first stop. The asshole would never accept freedom without Jayd in tow. Not after all the defeats he'd been served in Paris.

Damn. With an imagination like this, he should've been submitting scripts to Hollyweird.

At least he hoped it was all fiction, even as he kept up his visual recon of the area.

Could he pry away this pillar for use as a battering ram? *Negative.* Likely holding up part of the ceiling.

Waist-high planter pot? Excellent. *Check.*

Small marble fountain and perimeter statues? Also excellent. *Check.*

Iron wall sconces? Doable in an extreme pinch. *Check* again.

Christ. Why did he think this was going to become an extreme pinch? And where was a main hall full of palace-type knick-knacks when he needed it?

No time for ruminating that answer.

Very much time for holding off these cheeky *connards,* here and now. With any luck, they'd be in the mood to rock the rafters in return. Lots of loud boom-booms felt like such a perfect plan right now.

"Halt in the name of His High Majesty King Evrest of Arcadia!"

At once, the newcomers paused their advance.

Paused.

Just as quickly, the footsteps restarted. Double the pace. Triple the purpose.

"Listen up, assholes. You're trespassing, and there'll be serious repercussions. *Comprenez-vous* that shit?"

He finished with a self-congratulatory grunt. Yeah, he still had it with the vocal dominance. Bronson and Johnson, peppered with a little Statham, did it every time.

The Arcadians' newest guests didn't agree. Their subtle snickers spoke that truth clearly enough.

"Oh, sweet honeysuckle. Oh pwwwease don't inflict your wwwepercussions on us, Mr. Badass Soldier Man!"

"I'm not even weawwing my protective nut cup. What if he shoots off my family jewels?"

"Not the family jewels!"

Air rushed from Brick with speed he didn't think possible. "Jesus in a donut."

He exposed himself by rolling out along the pillar. He kept half his weight pinned against the stone, unsure if his suddenly flimsy knees would lend full support.

"Well, well, well. Speaking of rare jewels . . ."

He cut off the approaching man with a brutal snort. Part of him wanted to punch the pretty boy in his exquisitely carved kisser, but revenge like that was out when a guy wanted to bawl for joy of seeing a good friend.

"Ethan fucking Archer." He slapped the man hard on the back during their gruff hug. "What the living—"

"Careful, Brickmeister. That's a lot of nasty language in the house of—how'd you say it?—his oh-so-High Majesty?"

"Says the lord of everything nasty himself?" he retorted.

"Lord Nasty is good for a start." Zeke Hayes folded his arms, definitely a musclebound monarch in the making. "But I'm so working my way up to being the High Majesty."

Ethan stepped back, unable to hide the mischief in his blue-black eyes. "How about you stay happy with Psycho Zsycho for now?"

"And how about both of you telling me why the hell you're here?" Brick broke in. "Especially because the last time we spoke, I remember you roger-dodgering me—from *Seattle*—about standing clear from this cluster."

"Huh. Really?" The big dork had the nerve to mix of a puzzled frown with an innocent gaze. "All I remember is the part about saying your posse would always be there for you. I mentioned the same thing to Archer, and he agreed."

Ethan nodded, adding his smooth take to Z's audacity. "Leaving friends out in the wind isn't our style, buddy. You've got to know that by now. Besides, my folks own a cute little place on Mykonos. Rayna and Ava were all over the idea of a Cyclades sojourn."

They chuckled in tandem about that, though Brick couldn't muster an answering laugh. It would take a while to bring his tense rockets off fire, especially after flying the stress galaxies for nearly a week now.

He leaned on his better leg, relishing the chance for a power pose with his hands on his hips. "To take shit down by a notch or ten, I couldn't be happier to see you guys."

Zeke snorted. "Can't say the same, since I left Rayna in Hora with a credit card and an order to get whatever she wanted in lieu of our reservation at *Kako Koritsi*."

"Ca-ca what?" Brick charged.

"Means *bad girl* in Greek," the guy responded, shaking

the shaggy black hair out of his eyes with a fast wink. "Take it from there or don't take it anywhere."

Before Brick could pick either option, Ethan was thankfully true to form, refocusing everyone on the more important subject at hand. "Can we assume, since you're bellowing the monarch's name and running around like Cowboy Loki, that the Arcadians have at least taken your side in this shit show?"

Zeke grunted. "Prison Loki is probably better dressed."

"Shut up," Brick snarled.

"It's a solid point." Ethan eyed him from head to toe. "Thank fuck Ava's keeping her sister company in Hora, or you'd already be dragged off to whatever they've got here for a clothes store."

Brick pushed out another weighted breath. "Well, then, thank God for Hora and the power of shopping sprees." He spread his hands, struggling not to remember the last time they were splayed in this position. The moments before he'd reached and secured half of Jayd's gorgeous ass with one of them. "If there *is* a shopping district in Sancti, not sure I'd be a welcome sight on those golden sidewalks."

His buddies were practically synched on their perplexed frowns, though Z got the jump on first comeback. "You mean you haven't gotten the grand tour already? What the hell've you been doing the better part of a week?"

Ethan cocked both brows. "Or perhaps *who*?"

"Shut. *Up*." But there wasn't time or energy for the extra viciousness. Diversion was his best option now. "You do remember the part about the uniforms at Bourget taking some target practice at me, yeah?"

"Fuck." Just as quickly, Ethan dropped his forehead into a

tight frown. "Z? You said he'd only been scratched."

"Fortunately, that was the case with the dome." Brick brushed a couple of fingers across the tiny stitches in his forehead. "Wasn't so lucky with a couple of the drumsticks." With the same hand, he tapped at his shoulder and thigh. "But their whitecoats know their embroidery. The scarring won't be bad."

"Boo to the yah," Ethan commented. "That's good to hear."

"*Pfttt.*" Zeke grunted. "If I were you, I'd flaunt that fuckery, man. When you get Stateside again, the girls will be lining up for a spot on your dungeon dance card. Subbies go into heat over scars."

Ethan flashed a skeptical side-eye. "And you're the hot expert on subbie trends now?"

"Said one old married fart to the other?" Zeke rejoined. "Come on, all the girls talk and you know it."

Brick stepped forward. "Can we go back to the part about me getting Stateside?" The subject was so invigorating, he forgot about the throb in his leg. At this point, he'd forego a trip back to his infirmary room for the little cup of meds that Twylah had likely set out for him by now. "Whatever ride you guys used to get here, I hope it's still waiting for the return trip—and an extra guest."

The guys took such a long second to respond, he feared they'd say their pilot—or skipper, or whomever—was off the clock for a long while.

At last, Ethan stated, "We put down anchor in Sancti Harbor. The captain's holding tight."

"Good." Brick pivoted, gesturing for them to follow. If anything beneficial had come from his trip to Jayd's suite today—okay, likely yesterday by now—it was his improved sense of direction around here. "Come on. I think I know a shortcut— *Goddammit.* What the hell, guys?"

What else was he supposed to say in response to their next hesitation? Were they waiting for emails with their VIP bar code?

"What the hell indeed, buckaroo." Zeke shook his head. "You're going to leave just like that? No goodbye, farewell, *auf wiedersehen* to you?"

"After their docs patched you up?" Ethan concurred. "After what *you* did—what, exactly?—for and with their princess?"

Brick scowled. "The princess won't miss me."

Their instant—and buoyant—laughter shouldn't have yielded his matching jump of tension. But holy fuck, how it did. At once, he was grinding teeth and twisting fists again.

"Told you, pretty boy," Z crowed at Ethan. "You owe me a crisp Benjamin."

"A hundred bucks?" Brick lasered a glower at Ethan. "Why?" And then at Zeke. "And what'd you tell him?"

Never before had he seen such a wide smirk on Zeke Hayes's lips. "That Prince Charming isn't the only one who likes macking on the princess."

Brick jabbed his tighter fists into the ample pockets of his jumpsuit. "All right, ladies. Can we just get the hell out of here now?"

"Do. Not. Take. Another. Step."

Though the command lacked any native Arcadian, he knew an imperative from their most menacing prince when he heard one. Further proof of that truth—as if he needed any—were the unnerving sounds that suddenly filled the foyer. The distinct *snocks* of cocking gun hammers.

Samsyn was obnoxiously serious. He'd brought a small battalion as proof.

"Whoa, baby."

"Shit."

Z and Ethan finished the reactions with fast arm raises. Brick did the same, only to have his wrists grabbed, dropped, and slammed against the middle of his back.

Before he could quell it, a harsh grunt exploded up his throat. Nothing like severely strained stitches to make a guy enjoy being shackled a little more.

"That hurts, hmmm?" The prince seized the chain between the cuffs, which had to have been crafted in the days witches were burned at the stake, before leaning in from the side and shoving a thumb into the wound at the top of Brick's shoulder. "Not as much as I want it to."

Raw confusion kept him from concentrating on the pain. Brick flung it all at Samsyn with a stunned swing of his head. "Okay, what the hell?" he demanded. "You don't like me. I get that. But I was getting ready to clear out, all right?"

"We'll vouch about that, man." How the hell Zeke sounded like he was unhooking Brick from a bar fight instead of tetanus-inducing handcuffs was beyond belief. "He's antsy to be gone. Just let us take him and—"

"None of you *kimfuks* are going anywhere," Samsyn barked. "Except right this way."

Brick was jerked backward and then around. He stumbled forward as soon as a steel barrel jabbed the center of his spine. He breathed deep through his nose, positive his heart rate was about to spike and his head would jump on the resulting merry-go-round. He never knew which would hit worse about the panic attacks. He just prayed like hell that he'd be able to steady his feet and his self-control.

Self. Control.

Thank God it seemed the foremost goal for Ethan and Z, as well. Ethan never had him worried. The guy owned a rehab ranch on the ocean and did impossible yoga poses for fun. But Zeke, while one of the finest Dominants he'd ever met, was known in the ops world as a decisive thinker. That was the polite way of saying *loose cannon.*

Samsyn and his men pulled them along an all-too-familiar hallway, down a flight of steps, and then back into the palais commissary. Thankfully, Z remained Josey Wales-worthy in his steely austerity. Brick marveled at it for a few seconds longer than necessary, knowing it'd be supplanted by a smirk once Zeke saw him sharing any kind of space with Jayd. Even so, he swung his gaze around in search of her. That was the only part of him still able to move so freely, thanks to the cuffs and the continued clutches from two of Samsyn's men. He couldn't help wondering how Jayd would perceive it all. Would she rejoice or recoil at seeing him like this? Would she protest or praise her brother?

But where was she? Surely she'd beaten him back to the surface and had come right back here, eager to revel in the same sight that sparked a smile to his lips despite all the pain through his body.

The beautiful panorama with Trystan Carris at its center.

They'd plunked him into a basic steel chair, which might permanently become a part of him with all the ropes that bound him to it. He was stripped to his pale waist, now marred from the rough ropes. His legs were secured to the chair's legs in similar fashion.

Despite the harsh custody, the man's posture seemed lax. Practically insouciant. The observation might have been wrong, since Brick was still only looking from behind, but surely his instincts weren't that corroded. Then again, his last official mission had seen him nearly killed because of shitty logistical calls. Judgments that would haunt him forever.

Weirdly, the same kind of wraiths that now flew across Samsyn Cimarron's face.

Huh?

He gave the sentiment some voice with a questioning grunt. Though he didn't really expect an answer, it was baffling to keep studying Samsyn. He knew furious regret when he saw it, and the sonofabitch was glued hard to the prince's features.

And Christ, now that he expanded his view, across Evrest's face too. And Shiraz's. And most of the crowd still hanging out in here.

What the hell was going on?

Why wasn't everyone already three sheets to the nectar-induced wind? Or indulging in adrenaline hook-ups in the bedraped alcoves? What happened to the celebration that was already winding up when he'd left the room? Had someone harshed the overall mellow by already knifing Carris? Had the man himself said or done someth—

Fuck.

All those thoughts were axed as soon as he got hauled over to stand in front of the asshole.

"Fuck!"

He wanted to repeat it again and again. In his mind, he did. But his throat was nuked by ruthless shock. The same poisonous cloud that took out his knees and fuzzed his vision.

Because Carris . . .

Wasn't Carris.

What... the... living...

The man in the chair, with a build, a face, and even a smarmy snicker to match the man's, unleashed an open grin at Brick. The expression was wide enough to crack some crumbling latex glue at the edges of his cheeks, which fell atop a flexible rubber mask in his lap. The thing was similar to the kinds of façades that hit the stores at Halloween season—only instead of the president or the latest internet scandal star, this was a face condom of the shithead who'd begun to dominate his nightmares.

And would continue to do so.

Only now, Brick was living those midnight terrors. In more ways than he wanted to acknowledge.

"Shit on a shingle," Z grunted.

"Deep fake for the obscene win, anyone?" Ethan added.

"Hmmm. I approve of his concept." In a different time and place, Carris's stand-in could've made some bank as a celebrity look-a-like for the asshole. Everything about the guy's voice was an ideal match too. "Winning has a nice ring to it. And since it is fairly much the truth now..."

"Which means what?" Shiraz surged forward, overenunciating the last word until it sprayed across the dickwad's features. "*Faisi-crish!* Start talking now, *kimfuk*. As you can see, we have exactly done what you dictated." He grabbed the front of Brick's coveralls and hauled him forward. "He is here now, yes? Your beloved *bonami,* in the flesh. So start—"

"Okay, whoa the fuck there." The doghouse was no place from which to start a dog *fight*, but Brick was willing to lose a paw for it. *Bonami.* He knew that term now. Jayd and Emme had used it enough times with each other. "I'm not *any* kind of a buddy with this ass chunk. Do you honestly think—"

"That you are lying through your fucking teeth?" Evrest was the surprise Dirty Harry to his brother's Josey Wales. "Or do you have another colorful story for why you ran out of here when Samsyn and his team were on their way from the airstrip and then showed back up with a bigger gang of *soldasks*?"

A new snort burst from Zeke. "Can't speak to whatever the hell a *soldask* is, but we're *no* gang, man. And further—"

"*Pardonais,* Your Majesty." Thankfully, Ethan was swift with serving the courtly manners platter of this awkward tea party. "What my friend means to say is that we arrived here of our own accord, out of a concern to assist if our friend Brickham was in trouble."

"Well, that he damned well is," Shiraz leveled.

"But not because I'm hitting ragers with *him*!" Brick glared harder at the pretender in all the ropes. He loathed the asshat's steady nod of concurrence.

"Another outstanding point from the Yank," the guy drawled. "I intimated not a thing about sharing ragers with him, did I?"

The king didn't fling back any answers. Neither did either of his brothers.

Which opened the door, terrifyingly wide, for Brick's logic to go to work.

And for its conclusion to exit his mouth in a harsh spew.

"Shit."

Cuffs be damned. He stomped in until he took up all of the dickhead's personal space.

"Are they shooting straight about this?" he demanded of the guy. "You told them you'd talk if they brought me back here?"

"Hmm." The guy emulated his idol once more, tick-tocking his head with Carris's trademark insolence. "More or less . . . yes."

Brick scowled. "Why?" But the threat faded from his face as harsher understanding exploded in his senses. "Never mind. I already know."

God fucking help him, did he already know.

He wasn't conscious of blurting it aloud, especially because the length of his throat burned with bile. But somehow, once he looked up again, Arcadia's three princes were braced in a tense semicircle around him.

Their stares, already bright against their burnished skin, were incisive with suspicion. He had no idea what his offered in return. Dread? Fury? Fear? Nausea? Any or all would be disgustingly accurate.

Still, he dredged words to his lips. He had no other choice. "He was following Carris's orders," he croaked. "The cockbag wanted the Arcadian troops distracted, and then me out of the way, so he could have a clean path . . . to her."

To *her*.

The prize that had first slipped from the man's grip, just when he thought his hold was airtight. The treasure he'd tracked all the way to Paris, only to be denied once more.

The woman Trystan Carris was determined to own—no matter how extreme the cost.

Fuck. Fuck. *Fuck*.

Ancient steel bit into Brick's wrist as he moved to fight the screams of his mind by clawing at his skull, until being reminded of that impossibility. The pain was brutal, but that was perfect. Anything to put a dent in the torture device he'd been calling a brain.

But before that happened, the torment got worse. He was helpless to do anything while watching the same horror bite into Jayd's brothers. Their anguish made him wish for their anger all over again. But respawns were only good for characters in video game forests, not real-life guys struggling just to reconnect clear thoughts.

Thank God for Samsyn Cimarron—yeah, Brick meant it this time—who lunged right in at the ass chunk. With the guy's neck solidly lodged beneath a hand, the warrior prince let fly with a vicious snarl.

"Where. The fuck. Is he?" Samsyn didn't let up, his Josey Wales glare throughout the imposter's stubborn silence. "That is the first and last time you get the courtesy of the question!"

As soon as his knuckles visibly tautened, the imposter gulped. Well, attempted to. Just as quickly, the bastard reverted to a smirk. Christ, Brick had forgotten how infuriating an indoctrinated zealot could be.

"He is . . . nowhere," the man said with sickening serenity. "And yet everywhere." He canted his head the same direction. "Do you not know this yet, Your Highness? We are the Pura. Our very name means purity. And when you are pure, you can flow infinitely. Boundlessly. Beyond places you ever dreamed—"

"Yeah, yeah. And following the light will grow your dick a couple of inches. Hold up while I grab the branding iron and Kool-Aid."

Under other circumstances, Z's crack would've earned him at least a chuckle from Brick. But here and now, he could only send thankful vibes his friend's way while hoping his shutdown stuck with Cosplay Carris. The fucker's son-of-insanity shit was already stinking like the pile of dung it was.

Once more, he was glad to see the same sentiment stamped across the faces of the men around him. He was also damn glad that his two buddies were a part of that small crowd, especially as Ethan embraced his straight-to-the-chase DNA.

"Much as I'd love to make sure this sweet thing never pisses right again"—he quirked a grin when the imposter paled by four shades—"he clearly doesn't know Carris's whereabouts. So that means *we've* got to think faster and smarter."

Shiraz straightened his spine. "That is correct. We are wasting valuable time. We have to find Jayd before they do."

"*They*... meaning anyone in the damn kingdom." Brick dove off the psychological high board and said it. Why not?

Best case, it engendered a few shreds of the royals' trust. Worst, they took advantage of the moment to really toss him in the brig, likely located below their very feet. Also not a shitty thing, if Jayd had lingered anywhere near the spot at which he'd last laid eyes on her. But to share that key information, he also had to get bossy. What was there to lose? He didn't care about getting the gold medal anymore. Or being the plucky little engine or even the world's goddamned savior. All that mattered was getting to her before Carris. No matter what the cost.

"I might be able to help. But we've got to take this conversation elsewhere."

Clearly, the princes still weren't keen about heeding his play calls. Thank God, yet again, for Ethan and Z, reinserting themselves with determined intent.

"Brickmeister's a hundred percent right," Z asserted. "You might as well assume there are unwanted eyes and ears in here—besides the choad-wad obvious."

"No offense intended, ladies and gentlemen." Ethan spun

around in a move that would turn Bruno Mars into a jealous biddy. A small clump of Arcadian females broke into instant giggles, clarifying that they'd forgotten *offense* was a real word. "Precautions," the guy added, garnering himself another round of girlish titters.

Z hardly noticed. "You guys have anywhere that's been tidied out, tech-wise?" he asked the princes.

Shiraz snorted. "We are in the middle of the Mediterranean, not Tatooine."

"Any other time, I'd be buying you a beer for that line." Z cuffed Shiraz on the shoulder. "Or whatever gets your rocks off around here. But right now, lead the way. Archer and I are helping you out." He rolled his head, loudly cracking his neck. "By whatever wild reasoning of the cosmos, we have a special knack for lost women."

Samsyn tilted his own neck. Jogged a look that vaguely resembled a curious German Shepherd. "And how do we know *you* are not the eyes and ears we should be wary of?"

Brick stiffened his stance. "Both these men are legit. I'll stake my gonads on it."

What the hell. His balls would be worthless if they didn't find Jayd, anyhow.

Who the crap was he kidding?

If they didn't get her back, his balls would be a pointless subject. His heart and soul would be the more questionable survivors.

Or, quite possibly, the fatal casualties.

CHAPTER FOURTEEN

When the hell will you learn?

Jayd lost track of how many times the castigation torched its way from her heart to her lips. But she let the anger come again and again, thankful for its arid fire in place of the wet stings that kept threatening behind her eyes.

When. Will. You. Learn?

Before long, it became the marching drum for her steps, as well. The interrogation her mind could no longer ignore.

But also for which she had not a single response.

It had not always been this way. Not so long ago, she had all the answers, so easily given. All of her limits were so clearly defined. Never, she vowed, would she tolerate a man who led her on. Or treated her heart—and body—as disposable. Or used *his* body to take over so many of her senses . . . and all of her control. Certainly not one who *spanked* her . . .

And made her like it. Savor it. Need it.

To such terrifying depths of her being.

Not. Ever. Again.

There. A much better chant. It was a perfect fit for her faster steps. If only she could escape the runaway train of her thoughts with matching speed. Do away with the images that took over more and more of her mind's eye, even as she fled faster.

The first hurricane wallop of Brickham's cobalt stare. The matching force of his hands on her flesh and her blissful inner tremors because of it. The taut glory that overtook *his* body when she touched him in return. How he coiled for her. Hardened for her. Swelled in such magnificent places for her.

How that glory intensified when he started entering her . . .

Not. Ever. Again.

It was time to push those beautiful scenes aside. To glue them into a mental scrapbook and not take them out for a long while. Not until far in the future, when they would only make her wistful instead of mournful. When she could traverse a tunnel and not stumble over her own two feet in delayed grief.

Or was this advanced anguish?

And did it matter since the result was the same?

That since her vision was so blurred, she missed the little steel lip that protruded from the ground below? And that now she was on her ass in the dark dust, tailbone bruised and outrage spiked?

"*Rahmié Creacu!*" The syllables were nearly hisses, turning them into verbal snake strikes. But unless she was mistaken, snakes did not keep up continuous attacks.

Or elevate those aggressions into sneaking footfalls.

Steps that were *not* hers.

She confirmed as much with a frantic glance down at her feet before tucking them beneath her backside. She was prepared to jolt up and run, though used her knees to scramble back into a shadowed alcove.

Until her head and shoulders bumped into something with a loud *kwong*.

She shrieked but then gasped, suddenly curious about the fog that her breath formed along a large plate of . . .

What?

Her attacker's *leg?*

No. Not an aggressor. Well, not a real one...

She had just made acquaintances with a suit of ancient Arcadian armor. *Ancient* wasn't entirely correct, since the kingdom was not yet three hundred years old. She deduced this had been strictly a ceremonial outfit for someone, though its thick tarnish had taken over a long time ago.

The armor's condition matched the rest of the old spears, rifles, firearms, and devices of destruction in the chamber she had happened upon. None of it was shocking—Arcadians had been called to defend the kingdom since its inception, and a secret lagoon with an attached armory was a definite advantage to that end—but it *was* an odd discovery. How had she never known of this chamber's existence before? Did that mean Ev, Syn, and 'Raz did not, either? Or *Paipanne* and *Maimanne*? And if that were the case, where exactly had she wandered to in the palais—if she was even in the confines of the place anymore?

And *why* could she not shake the sensation that she no longer roamed around here alone?

Which meant her adventuring mode was still stuck in idle, succumbing to mounting trepidation. Her nerves rattled harder as her ears perked and pricked, aware of more sounds than just her breathing. Sounds that seemed not normal, even for this hazy underground...

Like inhalations and exhalations that did not match her own.

And, carefully timed with each of those breaths, the pads of surreptitious feet. And the rustles of a moving body...

"Brickham?" She mouthed it more than spoke it, though it had enough air to be heard. But it was an empty effort. The man's energy was her psychological balm. She was as sure of it as the sun on her face and the stars in her nights—and this new companion was *not* that.

Then who . . . ?

Possibilities whizzed to mind. More flimsy assumptions. Requiemme or any valid palais staffer would have announced themselves already. Same, in gruffer style, for her brothers.

That left her with three choices.

It could still be her imagination. Or it was one of Samsyn's scouts.

Or one of Trystan's.

"Shit."

That one remained beneath her breath too. She muffled it a little bit better by pulling her knees against her chin. But that did not prevent a deeper dread from invading her chest. Why did she sense that she might as well have shouted out the curse?

Perhaps . . . because of the pair of black-booted feet that slowly paced into her view?

Because of the way those feet halted in the center of this miniature armory, purposefully pivoting until their owner completed a rotation back to his original spot?

"Your Highness Jayd?"

Creator's sweet toes. Back to *her* original spot.

"Damn it. You've got to be in here! If so, then I really need to know." Ohhh, yes. The underground interloper *was* female, speaking in a smooth feline alto. "I mean no harm. I promise you, I'm here to help you. I swear it on my *maimanne*'s memory, may she have ease in the everlasting."

Jayd had already sworn not to trust this stranger with her pinky finger, let alone the emergence of her whole self from the nook behind the armor, but then the woman husked out the last of her pledge. The answering pangs of Jayd's heart provided the courage to slip all the way back out.

"I . . . am sorry about your *maimanne*."

The woman turned with grace that matched the purring undertones of her voice. Though the overall action was dancer sleek, her gaze was the exact opposite. She studied Jayd like a creature nearly possessed, her irises swirling with psychedelic shades of purple. Jayd was so fascinated in return, she forgot to be uncomfortable. It was not a wise call. Logic said as much, but she could not stop her innate curiosity.

Who was she?

Instinct supplied key details. If the woman was Arcadian, that would be the shock of the night. Her accent and black battle gear seemed distinctly American, down to the daggers and pistol in custom sheaths at her waist, but her feline movements evoked a European model about to walk a Paris runway.

Complicated. She seemed very complicated—and most unique.

Thoughts that vanished as soon as Jayd spotted the distinct tattoo beneath the stranger's left ear.

It depicted an eagle in flight, though the bird's wings transformed into lotus leaves.

It shot instant, enduring pains through her chest.

Horrific nausea through her gut.

Most of all, a thousand layers of disgust at her all-too-trusting heart.

She had been played—by a witch's awful spell. By a bald, blatant play for her sympathy. *Swearing* on her mother's ease in eternity? Who did that?

Monsters who had the Pura emblem tattooed on their necks, of course.

"*Yaleur*," she spat, stumbling back. "Liar. Get away from me, Pura scum!"

The woman moaned. The emission sounded . . . frustrated.

Frustrated?

"Shit." She smacked a hand over the side of her neck as if merely punishing a mosquito. "Okay, listen to me. This isn't what you may th—"

"Damn right it is not," Jayd spewed back. "Nor will it ever be!"

"Your Highness. *Jayd.* Will you let me expl—"

"I said stay *away* from me!"

Too late. Sweet Creator, she was too pitifully slow by half, unable to flinch back as Miss Pura Power Ranger caught her by a wrist and held tight, forcing her to stay put. And likely, after this was all over, to relinquish her rights to Ripley in Jagger's nickname catalogue.

If the Pura would ever let her see Jag again.

"Boopsy girl, we don't have a lot of time here. You've got to grab some chill and let me talk."

Jayd's arm went slack. She blink-blinked at the stranger, battling a new and bizarre thought. The woman was being . . . sarcastic. Puras were allergic to humor. She also used vernacular that Jayd had never heard from a Pura. For that matter, from any Arcadian.

That anomaly explained nothing. The woman still bore the mark of the *bonsuns* who wanted to rip Arcadia apart. She was still armed and on the loose, sneaking around in tunnels beneath the palais.

And for how long now?

If Power Ranger's radio had trouble with reception down here, maybe she did not know about Trystan's capture yet. If she did, would that make a difference? Jayd was disturbingly aware of everything the Pura stood to gain with her in their hold, whether her last name became Carris or not.

The woman seemed to process those details in the same five seconds that Jayd did. 'Twas either that, or she decided to nod knowingly for the twisted fun of it. She added a long sigh while slipping her hand away from her neck. Only then did Jayd notice that there were only three fingers extending from that hand, with long-healed burn tissue where her pinky and ring finger should be protruding. The mottled skin extended up the back of her hand and then disappeared beneath the cuff of her leather jerkin.

"So, you're on your toes. That's good. Damn good. And yeah, you have a right to the freak fit about this." She tapped her forefinger at the tattoo with a swift move that could have been part of a rap video routine. "Felt the same way when those bastards forced it on me three years ago."

Jayd bugged her gaze. "When . . . they . . ."

"Drugged me, strapped me down, and then marked me with this tattoo," came the unnervingly calm reply. "And yeah, you heard me a hundred percent correctly."

The woman canted her head, which made a long black braid fall over her shoulder. There were colored ribbons twined with her strands—the red and purple favored by the Pura. But were those also not by the woman's choice? This was beyond baffling. Jayd's eyes told her one thing, but her gut clenched with a hideously different truth.

"Boopsy. *Highness.* I wish I could stand here and be all *fair Verona* with more of the pertinent back story, but we don't have that luxury right now. You either believe I'm on your side and have been waiting three damn years for the chance to do so, or you don't. What's it going to be?"

So much for wishing her gaze was going to get back to normal.

"Th-Three years?" Jayd blurted, ashamed to be searching—and perhaps wishing—for any glitch in the woman's composure.

Instead, she got two more layers of unnerving revelation.

"You think the Pura Dumplin' Gang simply spun up this caper in a few days?" the stranger charged. "Uh-uh. This has been in the works since Rune Kavill started rolling their action."

"Kavill," Jayd spat. "Disgusting *prispoul*."

"Word, girl. But regrettably, a lot of *prispouls* are brilliant fuckers too. Kavill wrangled those kittens enough to orchestrate the bigger stunts like kidnapping Princess Brooke and bombing the Grand Bridge. He was also the mastermind behind the effort that nearly doubled their legion in a year."

Jayd grimaced. "Which still baffles my brothers and the high council. A recruitment like that is absolutely—"

"Impossible?"

"In a word?" She tried to laugh, but it emerged as a bitter huff. "Yes."

The woman gave up a matching sound, though her sour edge was dusted with something more. Raw virulence. "Because it wasn't just a recruitment."

Just six bleak words, in the woman's dark tone, were the only switches needed to blare Jayd's mind with comprehension. "It was . . . an impressment?"

Sharper shards of violet gleamed in Power Ranger's eyes.

"Guess that's the nice way of putting it."

Jayd frowned. "What is the not-so-nice way?"

"In my case?" She rubbed her three fingers over her tattoo again. "Being locked in an induced coma and then woken up and told I'd been kept alive only as a bribery tool against my mother." She blinked a few times, revealing glistening drops along her lush black lashes. "The mother, mind you, who *I* thought had been dead for years."

"Wh-What?" Shock turned Jayd's rasp into a stammer. She and *Maimanne* had definitely had rough patches over the years, including most of the last ten days, but imagining that she had been lied to about the woman being alive at all . . .

Pain gouged her heart and contorted her face. "Why would anyone do that? And would your *maimanne* let them?"

"Because she was told I was dead too."

"By the blessed Creator." Jayd wrapped her arms around the thousand emotions stabbing her stomach. "*Why?*"

The woman's face gained some new creases, though they were vastly different than the tension lines of before. For the first time, Jayd detected some true conflict from the decisive warrioress.

"We have to get going, okay?" she decreed. "Come on." She yanked on Jayd's elbow, hauling her toward the tunnel that extended off the other side of the weapons room. "We should've been on the move already."

"Get going where?" Jayd made the demand despite her compliance with the stranger's new guidance. "And why? You know that Carris has been apprehended now, yes? My brother Samsyn and his team—"

"Have done nothing to change anything," the woman cut in. "*You* know *that* already, yes?"

Jayd forced down a heavy breath as they entered a second chamber. Its linear footprint nearly matched the weapons room but was outfitted with basic armoires along the sides. At one point in time, the pieces were likely a sturdy storage solution for the soldiers who deployed from here. Tonight, Jayd was stunned that their footfalls were not causing the wardrobes to crumple apart.

"Yes," she finally confessed. "I know," she insisted. "I *know*."

And now, more than ever before, she did know.

To the extent that she *should* have known long before this.

Enough to not be traipsing down secret palais tunnels in search of men who wanted nothing to do with her anymore. And then finding them and letting them strip her naked anyway. Letting them tease her body the same way they toyed with her heart. And yes, letting them do all that when a hundred of Carris's men were still infiltrating all the corners of the palais, on the hunt for *her*. Even getting on all fours and begging them for it . . .

Stupid. Stupid. Stupid.

"Good. That's really good." The female next to her, obviously reining in her gazelle stride so Jayd could keep up, also had Jayd scrambling to connect the words to the correct subject. "Because there aren't a lot of hiding places around here that those bastards don't know about yet. And if I'm going to get you to one quickly, you've got to trust me implicitly."

"Done." As Jayd emphasized it with a small squeeze to the woman's shoulder, they synced determined nods. "Though at the risk of rousing the elephant in the tunnel, perhaps I should know your real name?"

"Of course," she murmured. "You can call me—"

"Darling."

The interruption, for all its drawling silk, might as well have been a monster's roar. It clawed the same reaction through Jayd's body, making her skitter back as if trapped in a nightmare with the creature.

In true nightmare style, the beast only seemed to get closer. Too late, she recognized it was because Trystan Carris had snuck up behind them.

But how . . . ?

She was also too late to squelch the question from her lips. The second it spilled out, Trystan tossed back his head with an amused chuckle.

"How indeed?" he crooned. "Do you and your brothers really believe yourselves the only ones with fancy spy toys and crafty American friends?" He backed up his meaning by nodding toward the Power Ranger. "Wonderful work, my dear." A funny *tsk* vibrated in his throat. "And just think, you once insisted you would never see things our way."

"That was a long time ago, *Seigndim*. Can we not speak of it anymore?"

Jayd's breath clutched once more. It was sucked in by the chaos in her chest, where rational thought collided with her darkest fears. But where else could it go as she fought to process this insane twist?

How had Trystan escaped from Syn's men? Or was he ever in their custody at all?

And was this really her brave, intrepid Power Ranger friend, referring to the monster with a high honorific of the Arcadian language—and doing it with a simpering smile that belonged in a housewives' magazine from a hundred years ago?

How was any of this actually happening?

Had her instincts failed her that horrifically? Had she truly fallen for a stranger's maudlin tale just because she wanted it to be true? Seriously, who in this world was actually held captive in a coma and then inducted into a rogue resistance gang to the point of being forced to accept their tattoo?

Apparently, the woman who begged her with silent desperation to believe it all over again.

Even as Trystan stepped over and forced Jayd's wrists together. Also during the moments that he wrapped and tightened zip ties around them.

Even after that, Power Ranger was relentless about her wordless pleas for Jayd's understanding. Jayd conveyed her answer by squeezing her eyes shut. Who could she believe anymore? And did it even matter?

Imbezak. Imbezak. Imbezak.

Imbécile. Imbécile. Imbécile.

Idiot. Idiot. Idiot.

She was well on her way to kicking herself in more languages, when interrupted by her own pained yelp. The ties sliced deeper into her wrists as soon as Trystan yanked on their middle joint, dragging her to stand against the cold stone wall. He did not force Power Ranger to do the same, though the woman looked as if she longed for nothing more. By the time Trystan stomped back over to her, defined quivers racked her whole frame. They intensified as Trystan pressed in on her with a predatory purr.

"You do not wish to speak of it anymore, darling?" He leaned in tighter, thumbing the underside of the woman's chin like a dog trainer about to snap a muzzle on his errant retriever. "My goodness, why? Those who do not remember the past are doomed to repeat it. Or so some wise person said, somewhere. Perhaps *you* remember who, Your Highness?"

Jayd barely lifted her head from her protective cower. It was no surprise to find the *bonsun* waiting, his sickening smile at the ready.

"How are you here?" she spat. "And if you truly think you are going to achieve *any* of your objectives like this—"

"*Jayd.*" The brutal slice did not belong to him this time. "You need to shut the hell up, girlfriend."

"Ahhh!" As Trystan crowed it, he kneaded Power Ranger's chin with growing fervor. "And here I was seeking wise people, when I already have one at the tip of my thumb."

A scream fulminated in Jayd's throat again. But she gulped it down, hoping it made its way past her frozen digestive tract. The ice invaded deeper as soon as she watched Trystan drag his thumb downward, marring her friend's flawless olive skin.

Her *friend*?

She grimaced, forcing herself to accept the admission. The woman was as much a fly in Trystan's damn web as she. Trapped and struggling—especially as the man caressed across her tattoo. When his fingers covered the mark, he pressed in with deliberate force. The woman trembled, appearing ready to throw up. Jayd shook in abject empathy.

"Hmm. What lovely sounds you make, darling." He ran his tongue across his bottom lip before stretching out his other fingers, wrapping them against the front of her neck. "Perhaps my kinky little *salpu* wants to show our princess *all* the ways we have fun in the Pura?"

"No!"

Jayd longed to join her shriek with the woman's but bit the inside of her cheek to stay silent. Something told her that any interference at this point would only make things worse for her terrified friend.

Creator's mercy.

What if the coma prison and the involuntary tattoo were only the beginning? Was she not, in so many ways, already peering at that evidence? In every inch of the red marks along the woman's neck. In every pitch of the rhythmic sighs that tumbled from her lips. Self-soothing mechanisms . . .

Which she was denied from the moment Trystan closed his hand back over her neck.

"Shame, shame, dearest," he emphasized in a silken murmur. "You *know* you must have permission to scream. You also know how I detest little girls who disobey me."

"*D-Désonnum, Seigndim,*" the woman rasped. "*Désonnum beaupek.* I am very, very sorry."

Jayd hauled up her shoulders. Stiffened the set of her head. "Carris! *Damn it!* She says she is—"

The *prispoul* bellowed a laugh. "I know what she said, princess. But with naughty darlings like this, one just never knows about certain kinds of . . . boundaries."

He demonstrated by twisting his hold even tighter. And then by unsnapping the woman's jacket to the point that allowed him easy access to her breasts. Expertly, he reached in and found her nipple. Brutally, he twisted on it.

"*Seigndim!*" the woman cried out, panting hard to keep it from pitching to a scream. "P-Please! Just please . . . do not . . ."

"But darling, why not?" Trystan growl-hummed. "Isn't this exactly what you crave? All of this—how do the kids say it over in the States now—the rough stuff, right? Come now, little *salpu.* Does this not make your blood race? Does it not soak your *chanli* for any stud who will dole it out?"

"N-N-No. N-N-Not anymore," the woman rasped. "P-P-Please . . . stop."

"Creator's blessed mercy. *Carris!*"

The *bonsun* swung out a new glare. "This concerns you *not*, Highness." He snarled the last of it so violently, the one word could have been two. "Unless you would like to start modeling courtly restraint with a gag between your pretty lips?"

She fought a new wave of nausea. "Are you just liking the sound of that promise, or do you plan to make good on it?"

"What?"

Despite how Power Ranger splurted it with him, Jayd stayed focused on the only face that mattered right now. The gray matter belonging to the only mind she had to sway.

"You heard me," she declared. "You heard me loud and damn clear, *prispoul*. And yes, I *am* a hundred percent serious."

"No," her friend cut in from between her teeth. "No you're not, damn it!"

She waved the woman into silence but did not look if there was compliance. She did not dare look away from Trystan now. Not with the ruthless focus he was not letting up on. Not with the heavy dose of bemusement that entered his speculative glare.

"It makes all the sense in the world, right?" she queried him. "You are still damned and determined to go through with all your . . . grand plans . . . for me, yes? So, Lord Trystan, why not begin now?"

She had to clench her stomach to keep its contents from spilling along with the title he did not rightfully possess, but her purpose was achieved. She had his attention. He even withdrew his hand from Power Ranger's jacket. His hold eased on her neck.

As soon as Jayd gulped, he let up on the clamp altogether.

"It shall be an even trade, all right? Me for her. Plain and simple."

But who was she trying to fool? This was nothing near plain or simple. Part of her wondered—hoped?—if this was all real. If her lips were even suggesting it. But ohhh yes, she had. And that meant standing by the offer, no matter how terrifying or debilitating. It meant keeping her word, no matter how daunting the mission.

Doing the right thing isn't always doing the easiest thing.

Unbelievably, she owed that one to 'Raz. Creator's mercy, her adorable brother and all the motivational posters with which he loved wallpapering his office.

THE RIGHT THING IS NOT ALWAYS THE EASIEST THING.

GREAT ACHIEVEMENT IS ACHIEVED BY GREAT SACRIFICE.

THE GIRL WHO GETS THE BOY ISN'T ALWAYS THE LUCKY ONE.

All right, 'Raz hadn't gotten around to ordering that last one yet. That didn't negate the pound of its truth in every damn pore of her five feet, three inches.

But she could still do this.

She *had* to do this.

"Plain... and simple." As Trystan echoed it, new chills raced each other down her spine. He was warming to the idea, which should have thrilled her. But inside, she was swearing in agony just like her American friend.

"No. Fucking hell to the fucking no! Your Highn—"

"Plain and simple," Jayd interjected, loud and bold about the enunciation. "Set your *darling* free, and you get the Jayd Cimarron full-access pass. That includes everything you see here"—she slid a hand from the top of her head to well past her knees—"as well as cordial introductions to everyone I know in the palais."

And there it was.

The campaign promise she could no longer rescind. The marketing pitch Trystan could no longer ignore.

The man indicated as much by turning completely from Power Ranger, his gaze fixed on Jayd's little nook in the wall. But the moment she thought he would rush forward and force his greedy hands—and fingers and tongue and mouth—all over her personal space, he did nothing of the sort. He remained an arm's length away. Perhaps more. He kept examining her, as if waiting on rhododendrons to start growing out of her head or something.

"Just *how* many introductions?" he queried.

"A hundred at least." She shrugged, giving away what an easy fact it really was. "Possibly one-fifty." That was likely a low ball too, though she was not so transparent about it. Clearly, the first number was already his wildest dream come true. At least she thought so. His face vacillated between several unreadable expressions before he spoke again.

"And you are *really* ready to do all this?"

"No," snapped the woman behind him. "No she isn't and no she won't!"

"You would truly trade yourself out like this?" he went on as if she had just chirped like a cricket. "For a person you barely know?"

"I barely know *you*, Trystan. But sometimes, things simply

have to be done." She attempted to stay serene, but her fingers rebelled and started tapping against her thighs. "I may only be half a Cimarron, but I know the meaning of dutiful sacrifice."

Another indecipherable look from him. This time, Jayd wondered why he looked on the verge of a soft laugh. Maybe a not-so-soft one.

"Sacrifice," he echoed. "Aha. The dutiful kind, at that." More of those strange, mirthful tugs at his mouth. "Is *that* your passionate lesson from Paris, then? The things that your handsome soldier boy imparted?"

She hissed hard through her teeth. Even that melodrama was better than exposing her tears to the *prispoul.*

"Leave Brickham out of this," she charged. "Far, *far* out."

"My complete pleasure."

He emphasized it by raising his arms like a super preacher committing to a *hallelujah.* He brought them back down to brace his hands on the sides of her little indent in the stone wall. When he added a defined lean, there went her personal space. She had no place to turn now, forced to accept the hot brush of his breath as he pushed even closer.

"But believe me, beautiful girl"—his murmur dipped into a register that reminded her of cockroaches on a butter stick—"fucking me is going to be so much better than your sacrificial duty."

"Fucking you is what she'll do over my dead carcass."

Jayd gasped. At first, the sound vibrated with nothing but jubilant shock. It was the same jolt, connective and explosive, no matter where she was when Brickham re-entered her atmosphere. The power surged down her body and stormed across her mind, even as she struggled to process that the man was actually here. Never had he sounded like this. So violent and vehement. So ready to destroy something. Or someone.

At once, Trystan focused on retaliation. By reaching in and releasing his butter-coated bugs on *her*.

Before she could let out half a scream of protest, the *bonsun* pinned her in with brutal grabs at her arms. When she fought to maneuver her legs and kick him back, he drove his booted foot into both her shins.

Her matching yelps were like the double-click on Brickham's rage button.

He was an earthquake, noiseless but devastating.

He was a volcano, potent and daunting.

He was a tsunami, unwavering and unstoppable.

He took away every molecule of her breath.

Especially when Trystan altered his hold, pulling her out and around in front of him—and she realized there was something worse than being used as the monster's new hostage.

Something like realizing that earthquake-volcano-tsunamis thought it completely okay to rush their enemies with no weapons but handcuffs.

Giant, dungeon-sized handcuffs.

Which they happened to still be *wearing*.

The same handcuffs that were turning Brick's wrists to hamburger as he moved into a deep crouch. As he swung his arms in an insane pseudo-battle stance. As he glared like his curled hands were wielding a battle ax.

Until it became an imaginary scimitar.

The cuffs chinked loudly as Brickham adjusted his pose for the new "weapon." Jayd could not help her disbelieving shriek. The man's lagoon swim must have infected him with the go-crazy-or-go-home bacteria. She tried telling him as much, screaming even louder. She had no idea what she looked like. Before now, she had only used this condemning gawk on Samsyn during his stupider stunts.

But Brickham focused solely on Trystan. He was daunting. No longer a force of nature. More like a *natural disaster*.

Except with the storm doors already locked into place.

No way was he getting out of those shackles soon. The bonds that had started to bloody him. That definitely, certainly limited him.

The sooner she recognized that, the better.

Her mind was cooperative, drinking down the cold grief, but her heart screamed and fought the defeat. It pumped wildly and violently, until her whole body bucked once more at her filthy captor.

"Ohhh my, my, my goodness!" Trystan exclaimed. "Little princess palooza! I never knew you had all *this* in you. What a fascinating thing to discover about one's future fuck doll."

The words were not Jayd's downfall.

Brickham's cascade of flammable reactions were.

Screaming his name was no use, even as he barreled straight for them. Balling up her hands and trying to pummel him back was an equal trip to the futility zone, as Brickham swung around and sidestepped to the right.

But Trystan was just as swift on the mark, seeing the headbutt attempt before Brickham could even start it. Jayd was already forced to spin in tandem with him, her feet twisting and her shins throbbing, before they locked down in their new position.

Back to square one. In so many more ways than that.

Like his name pouring off her lips, a pointless attempt to stop him from sweeping to the side. To halt him from prepping for the headbutt that really only worked for guys named

Bond, Bourne, and Neo.

But what about blatant fake-outs?

Brickham executed his so smoothly, Jayd was now the jumpy one. She was not conscious of Trystan doing the same thing, though surely that must have been the plan. In his moment of distraction, Brickham found the important chink to expose. In a pair of astonishing seconds, she was hauled off her feet, out of his grip, and clean out of the way—

Just in time to watch Brickham crack the top of his skull to the center of Trystan's brow.

"*Yeeeoowww!*" Trystan bellowed.

"*Imbezak!*" Jayd yelled at the same time. "Creator's *balls,* Brickham. What do you think—"

A swoop of dizziness consumed her for too long a moment. 'Twas her own fault, a result of trying to scramble free from the fray. But in the process, she had forgotten Brick's real size. Her successful effort meant a significant tumble from his massive arms. Thank the saints, a second man was on hand to grab her by the waist.

"Easy, Highness," said that soldier in a very American baritone. She flashed back a fast glare, withholding her curiosity for the more necessary message of the moment.

"You see the *handcuffs* he is wearing, do you not?"

The guy returned an intense, ocean blue scrutiny. "He knows what he's doing, okay?"

"And if he doesn't, he's got a bit of backup." His comrade, the giant with the tree-thick arms, issued that while deftly cracking his knuckles. His neck. His knuckles again.

"And when, exactly, do you two make that call?"

She seethed out enough of it that they knew she was serious. Yes, despite the jaw-dropping number of hits Brickham had already landed on Trystan. She had retained enough from Syn's fight-like-a-boy lectures to know a combat like this could flip its fortune any second.

Just like it did, before the ink was dry on the thought in her head.

"Brickham!" she screamed. But the awful writing was on the bloody wall.

Literally.

Clearly, Brickham knew more on a tactical level than Trystan could hope to understand. But sometimes tactics mattered not. As soon as Trystan saw an opening for a side-sweep, he took it.

Once Brickham was toppled to his back, the Pura *bonsun* moved in with a ferocious war cry. Brickham's two-handed blows were not as effective without gravity's help. After debilitating Brickham with a well-placed kick to the vulnerable shoulder wound, he knelt on Brickham's chest and scored a solid jaw punch. Then two. Then three.

He had to be stopped.

He had to be stopped *right now*.

"Holy shit." Brickham's American pals spat it together as she pushed them back and raced across the cavern.

They repeated it, louder and harder, as she launched herself onto Trystan's back.

She had no preplanned thought. No logical plan. So much for remembering the tactical parts of Syn's lessons—though something must have stuck, because she dug her teeth into the crook of the *bonsun*'s neck with a great deal of determined purpose. And savage satisfaction. Oh, especially that.

"*Yeeeoowww!*"

It occurred to her, while feeling like a she-knight being

bucked by a smelly dragon, that Trystan actually had the battle cry of a castrated crocodile.

The thought made it easier to hang on while he writhed again. She kept the cling even when he twisted from side to side, clipping her on each thigh bone with backward-elbow drives. Jayd fought back with her knees, ramming the neighborhood of his kidneys as hard as she could. Since Trystan's growls were more labored this time, she took heart that she was getting *something* right—

Until a dozen daggers drove into the right side of her rib cage.

A scream blasted through her mind first. But when it craved an explosion on her lips, no sound cooperated. Her lungs were downed by the blades too.

Her lungs…

What in the name of the Creator…

She dropped a hand from Trystan's shoulder to investigate. There was not a single knife hilt in her side. So why did every breath feeling like a dissection?

The pain consumed her. Drained her strength until she crumpled to the ground.

"Jayd!"

Brickham's shout, full of more raw wrath she had ever heard from him, blew up the cavern.

"Fuck. *Fuck*. Jayd!"

"*No*, damn it. Stay down!" The second yell had her peering around, struggling to connect logic to confusion again. It was beyond difficult with her body still drowning in this bucket of pain, especially because the order did not belong to either of the formidable Americans behind her. Unless one of them had suddenly switched genders…

Wait. She remembered now.

Power Ranger.

The woman had not run away!

The realization brought new stings to Jayd's eyes—this time in unbridled joy—even as the air over her head became a whirl of frightening zings and metallic tang. But she was certain, had a gun really been fired, they would all be deaf from the awareness.

She had definitely not gone deaf.

Because she heard, with clarity that made her gut clench, the double *thwunk*s of steel driving into firm flesh.

Into Trystan's body.

Rahmié Creacu, so close to one of the kidneys *she* had been after.

As she shoved up onto her elbows, she repeated the oath in a stunned whisper. Trystan did the same, nearly at the same time and with the same inflection, until the cruel interruption from his convulsing throat. His groan was naught but ugly harmony and choking resistance. His face was covered in sheer disbelief.

The look persisted even as his knees gave way and blood seeped from the bases of the two crossbow bolts in his side. Soon, the thick red drops were loud splats against the hard clay.

Trystan saw none of it. He shook his head slowly, as if adjusting it to the proper angle would somehow click everything back into focus. Though it was clearly not helping, he persisted. He kept up the effort even while collapsing onto his side. Not once did he rip his dazed condemnation from the woman who stood a good twelve feet away, an old but functional crossbow still secure in her grip.

Trystan reached a trembling hand toward her. She moved not an inch.

He moaned but decided better of it, as a suffering crocodile wheeze took over his breathing rhythms.

She still moved no muscle in her stance.

He opened his mouth, working his jaw as if to form words, but only one long syllable emerged. "Lllluuuuu . . ."

"Holy. Shit."

Brickham's interjection rode nearly the same decibel level. His rasp delayed Jayd's double-take by several seconds. Moments that proved how seconds sometimes truly counted. The force of nature had already sprung back to his feet and now advanced their way, his prominent features etched in shock.

A lot of it.

"Holy *shit,*" he repeated, sounding like he had been socked in the stomach with a cannon ball.

As if forcing sound around the edges of that ordnance, he grated, "Luna? Luna *fucking* Lawrence?"

This time, the Power Ranger did move.

CHAPTER FIFTEEN

"What in the living—"

"The *living*? You sure about that, man?"

Z's and Ethan's mutterings were comforting but disconcerting. Brick admitted the first while pulling in a long breath and then fought to dispel the second while whooshing everything back out.

It wasn't working.

Because he wasn't going crazy.

On the other hand, *he wasn't going crazy*. And yeah, in this moment, that was really as scary as it sounded.

"Christ had crackers."

"In bed. With cheese squirts on top."

Or maybe the crazy was so deep in here, those two dorks had joined him in wading through it.

Few other things could explain him wanting to hug them and smack them down at the same time. He ordered those bickering instincts to join the other demons that were already skirmishing in his psyche.

Carris was down, which meant he could get to his Pixie. But that meant garnering the goodwill of the woman still cuddling with the old crossbow, still looking like she was going to aim a bolt for him next.

The woman he still gawked at like a ghost had materialized from thin air.

Because visual backup from his boys or not, that *had* to be the case.

In his life, he'd trained for a lot of batshit circumstances. That included walking through actual bat guano. But his instincts had nothing for him now.

"Fuck me to Christmas."

Dollars to donuts, that wasn't the right thing to say either. But no way was he yanking out an apology. He stood behind every stupefied syllable of it. Yeah, and the flash-banged expression that likely tagged along.

"Brickham?"

But Jayd's query, soft and shivering, was more jarring than a dozen flash grenades. Even with a loaded weapon still pointed his direction, he was compelled to swing his gaze down, checking on her.

Shit.

His pixie princess looked more like a stomped fairy. Her complexion was wan. Her breaths were ragged. Despite how Carris still snoozed, she was in some real pain. He could already tell that.

"Brickham?" she prodded again. "What is going—"

"You're supposed to be dead."

Zeke to the rescue, voicing the charge that couldn't make its way to anyone else's mouth. No surprise there, though. In another time and place, the guy had been Luna's dream date in the Bastille dungeon. But he'd never taken things so far as to add sex to the dynamic, despite every vibe Luna had broadcast to the contrary.

Brick had joined many others in secretly thanking the guy for not going there—in plentiful amounts back then but a thousand times more right now. Talk about a factor that would've made this jolt even messier. Not that it wasn't a giant ball of what-the-fuck already.

"Holy. Shit." At least Luna relaxed her grip on the weapon. Not to the point of lowering it completely, but at least Brick wasn't stressing about a rusty bolt through one of his aortas. "Of all the dank caves in all the tiny islands in the world, you clowns decide to walk into mine?"

Zeke matched the woman well in the scowl department. "*Not* the main issue right now, girl."

"Depends on where you're standing, doesn't it?"

Thankfully, Luna didn't add a cute twirl of the crossbow as emphasis—though Brick wondered if she was even conscious of the weapon anymore. Distinct emotions now sharded her eyes. Just like her days of hanging out in Bastille, desperately looking for the Dom who would take her away from the world, those violet depths gave away the pain beneath her sarcastic veneer. Wounds that never really seemed to heal, no matter how many times she tried, with so many of the club's Doms.

Only one guy seemed to be making any headway with the woman—but just as Tait Bommer had made that connection, his team undertook a rogue mission that went horrifically sideways. Everyone got out alive, but only because of a surprise operative in the mix. Luna. In the end, the woman gave the ultimate sacrifice for that effort.

Or so they'd thought.

"So did you bring the whole Scooby Gang this time, or just these two dorks?"

Clearly, they'd thought wrong.

The woman's fresh ignition of her signature snark wagon gave more glaring proof than if she'd whipped out a giant-sized photo ID. But there was more that gave her away. The scrutiny she tried to disguise with her words. The way she studied every tiny move they made, as if one of them were about to reveal they were hiding more men in their nonexistent coattails.

No. Not more men.

Just one man.

Who obviously wasn't going to appear.

It was one of the few times, in all his experience as an elite missions operative, that Brick hated having the answer in advance.

Zeke and Ethan were on his bandwagon before he asked. Their waves of discomfited energy were as thick as twenty-foot breakers of Pike Place clam chowder. And damn it, he was weirdly certain Luna had heard that thought too.

There were new slivers in her stare, not so hard to read anymore. He'd seen them too many times before, in the mirror . . . when he ached for home.

"Nobody else is with us." Again, Zeke came through like the surprise stringer from the bench. Since Brick was feeling more and more like a number on the injured list, he gladly stepped back to let the guy fully address Luna. "But shit, do I know someone who's going to barf on his phone when he sees you on Faceti—"

"No." Luna punched it out so vehemently, Brick joined Jayd and his buddies in a group jolt. But she only punched the trigger on her denial to Z. "No," she repeated, quieter on volume but *dis*quieted in tone. Brick wasn't sure he'd seen the woman so unraveled without being flogged into subspace first. "No Facetime, Z. No . . . anything. You can't let him know. I'm begging all of you . . . Just please, Sirs. No."

Z took a long moment to step back, mentally wading through what the woman had said. Brick didn't have that luxury. He whipped around, frantically locating Jayd again. Scrambling through both seconds he had after her pained gasp.

Two seconds to communicate a thousand impossible things.

It's not what you think.

It was never like that. Not with her. Not how it was with you. Not how it is *for me with you.*

Pixie . . . please hear me. Please . . .

His telepathy was cut short by a new growl on the air. But this time, not Zeke's.

Ethan strode forward, his wide gait eating up space. "Begging isn't always the key to getting what you want. You should know that more than anyone else, Luna."

The angles of her elegant face became a new contortion of desperation. "This has nothing to do with what I want and everything to do with your safety. *And* his."

"His who?" Ethan demanded.

She grimaced. "Damn it. You know that already."

"And we all know what assuming does to everyone, girl." Ethan stiffened. "So yeah, we're going to go there. We *will* be saying it. *Tait Bommer*. The man who paid for your funeral and all the upgrades on your tombstone. The guy who wept on your grave for hours and then practically fucked up a string of missions because of his memories of you. The friend who had us wondering about setting up a suicide watch—"

"*All right,* man." Brickham swung up his hands, almost looking ready to swing at a curve ball. Appropriate, given the insanity of this new twist. "That's enough."

"Is it?" Ethan swung his glare back around to Luna. "Because what's really enough here? Did you even know all that, Miss Lawrence? Did you even *care* about all that?"

"Fuck. You."

Luna punctuated the first part by hurling the crossbow to the ground. She spat out the second while a bolt discharged, hitting the ceiling before impaling the packed mud directly behind her. While they all gawked at the stranger-than-a-movie-moment, she pulled in harsh air through her nose.

"Yes," she finally declared. "*Yes,* damn it, I *did* know all that—two entire months after it happened. Because, you see, for six of those eight weeks, the coma I supposedly died in was the prison I was forcibly kept in. And if you think the Pura don't have the resources to make all that shit happen, think again."

"By the blessed Creator."

Jayd's insertion, heavy with fear and sympathy, was better than anything Ethan could have mustered. Fortunately, the guy nodded with the same acknowledgment.

"Go on," he encouraged, more good cop than bad cop about it now.

"I did gain consciousness a few times," Luna offered, back to that voice of raw but strained emotion. "I remember him—Tait—being at my side. His hair between my fingers. And all the things we said..." She choked, but it quickly became a rough cough. "The other times weren't as wonderful. Once, I was on a plane, I think—it was loud and cold. But at least there were people there. People with comforting faces and soothing voices. After that, I woke up a few times in the box, and—"

"The what?" Zeke sounded as incredulous as Brick felt and Ethan looked.

Luna waved a dismissive hand. "My word for it," she stated. "I was simply so happy when they let me out of it, I didn't want to know its official label."

But while Brick nodded hard, flowing his commiseration to her in every way he could, Ethan was back to being strict enough for a powdered wig and velvet britches.

"So they let you out... and you made no efforts to contact

Tait at that time?"

Luna nailed him with her crossbow-tossing glare again. "I said they let me out of the *box*. Not anything else."

Brick pivoted, purposely setting up his stance like a symbolic bridge. "Prisoners have to be grateful for mercy, in any small way they get it."

Luna sent him a thankful nod before going on. "After a couple of weeks, they finally trusted me with a smart pad. Everything was blocked except for internet searches and some lame games. You want to know how strange it is to read about your own death between Google hits for Seattle's best Italian restaurants and that girl from the wizard movie with the crazy glasses?"

"*Rahmié Creacu.*" Once more, Jayd's rasp felt like the flow of warm compassion that the air needed. "I cannot imagine . . ."

"Well, I *can*," Ethan objected. "But what I don't get is *why*." With Brick's and Z's nods of support this time, he drove an intense scrutiny into Luna. "These douche nozzles went through a lot of effort to keep you alive and reined in. For what?"

Luna's demeanor straightened. She actually seemed grateful for the questioning now. "For keeping my mother in line."

"Your mother?" Z demanded. "You mean the one who is *also* supposed to be dead?"

"Along with my father, yes," she said. "Darlene and Owen Lawrence. My loving 'parents.'" She air-quoted the word with hard finger stabs. "Their names are even on my birth certificate."

"But they are *not* your *maimanne* and *paipanne*?" Jayd queried.

"Not according to the woman to whom I was finally introduced." She stuck out her arm and swiped at the digital watch on her wrist. After two determined taps, a photo took up the screen. One swipe later, the device blasted the image onto the cave's wall.

The photo of a semi-smiling Luna, her arms draped around a woman who could nearly be her sister.

"Damn." Ethan and Brick muttered it together.

"What the hell do they put into the water around here?" Zeke added.

Luna rocked back, emulating her expression from the photo. "My *maimanne* is pretty awesome."

"And . . . familiar." Though a stitch in Jayd's side broke up her voice, she was confident about the assertion. After an unsuccessful attempt to push to her feet, she stated, "She seems *so* familiar to me . . . but I cannot recall . . . *Oh!*"

The burst spilled from her as soon as Luna swiped her watch again.

There was another image of the dark-haired beauty who'd just been smiling in her daughter's arms.

The woman was younger in the second shot. She was also standing by the side of an elegantly attired royal. After a few moments, Brick recognized the woman in the ornate clothes and sparkling tiara.

Queen Xaria.

With a somber look, Luna tapped her watch to kill the picture on the wall. With the same demeanor, she turned to fully face Jayd. "My mother, Elarah Lawke, was *your* mother's closest confidante for years."

At once, Jayd compressed her lips. Darkened her gaze. Dropped her hands into taut balls. "And the bitch who sold those tapes to Fortin and Trystan."

Luna hiked up her chin. "No. The woman who was blackmailed into giving the tapes over—on top of other palais secrets those cocksuckers ordered her to fetch for them over the years."

Jayd spurted a sound that started as a bitter laugh but ended as an agonized grimace. Again, Brick winced along with her. All of her actions and reactions were evidence of at least one cracked rib, but her pain billowed from deeper places right now. Places reflected in every new clutch in her throat and hitch of her shallow breaths.

"Why do I find it impossible to believe a word of that?" she finally spat.

"And why do I believe every last syllable?" Ethan said.

"Yeah," Zeke uttered. "Me too."

As they rendered the conclusions, Brick carefully watched Jayd.

She wasn't happy, that much was clear. But her composure, regal and guarded, gave him hope that his tongue wouldn't be ripped out when he offered his own take.

"She was blackmailed," he reiterated. "And it worked—because *you* were the assholes' bargaining chip." He knew he'd hit the truth gong before watching it reverberate across Luna's face. "They were likely watching you for years, probably as far back as your romps with dickwads like King and Mua—"

Z's low snarl signaled his takeover on the narrative. "You mean until their slave girl candy store got shut down when they superchipped the wrong soldier? Yeah, sorry not sorry, kids."

Ethan expelled a snort as proxy for a nod. He looked at Luna, whose complexion rivalled Jayd's for drained color. "Those bastards had probably already collected a down payment from the Pura for you."

"So I figured." Luna emulated his rough sound. "But nothing like an indie contract with the FBI to fuck with a few well-laid bad guys' plans for a while."

"Just a little thing like that." Ethan huffed out a smirk. "By the way, just to make it official from me, thank you. Everything you did that day was—"

"Uh-uh." Luna swept up a firm hand. "We're not going there right now, okay? You all don't have the time for mush breaks."

"She's right," Brick inserted. "We all need to beat feet before consciousness knocks again for Sleeping Shithead."

As if his head jog toward Carris extended an actual bonking stick, the bastard grumbled, moaned, and fluttered his eyes.

"Hrmmm. Fuckkk meee. Whaaa..."

As if a grenade had been chucked into the cave, everyone moved at once.

Zeke, already pounding up the tunnel to run a safety recon for them.

Jayd, using her feet to scuffle farther away from Carris.

Brick, lunging over to scoop her up as best as he could in spite of the damn shackles.

Ethan, pushing the other direction to reach for Luna's hand.

But Luna, already circling back to gather up the crossbow again.

"Go," she ordered, already reloading a bolt and pointing it down at Carris. "Do. It. *Now!*"

"What the hell?" Ethan gritted.

"Goddammit, Luna!" Brick spat.

"*No.*" But his pixie got the award for the best version. "By your nipples and mine, Luna Lawrence. *No!*"

Yeah, that part pretty much cinched it.

If only Luna was that attached to her nipples too.

But everything about her return glare at Jayd, with lips parted and violet eyes ignited, said she was ready to give up even more than that.

Why? Brick barely held back from bellowing it aloud at the woman. There was a difference between stubborn and stupid. Fuck him six kinds of sideways, why was she opting for the latter?

The same question was painted across Jayd's features as she turned back to Luna. It developed into a pleading wince, which Luna mirrored. Brick looked on, stunned by seeing so much vulnerability across the woman's features. Though Luna had been through hell and back, the last three years had actually tenderized her in some ways. Many more than in all her sessions in the dungeon combined.

But when her take-no-shit mask returned, it did so with unforgiving vengeance.

"Get out of here, damn it," she ordered, specifically to Jayd this time. "I'm sorry. I really am, okay? But I can't go with you now, girlfriend." She cocked her head back, as if willing tears to the back of her skull. "It was stupid to think I ever could."

"No." The word was a renewal of vehemence from Jayd. She clutched at her ribs with one hand while beseeching toward Luna with the other. "Please!" she begged fissuring Brick's heart in new places. "We cannot just leave you here!"

"You can," the woman asserted. "You have to, okay?"

"But I *believe* you now. I do. Truly!"

"I know, Your Highness." Another head shake, though

slower this time. It was a motion of deep decision. Of firm resolve. "I know."

"Then why—"

"Pixie." Brick issued it as an order more than anything, attempting to wrap her in a weird but comforting hold. But the whole time, his gaze stayed locked with Luna's. He saw everything about her, right in those brilliant violets. Her strict mission. Her grim purpose. Her soul-deep commitment. "We need to go now, Jayd. I'm not asking."

He tugged on her harder, giving her form some momentum so he could fully pick her up. Jayd let out a sharp yelp, abandoning her royal control in favor of trying to punch out his ear drums with her fierce frustration. She already drove in the point by socking a fist to the middle of his chest.

"I already said I'm not asking," he growled while turning for the exit. "Now don't make me throw you over my shoulder too."

Goddammit, how he wished he didn't really mean it. Or if he did, how it could've been just some frolicking dungeon play before he carried her off to a fucking bench and buried himself, body and soul, inside her fiery heat. Or hell, even into a vanilla bedroom, where they could wrap themselves around each other for hours.

How he wished he was carrying her anywhere but back to a reality of harsh truths—and away from a cave of harsher ones.

A cave that was now overflowing with haunted house echoes.

Echoes that crawled, grisly and graphic, to surround them in the tunnel.

Male screams, begging for mercy.

Steel bolts, exploding one after another after another.

Hoarse rasps, of a human fighting for their last air—and their soul's mercy.

★ ★ ★

The sounds of anyone's death, even those of an asshole who'd bred chaos and fear for so long, weren't easy to forget.

Unless there was a worse sound to drown it all out.

Like the mewls of a princess being overtaken by her own memories of the occasion.

"N-N-No. *No*. Please!"

And the wild thrashes of her bed sheets as she fought her way back to consciousness.

"D-D-Don't," Jayd mumbled into her pillow. At least that was what Brick assumed before pushing up from the floor next to her bed. Sure enough, his sights breached the mattress as his pixie rolled over, smashing her face deeper into the down cushion. "Trystan. N-N-Nooo. Stop it! Please! Stop it, or she will have to…"

"Jayd."

"She will have to… but she cannot! She—she—"

"*Jayd.*" He raised up on his knees and gently nudged at her hunched shoulder—the same way he'd rocked her every night for the last week. "Sweet girl, wake up."

When she only rolled onto her back, still thrashing at the covers and fighting at the dream, he leaned over and picked up one of her hands. As soon as he pressed a kiss over her knuckles, she started rousing.

"Brickham…"

"Right here."

He pushed up until he sat next to her. This wasn't exactly

obeying her brothers' rules about keeping his hands to himself from the air mattress on the floor, but it wasn't snapping them clean either. It was middle ground—the perfect assignation for how *everything* had been for the last seven days.

The French troops had gone home, since all of them could account for their whereabouts during the estimated time of Trystan Carris's mysterious murder. Zeke and Ethan were gone too, back to Mykonos after receiving glowing character endorsements from all three of the Arcadian princes.

But Brick's clearance had been held up, for all the obvious reasons. Arcadia and France had an expedition treaty, so there was that. After the French authorities cleared him, there were all the questions from the island's high council about how he knew where to find their princess so fast during the terrifying hours of Carris's incursion. Though technically, by the time everything was over, she was no longer Princess Jayd. She was just Jayd Cimarron, newly de-crowned but very much alive. A true survivor.

Since then, questions had been flying at both of them on the daily. How much had Jayd known—or not—about her true lineage? How much did either of them know about what the Pura were going to do with that intel? How much did either of them know about Carris's ultimate and astonishing plot twists?

Somehow, in a variety of miraculous ways, they managed to weather the storm. By day, they answered all the questions and attended all the hearings. By night, they laid low in Jayd's suite and thanked her all-seeing Creator for the extra time they'd been gifted yet again.

So yeah . . . middle ground.

A holding pattern they were determined to savor, second

by precious second.

Even these kinds of moments. The uncertain limbos in which his pixie hovered between the ordeal of her nightmares and the pain of her reality.

The seconds in which a gob of strange fears filled Brick as well. Shit that almost brought on the next-level crap. The lungs that refused to work. The mind that switched off. The attack from his own damn nervous system . . .

But then she opened her eyes, refocused her gaze, and really saw him. And smiled because of it.

And the world was right again.

"Well, hello there, Sir."

He lifted her hand to his lips again. "Hello there yourself, beautiful."

Her smile sobered when she glanced to the window, observing the moon and stars reflected by the calm ocean waters. "Damn it," she whispered. "I did it again?"

Brick bent over, this time to tenderly take her lips. "You're only one week post trauma, Pixie, with two significantly bruised ribs on top of it. It'll take time for things to heal."

A labored breath escaped her lips. It was just as much effort for her to swallow, as he saw when she rolled her head to the side. "But we are running out of time. You know it as well as I do. This is borrowed time, Maximillian. A wonderful dream for us . . . but a dream nonetheless."

Brick scowled. He was beyond tempted to add a snarl, ordering her back from the fascinated fixation with the star-covered sky and the moonlight-drenched ocean. But damn it, he was as mesmerized by *his* view now. Or maybe that was a lame-ass excuse for his actual truth. For the straight-up he knew *she'd* just spoken, in so many words.

Still, he dipped over her a bit more and whispered, "What are you talking about, sweet girl?"

She flung her head back to center, which caused her thick black spikes to spread against the pillow. From his perspective, in the dim light of the room, the points looked like the tines of an elegant black crown.

They looked absolutely perfect.

She was the queen of the shadows.

Of *his* shadows.

She lifted a strangely quixotic smile. "Have you ever heard the story about the secret prince of France?"

Huh?

That one was easy enough to stow away before he replied, "Ermmm . . . no." Not so easy to quell was the urge to stretch out next to her and then tuck in for some cozy spoonage as she relayed her royal tale.

"I thought perhaps you might have, since his name was also Maximillian," she began. "He was born in the middle of the eighteenth century, supposably a bastard of King Louis the Fifteenth. But all of that was kept a secret from him at the order of Louis the *Sixteenth*, until the breakout of the Revolution in seventeen eighty-nine."

"When the mob seized the records and went after him with the axes?"

His pathetic attempt at levity changed nothing about her faraway gaze. "Well, that was just the thing . . ."

"What? The mob or the axes?"

"Both," she supplied. "But neither."

He arched a brow. "Am I going to need a Schmoop study page for this?"

Again, she went on as if his jibe didn't exist. "The peasants found his parents and brother with no problems. There are clear records of their executions."

Well, there was a cue to sober things the hell up. "And the secret prince himself?" he asked quietly. "Where is he in all the records?"

"He . . . is not."

She coupled that declaration by raising her gaze back to his. While Brick was eager to accept her offering, he felt like an alcoholic given an empty wine bottle. Her gaze was just as bleak, a shadow queen with no court, her aquas subdued to the shade of turquoise in the rain.

"There are many stories about what happened to him. That he was burned to total ash by a rogue faction of the rioters. That he dressed up as a servant and somehow escaped. That a servant helped him another way, by invoking a gypsy spell that made him vanish from time altogether."

Brick hiked both his brows. "Well, there's some originality."

"Except that it could be just as true as the other theories." Jayd underlined her point by sliding a hand beneath his with matching emphasis. She curled her fingers up, meshing their fingers with force that made him double-take. The extra squeeze was already causing her grip to quiver. "The thing everyone *does* agree on is the ending. He disappeared that day and was never to be heard from again—not even when Napoleon restored the château back to the family's name." She paused, concentrating on pulling in a stuttering breath. "He simply never came back."

Brick started on a rickety inhalation of his own. Never made it all the way in, though. "Jayd—"

"He *never* came back, Brickham."

He dragged his free hand across his skull. "Okay, so the

moral of the story here is . . . what?"

"Not applicable." Her answer was too quick. Too clear. Too dismissive. Too much of a tone he could imagine her using on Carris, not him. *Fuck.* "There *is* no moral, Brickham. That is exactly the point." She let her hand slip free as she scooted back, arranging her pillow against the headboard so she could lean into it. "Sometimes a dream is really just a dream. And you can join the world and its grand stab at purpose, wasting time in picking it apart for meanings that are just not there, or be glad and grateful that you had the dream at all."

For long seconds, Brick was motionless. Bolted to his spot on the edge of the mattress. More unnerving symbolism, since he again felt like the guy on the fringe of the party, lost about whether the game was charades or spin-the-bottle. Worse, he wasn't aware of the etiquette. Was there a limit on how many times he could ask the hostess what the hell she was talking about?

But then he paused.

And thought about it.

Then some more.

Shit.

He wasn't lost about any of this. He was just wishing to be.

Double shit.

Even then, he forced himself to dig even deeper. To fire up his mental jackhammer and push it into the thicker clay of his psyche.

Triple shit.

Not only was he not lost, but he knew exactly where to drop the pin on being found. The one place he never expected to be. The sole destination he'd told this woman, over and over again, to never seek him in.

So . . . she wasn't. Despite how the effort was filling her eyes with rain, her voice with mist, and her words with shadows, she was honoring every boundary he had ever set. Every fence he had ever ordered her not to climb.

All the walls that now became all his regrets.

Fuck.

As soon as it tumbled from him as a dismal mutter, Jayd rustled beneath the covers again. But it was only to tuck her hands in, not out. Her shoulders shivered a little, perfectly emulating the nervous tremors in his gut. Just in time to give physical support for the lurch of his heartbeat, a massive wave suddenly crashed along the palais shore.

"Pixie."

"Hmm?"

Her tone was worse to take than before. Clear and dismissive were replaced by quiet and noncommittal. He thought he'd been tossed in hell when they realized both she and Carris were roaming free through the palais. But there had been an instant plan for that. Detailed actions of what they could do.

But *this* . . .

There was no conceivable field of weeds to describe his mind about this.

"What if someone doesn't want the dream to be over?"

Well, that felt like a terrifying jumping-off point if there was one. Until her soft, bitter chuff filled the air, bringing his instant *splat.*

"Dreams do not work that way, Brickham. You know that as well as I do." A new shrug vibrated her shoulders. "They are what they are. They end when they end."

"But what if . . . they change?"

He took the leap again, which was no awful than the first. But this time, he added a new factor. The plunging intensity of his gaze. The stare he refused to relinquish until she felt its intensity and raised her own.

When it finally worked, nearly a full minute later, he almost pumped a fist in triumph.

"You mean like when they become nightmares?"

Thank God he'd held back the victory parade.

"No." He unbolted his ass, ordering himself to slide closer to her. As he reached up, wrapping a hand around hers through the comforter, he clarified, "I mean like when they *change.* When they become . . . bigger. When they become . . . better."

Jayd shirked his hold by pulling her knees up to her chest and then tucking her hands between them. Brick only grinned. Silly girl. Hadn't she seen enough proof of his tenacity to know it didn't exactly work that way with him?

Of course she did. He saw it now, as her chest pumped faster. As a rapid pulse began to drum in her neck. But most especially as she ducked her head again, attaching her stare to the twin hills of her knees.

"Brickham."

He cupped one of those hills beneath the firm curve of his hand. And then the other. "Yes, sweet girl?"

"You are scaring me."

"I know." It was gruff with his sincerity. "Because I'm scared too. I haven't stopped being scared for the last week."

She wiggled once more, trying to shake him off. When he persisted his hold, she dropped her head deeper, adamantly shaking her head. "You had buttons pushed," she retorted. "That is all. You were locked in shackles from the dark ages—"

"No." He reached in until his fingers bracketed her chin

and jaw. With a masterful nudge, he compelled her face back up. He held her gaze with the same don't-you-dare-brook-me force. "I was petrified from the second you walked away from me at the lagoon."

He watched, holding his breath, as emotions battled for control of her expression. As he expected, she pulled in breath to start sacking him again, no doubt with his own panic room problem as the perfect lead-off.

But just as fast, she clamped her lips shut. His hope skyrocketed. She was feeling him again. Maybe not everything yet, the way they were bound before, but enough that she knew he wasn't referencing the tight confines of the grottos around the lagoon.

He was talking about a fear that hadn't gone away.

A terror that had doubled when he had to think of her falling back into Carris's captivity.

An anxiety that hadn't gone away in seven damn days.

She had to see that now too. The same way she always saw straight into *him.*

As their gazes held, he knew she did. And as tears welled in her eyes, bringing back the lush aqua light in their depths, his heart swelled until it shoved at his lungs. He didn't care if they were pressed to the size of peas. He'd deal. As long as he had more of *her* in all the places that mattered...

You feel it too... don't you, Pixie?

Oh God, how you feel it too.

Say it, princess.

Please say it—and then beg me to stay again.

Because this time, I might say yes.

"Brickham..."

"Yeah?"

"I really think I need to go back to sleep again."

His heartbeat halted. His teeth locked. His lips went dry. He dropped his hand away from her face.

"Uh . . . okay." He managed a stiff nod. "Sure. I understand. In the morning, we can—"

"Pretend this conversation never happened."

With her queenly spikes circling her head on the pillow, she eyed him as if really making the request from an anointed throne. The shadows returned to shroud her, despite the unchanging brilliance in her opalescent eyes. Their intensity was like a taunt now, like rare jewels beneath museum lights. Reminding him of a splendor he'd turned away. A treasure he'd knowingly turned down.

The only gem he longed for now.

"*Désonnum,* Brickham. That was most blunt of me." She leaned and swiped the back of his hand with the tips of her fingers, almost as an afterthought. "And I am most grateful, in so many ways, for how you have extended your stay in order to care for me a little."

But I want to care for you a lot. *Don't you get that, woman? Don't you feel it? I want to care for you every damn day, until—*

"But I understand so much more now, especially about accepting our ultimate reality here." She patted the back of his hand again. Christ, like he was some puppy to be soothed. "You have a life to return to. A business to run. A life to lead. The idea of changing all of that for some female you have known for less than a month . . ."

He chided her with a stern look. "You mean a *princess* of her people, who'll be returning to her royal duties soon?"

She released a heavy sigh. "A princess who will be thinking of her magnificent king and *his* empire."

Brick huffed and rolled his eyes. “Right. That oh-so-mighty kingdom where the castles are flipped upside down.”

The statement did nothing for his ultimate purpose right now but was worth it for the payoff of her giggle. “Dungeons on the top sounds like a fine idea to me.” But all too quickly, her laughter faded. “I shall certainly be adding yearly visits to Seattle in my travel schedule, you know. Perhaps, if you are not too busy with others vying for your attention, we can—”

“Sure.” He nearly spat it as he lurched to his feet, ignoring the rubber in his knees and the nausea in his gut. “Yeah, that sounds…”

Like the worst idea he’d ever heard.

Like the most unacceptable arrangement he could conceive.

Like a living hell that was never, in a thousand years, going to work.

The surety only twisted its blade deeper as he settled Jayd beneath the blankets and then stroked her forehead until she fell back asleep. It started its full evisceration as he watched her well past that point, running a knuckle down the proud slope of her nose, across her sculpted cheeks, and around the sweet curve of her jaw.

By the time he touched the steady thrum of the pulse in her neck, he was officially, thoroughly gutted.

And now, consumed by new resolve.

The heart that created that beat… the life in it, the love in it…

Nobody would protect them the way he could.

Nobody would love them the way he did.

Which meant things had to change. *A lot* of things.

He was willing now. He was ready now.

And yeah, that cliff was still damn scary to contemplate. But to dream as big as the sky, he had to be willing to leap—and fly.

CHAPTER SIXTEEN

Pretend this conversation never happened.

What, by all the saints and stars, had she been thinking?

It had been *exactly* the conversation she wanted from him. Had begged the Creator to materialize for them. But when a whole week went by without Brickham so much as hinting he wanted to reevaluate their relationship, what there even was of it, Jayd had indulged herself a good long cry before resetting her mind for a life without Maximillian Brickham. Yes, to the point that she reread that silly French folk story about the secret prince who shared his name. To the point that she spun it into a little morality play of her own. Yes, complete with the psychological T-shirt and a mini motivational bible to tote around.

To the point that when Brickham *did* finally hint at sticking around here longer, she had obeyed her script instead of her heart. Gone completely on autopilot, rather than strapping on her parachute pack just in case the flight got shot out of the sky again.

She threw the whole bible at him.

And this time, damn it, he listened to the stupid sermon.

The next morning, he even took the rest of the thing to heart. For that matter, it seemed, to the depths of his soul.

By the time she returned from the infirmary, where the recheck on her ribs had been quick but painful, the man was briskly packing his small tote bag. He was scheduled on the next flight out of Sancti, which would take him to meet up with his friends on Mykonos before the long journey back to Seattle.

That was when breathing *did* become difficult again.

To the point that she had to leave the room as he gathered up the few things from his stay in her land. The casual shirts and khakis he had been able to purchase from the palais clothier. A few books that Syn had gifted to him, apparently after he passed the kicking-bad-guy-ass-in-handcuffs test. A patch with the Cimarron crest, bestowed by Evrest after he passed the hands-off-the-injured-princess test. 'Raz had not been so demanding about his conditions, simply gifting Brick a blank journal. Remarkably, it seemed to be the most well-appreciated boon of the bunch.

With a frightening pang, she wondered what he would think of hers.

But she would never know that answer.

She took care to sneak back in when Brickham went to collect his stuff from the *tuvalette*. By the time he emerged with his toothbrush, razor, and hair shaving kit, she was already back out in the living room, feigning nonchalance with a game on her phone. He would not know about her present, along with the note she hastily scribbled to go with it, until unpacking it from the deep burial spot in his bag.

Once he gave the tote a final zip-up, he strode out to the living room with purposeful strides. Ohhh, yes. The walking version of approaching thunder, so long and forceful and—

Not nearly as magnificent as his kiss.

His massive sweep of a tree branch arm. His grip, cupping her bottom in lieu of her ribs, still able to hike her a good three inches off the floor. And then his lips on hers, force-of-nature fierce. His tongue along hers, act-of-God illicit. His moan in every crevice of her mouth, so heaven-and-earth moving.

Until, just as quickly, he let her go.

Before he turned without another word—and left.

Pretty much as she had decreed to him.

Making her vow to never make her own bible again.

Not that, within the next four weeks, she never peeked back at the one she already *had* made. Not because the recall brought mental reinforcement or even a good wallow of sorrow. Because it brought so much more.

Memories.

Of the way Brickham had gazed at her in the shadows of that midnight.

Of the way he embellished her story with so many attempts to make her smile.

Of the way, in the end, that he saw into everything she wanted to say because of it, though most of it was not what he wanted to hear. The way he honored her with his seriousness, even when he was trying so desperately to change her mind.

Even when she was being nothing but stubborn in return.

Even though it clearly killed him to back down.

Even when she should have offered him anything to stay. Even for just a little bit longer. *What could they have done with just a little bit more time?*

"Highness?"

She tugged her head up and glanced dutifully out of the town car's window. "Yes," she chimed. "Hello. Hi. I am here!"

Requiemme chuckled, despite having been on her third or fourth repetition of the hail. "Are you certain?"

"Yes." She tried not to be snappy about it. "Of course. *Honestly.* I promise."

She meant it. She had to. After all, if she had to stuff Brickham away for a while, one of the best distractions was getting to return to some princess duties. The medical team had not cleared her for distance travel or even full days yet, which meant sticking close to home and assisting Evrest with ceremonial and community events. Not usually the most glamorous assignments on the roster, but there were only so many books, phone games, and palais redecorating projects she could tolerate. This way, she was out in the sunshine and doing worthy work for her people.

"All right, then." Emme extended a tube of lipstick and a small powder compact. While Jayd polished off appearances with the help of the pull-down makeup mirror, her maid added, "I see that the energy nectar has definitely kicked in."

Jayd giggled. "You think?" She stole another glance outside, at the well-kept street in a higher-end section of Sancti. "Well. Ending the schedule with some swanky flair, hmm?"

"'Twould seem so," Emme supplied.

"So what do we have?" she asked. "School appearance, perhaps? Please tell me it is *not* a culinary academy."

"Thank the Creator, no." This time, the woman's laugh was strained. They had taste-tested some stew creations at a cooking school last week and both ended up flat on their backs for a day. Later, they learned a student had confused regular milk with expired buttermilk. "This is a preopening tour of a new business. A newcomer to Sancti, trying something new."

"A *pr*eopening tour?" She scowled. "Of something new *how*? And why on earth are you smirking like that?"

"Do I have to have a reason to smile?"

"I said *smirk*, not smile. Emme—"

"Ah. Here already!" As soon as the driver swung open the door, her friend waved with fluttery fingertips. "Have a *wonderful* time."

"Wait." Jayd ducked her head back into the car. "You are not coming along?"

"Fairly certain I will not be needed."

Her maid waved again, though this time at a spot past Jayd's shoulder. When she followed that visual cue, it was to collide her stare with a pair of the most welcome faces in her world.

"Well, I do declare!" she joked, spinning and rushing to where the two men stood. "Jagger Fox and Ozias Demos. Trouble has come to the neighborhood!" She exclaimed most of that into the solid expanses of their shoulders during their exchanges of tight, happy hugs. "I thought you two were on some kind of spirit quest in the outback. Though you were not truly fooling anyone with all that, you know. Kinky fuckery by any other name . . ."

"Ahhh." Oz stepped back with a hand over his heart. "That's it, Jag. Our jig is up."

Jagger stepped over and sidled next to his man, tucking his head along Oz's shoulder. "To be honest, I never thought it would last this long." He winked at Jayd. "You must be staying very busy."

"As much as I possibly can."

She fought her damndest to match his buoyant tone, but the guy was still one of her closest friends. Why pretend to be intrinsically happy when she was truly not? Oh, yes, contentment was usually attainable—but soul-deep happiness? Not yet. Not when she still ached this much for a man who was so many miles away. For a dynamic she could not imagine having with anyone else . . .

"So, I guess you two are staying busy too?"

"As much as we possibly can."

While Oz accented his innuendo with dancing eyebrows, Jagger added, "Between the busy, we have been spending a lot of time right here."

"Here?" That was curious enough to pull her giggles short and tug her stare higher. "Doing what?"

Oz deferred his new grin to Jag—who deferred *his* right over to *her*. His expression seemed to take on a strange shroud as he finally declared, "Helping to build a dream."

"A . . . dream?"

What if someone doesn't want the dream to be over?

She ordered the words away from her mind and their impact out of her heart. Not everything in her world had to keep reminding her of Brickham. One day, hopefully soon, that would be an easier deletion to make. For now, she concentrated on the new surge of happiness that dawned in her heart.

"Jag . . . Oz . . . are *you* the new proprietors setting up shop over here?"

She openly admired the building behind them, which was a newer build in Sancti. There were three floors total, each with a dedicated stairwell entrance from the main door. A glass elevator tube went up one side of the building too. Every floor had lovely stained-glass insets, leading her eye to a cascading water feature that angled down from floor to floor. At the bottom, the flumes emptied into a diamond-shaped reflecting pool that was surrounded by benches beneath manzanita trees.

"It is a stunning venue," she marveled. "How wonderful for you two! I should have been faster on the uptake when Emme flashed the Cheshire Cat leer and then said I was meeting with a new resident in Sancti. I just never imagined it would be—"

"Okay, damn. Hold up that furphy-mobile, little Sheila." Oz grinned. "We're not the droids—or the proprietors—you're looking for. Though I must admit, Sancti's growing on me more by the day . . ."

He trailed off into a series of mushy kisses with Jag that had Jayd wondering whether to applaud or groan.

She eschewed both to simply ask, "So can you lovebirds just give me an idea of what floor to head for, *lüt vous plait*?"

Since Ozias now cinched his boyfriend by the nape, he used his free hand to hold up three fingers. With a husky laugh, Jag broke free long enough to reiterate it. "Up on floor three, Ripley."

The nickname had her smile stretching even wider. "*Merderim,* trusty partner in crime."

"Ohhh, no," Jagger volleyed. "Tonight, you get to have *all* the violations."

Oz snickered. "Lucky girl."

"Huh?" She gave it twice the thrust of the first time.

"Would you just get your sassy arse up those stairs?" Oz quipped. "He's been waiting too long."

"He who?" she asked.

"And our little princess is looking ever so cute." Jagger gave her a sultry once-over as Oz snuggled into his neck. "So Marian Librarian in that swing skirt. But he will love those Mary Jane heels most of all."

"He *who*?"

But by the time she burst it as an outright demand, her friends were wrapped up in each other once more. For a second, Jayd was just wistfully mesmerized—until an unsettling force took over her senses.

She glanced up and then around. Was it *dejá vu*? Perhaps, but not likely. She had definitely never been to this part of Sancti before. But the feeling continued, now tied into more organic sensations. She studied the sky, wondering if a sudden storm was about to hit. Not a single cloud lingered in the thickening lavender of twilight. The trees barely moved.

But *Maimanne Naturelle* was still speaking to her.

Or was it . . . *Paipanne Naturelle*?

Technically, she had just made that one up—though in the primal parts of her, buried deep between her animal instincts and her soul's songs, she connected with the presence as if it were masculine.

And she felt it connecting back.

Watching her.

Reaching out to her.

Was it the *he* who was up on the third floor, waiting for her?

And if it was, should she be afraid of going up to meet him alone? Did she need to set up a safe call thing with Requiemme, perhaps? Four weeks of missing the hell out of her Sir had made her a very curious girl about the world of Domination, submission, and power play. She knew all about safe calls now, which ranked on the milder side of the subjects to which her studies had taken her to. Subjects that pounded across her mind like scary hail as she continued to vacillate in the building's pretty courtyard.

At last, she shook her head firmly, deciding against the safe call. In the same moment, she came to other decisions.

She had gone cuckoo. At the very least, persnickety and paranoid. Next thing she knew, there would be voices in her head along with the daunting pressure in her senses. But her reasoning was a case of *imbezak* on crack. This was not the Adam nor Eve District. This was not even the sketchy outskirts of Faisant. Moreover, Emme was right here with the car and a burly driver. If anything went wrong, even during this courtesy stop-in…

Nothing will go wrong.

Nothing will go wrong.

The mantra provided a catchy off-beat to her steady footfalls up the stairs. By the time she reached the top, she was a little out of breath but a great deal better in the head. The power of affirmations was a mightier force than she imagined…

Until it was not.

Until she opened the big door in front of her and beheld an ornate desk in front of a wall that was wallpapered in black and gray *fleurs de lis.* The only thing interrupting that pattern was a black medallion, at least a meter in circumference, hanging from thick gold chains. Embossed into the large sphere was a distinct design that she had beheld for the first time only last month. In the heart of Montmartre. In the moments before her eyes were opened to a whole new world of interpersonal dynamics.

Before Brickham had shown her exactly what the BDSM triskelion stood for.

Brickham.

She stepped inside despite how her pulse sprinted, her chest throbbed, and her body shook.

She walked toward the desk, illuminated from beneath in purple and from above in red. There was no banishing him from her thoughts anymore. Definitely not here. Absolutely not now.

Brickham.

He was a cataclysm in her mind, forceful and sensual, taking her hand to guide her through colored depths just like these. Leading her into a room with smells so similar to the ones around her now. Polished leather and fruity lubricants. Earthy rope and unforgiving steel. So many heady intoxicants . . .

Except for one.

The most important one.

The aroma of sex.

Of hungry mouths as they moaned and tasted. Greedy fingers as they groped and penetrated. Slick skin as it glided and undulated, smacked and fucked . . .

Brickham.

Brickham!

For the first time in four weeks, she couldn't battle the word on her lips anymore. It spilled from her lips as heavy tears brimmed from her eyes. The drops poured down her cheeks and then salted her lips.

And once it was there, spoken into existence in this dark and beautiful place, she never wanted to stop it again.

She sobbed it. Pleaded it. Snarled it.

But most of all, loved it.

Over and over again.

Until she fell to her knees in front of the desk, unable to stop saying the perfect, powerful syllables of the perfect, powerful man who had left this island and taken her whole damn heart with him.

Clang.

She startled but gave in to no shriek. Whatever had fallen to the floor in front of her was not that large. Probably an ill-fastened part of an overhead light. She was grateful for it, actually. The owner of this place was owed a visit from his royal family that did *not* start with his princess in a blubbering heap on the floor.

But as she rose to rest on her haunches, still swiping beneath her eyes, her vision finally cleared.

And her breathing fully stopped.

As she recognized the exact source of her bizarre sensations from outside.

She had been summoned by a force of nature.

The towering, devastating mountain of a man who loomed over her, giant hand still outstretched because of the object he had allowed to tumble from it.

A heart-shaped cookie cutter. With a hand-scribbled note now taped securely to it.

Steel hearts were meant to be filled by those they cut.

Her note. The one she had tucked into his suitcase along with their special memento.

"Brickham."

It was her most wobbly inflection of the whole litany, but she cared not. It was the last time she planned on saying it, and the earthquake in her voice felt like a perfect fit with this surreal fantasy. Part of her expected to wake up any second, still back in the town car, being nudged into consciousness by Requiemme. But that brought an odd sense of freedom.

If this was her dream, then she could say and do whatever she damn well wanted.

"Oh . . . *Sir*."

And oh, how she truly wanted to say *that*.

Just before she indulged the *doing* part.

She began by hooking her first two fingers into one of the holes in his sinfully soft black jeans. When she found a perfectly placed rip in one of the legs, she curled her other hand into it. She now had leverage to inch her way up his body. All of his hard ridges and mighty muscles felt so blissfully hard and *real*, enough that she pressed herself as tightly against them as she could during her sensual climb.

As was the way in wonderful dreams, he wore no shirt at all. So once she climbed high enough to explore him there, she did. The molded ridges of his torso became trembling response zones to her splayed fingertips. His snags of breath puffed out in matching time, wordless urges for her to keep touching him like this. So she did. Endlessly. Greedily. Marveling, over and over, at the perfection of him. The flawless magic of *this*.

"Creator's glory." She found air of her own to mold into words. "Brickham. My Sir," she worshipfully uttered. "You are so—"

And then, even words were impossible—as her mouth was suddenly smashed beneath his, taken in a torrid kiss.

Taken? Oh, no.

He was not just taking her. He was conquering her, forcing her to take the whole sweep of his plunging tongue. He was consuming her, sucking every decibel of her moans and pitches of her passion back into the savage depths of his mouth. He was penetrating her, ravaging everything she gave him like a possessed demon.

Like a man who had not kissed his woman in four weeks.

"Oh," she blurted as soon as they found the mental capacity to drag apart. "Oh, my Sir. You are so . . . *real*."

Brickham, who had already found both her butt cheeks with his wide hands, dug his grip in deeper. He hitched her off her feet and then carried her over to the desk. "Real is very much the idea, Pixie." After placing her on the desk, he spread her legs so he could settle between them. But his gaze, as intense and vibrant as the rising storm she had sensed outside, never left her face. "As real as I can be for you, each and every day, from now on."

He leaned in, kissing her softly this time, but Jayd hardly comprehended the peck. As soon as he was done, her whole jaw dropped open.

"Wait. Oh, by the stars, just wa—" She slammed her hands to the broad planes of his shoulders. "*You* are the proprietor who called the palais for a pre-opening visit?"

He tick-tocked his head, flashing the mischievous smirk that always turned her heart inside out. "If a text message to Requiemme on the sly counts as a call to the palais, then, guilty."

She narrowed her gaze. "But she also said you were a new resident of Sancti."

"Also guilty." He was more subdued about the magic smirk this time. "But also beyond happy. It's awesome here. I found a little place on the beach, not too far from here. Pods of dolphins swim by every morning, and—"

"Wait. Just wait once again, Maximilian Brickham." She was glad she had not moved her hands. That made it easier to rearrange her grip, with one hand clamped on his nape and the other gripping the back of his head. "You have a *life* back in Seattle—"

"No." He reared his head back, purposely working his skull into the cradle of her hands. He even rolled his head from side to side, playing his pressure against hers without surrendering the serious mien across his features. "I had an *existence* there, Jayd. A pleasant one, to be sure, but not the fire or passion that should define a *life*."

She slid her hands back to his shoulders. "I still do not understand. You built Bastille from the ground up. You have cultivated that business, a special place for people to go . . ."

"And it's still there," he explained. "As is the club that Z and I helped to rev up outside of Vegas."

"So even more people who owe so much to you," she persisted. "Friends who care for you. People who think so highly of you!"

"People who *aren't* the woman I'm in love with."

For the second time this hour, Jayd could not remember where she put her breath. First guess? It had plummeted to the region of her toes along with every brain cell in her head. But that was not possible either. Fate fired up the next moment, sparking a fireworks show that filled her senses with every conceivable description she could find for shock, awe, and joy.

By every angel in the heavens, especially that.

Still, she compelled words to her lips. Words that she needed, despite already feeling every assurance the man was sending with his gaze, his smile, his touch, his devotion.

"Wh-What did you . . ."

"I said that I'm home *here*, little pixie. That nowhere else across this globe, or even this galaxy, will ever be home again—without you." As he pushed in closer to her, gently pulling at her to do the same, Jayd was certain he could hear and feel the wild thuds of her heart. She rejoiced in the answering thunder of his as he murmured, "I said that I'm in love with you, Jayd Cimarron. I can't believe that's true, but it is. Before you stared me down in that damn alley, I never thought anything like this was meant for a guy like me. I was shackled to my past and every awful fear from it."

She wrapped her arms back around his neck. "The fears

from what happened with Asha."

His lips compressed. His dark blues were even stormier. "Yeah."

She kissed him then—but naught with any expectation. Just as he had done for her so many times, she did it with one purpose alone. To console him. To heal him.

"And that is fine, you know. It will always be a part of you, Brickham—a part you can tell me about tomorrow, or the next day, or never—but I do not have to know all about it to honor it in you. To love it in you . . . as I love all of you."

He blinked at her, allowing her to see the unmistakable sheen that formed in his eyes. When he dipped in and kissed her again, flowing his tongue languorously with hers, she accepted the salty wetness that seeped between their mouths as well.

Many minutes later, when they pulled back far enough to soak up the wonder of each other's stare once more, she finally dared to smile at him with a new intent on her face. A decidedly naughty one.

"So, Mr. Brickham . . . does your princess get a grand tour of your pretty new dungeon now?"

His gaze was still agleam, but this time, it was pure happiness that he beamed her way. The exhilaration of a man about to start a new adventure, looking back at the woman who could not wait to embark on it with him. Who knew what that journey was going to bring them? They already had a high bar to reach.

No matter what, Jayd knew one thing for certain. She was all-in—for every single moment of it.

But first things first . . .

"A grand tour, hmmm?" Brickham helped her off the

desk, looking as gallant as a duke in naught but his gorgeous jeans and godlike flesh. “Now how did you know I was thinking exactly the same thing?”

Jayd threw him another coquettish grin. “Great minds?”

As Brickham pulled her deeper into the shadows of their new fantasyland, he leaned in and kissed her with agonizing tenderness . . . and eternal promise. “I’d like to think . . . bound souls.”

ALSO BY ANGEL PAYNE

Honor Bound:

Saved
Cuffed
Seduced
Wild
Wet
Hot
Masked
Mastered
Conquered
Ruled
Bared
Bound

The Blood of Zeus Series:
(with Meredith Wild)

Blood of Zeus
Heart of Fire
Fate of Storms
Bridge of Souls

Shark's Edge Series:
(with Victoria Blue)

Shark's Edge
Shark's Pride
Shark's Rise
Grant's Heat
Grant's Flame
Grant's Blaze

The Bolt Saga:
Bolt
Ignite
Pulse
Fuse
Surge
Light

Misadventures:
Misadventures with a Time Traveler
Misadventures with a Duke

Cimarron Series:
Into His Dark
Into His Command
Into Her Fantasies

Temptation Court:
Naughty Little Gift
Pretty Perfect Toy
Bold Beautiful Love

Suited for Sin:
Sing
Sigh
Submit

Lords of Sin:
Trade Winds
Promised Touch
Redemption
A Fire in Heaven
Surrender to the Dawn

For a full list of Angel's other titles, visit her at AngelPayne.com

ACKNOWLEDGMENTS

It's surreal to believe that the guys have found their way to book twelve—and for the Cimarron kids, book four! What a wonderful ride it's been to bring you these stories.

None of it would have been possible without some incredible readers and their nonstop passion for this world. Some of you have even taken on the heroic call and have become beta readers and advanced editors, helping to weave the labyrinth of these plots before anyone else. I'm beyond grateful to you all: Corinne Akers, Ellie McLove, Jacy Mackin, Kika Medina, Melisande Scott, Riane Holt, Trish Bowers, Val Draze, Victoria Blue... and probably a thousand more! Forgive me if I've left someone out. The brain—and heart—are so full!

Special thanks to Tracy Roelle, for putting in the extra time, expertise, and love for the guys.

Scott Saunders: you are the editor from heaven. Thank you for all your insight for each and every word on the page and for taking such good care of the stories from my heart and soul. I cannot begin to convey my thanks for your presence in this journey.

There would be no sassy Caressa/Carey without the one and only *original*. Carey Sabala, you're my lifeline to sanity on so many days. Thank you for always picking up the phone!

A writer's world is a lonely place without the friends who are "sister close." Gratitude is boundless for those in my

world: Jenna Jacob, Victoria Blue, Meredith Wild, JL Drake, Stacey Kennedy, Katana Collins, Julie Kenner, and Shayla Black. Thank you, goddesses, for always being there!

This duet wouldn't have been possible without the team at Waterhouse Press pushing for it and believing in it. Thank you so much to: Meredith, Jesse, and Jon in executive leadership . . . Robyn, Haley, Jennifer, and Keli Jo in marketing and the shop . . . Kurt, Yvonne, and Amber in creatives & tech. You all are so amazing, and I feel so blessed, every day, to work with you!

Last but never least: I love you, my amazing fam! Tom, Fortune (and LaLa and Claire!), you all give me the sustenance I need to do this stuff each and every day! Thank you!

ABOUT ANGEL PAYNE

USA Today bestselling romance author Angel Payne loves to focus on high-heat romance starring memorable alpha men and the women who love them. She has numerous book series to her credit, including the action-packed Bolt Saga and Honor Bound series, Secrets of Stone series (with Victoria Blue), the intertwined Cimarron and Temptation Court series, the Suited for Sin series, and the Lords of Sin historicals, as well as several standalone titles.

Angel is a native Southern Californian, leading to her love of being in the outdoors, where she often reads and writes. She still lives in Southern California with her soul-mate husband and beautiful daughter, to whom she is a proud cosplay/culture con mom. Her passions also include whisky tasting, shoe shopping, and travel.

Visit her at AngelPayne.com